Praise for the *New York Times* bestselling
CITY SPIES

"Ingeniously plotted, and a grin-inducing delight."
—*People.com*

"Plotted with an enjoyable amount of suspense, Ponti's story features a well-drawn cast of kids from around the world forming a chosen family with sibling-like dynamics. A page-turner suited to even the most reluctant readers."
—*Publishers Weekly*

"A well-paced story laced with suspense, wit, and entertaining dialogue. Events unfold within colorful Parisian settings that include the Eiffel Tower, the Catacombs, and a deceptively shabby-looking hotel run by British Intelligence. Laying the groundwork for a new series, this brisk adventure features mysteries, intrigues, and five clever young heroes."
—*Booklist*

"Books like this are the reason why kids love to read."
—COLBY SHARP, Nerdy Book Club

"A must-read for anyone who loves adventure, intrigue, mystery, and humor."
—STUART GIBBS, *New York Times* bestselling author of *Spy School*

"Beware, *City Spies* may keep you up all night—reading!"
—CHRIS GRABENSTEIN, #1 *New York Times* bestselling coauthor of *Max Einstein: The Genius Experiment*

ALSO BY JAMES PONTI

The Framed! series
Framed!
Vanished!
Trapped!

The Dead City trilogy
Dead City
Blue Moon
Dark Days

The City Spies series
City Spies
Golden Gate

BOOK
3

CITY SPIES

FORBIDDEN CITY

BY JAMES PONTI

ALADDIN
New York London Toronto Sydney New Delhi

💡ALADDIN
An imprint of Simon & Schuster Children's Publishing Division
1230 Avenue of the Americas, New York, New York 10020
First Aladdin hardcover edition February 2022
Text copyright © 2022 by James Ponti
Jacket illustration copyright © 2022 by Yaoyao Ma Van As
All rights reserved, including the right of reproduction in whole or in part in any form.
ALADDIN and related logo are registered trademarks of Simon & Schuster, Inc.
For information about special discounts for bulk purchases, please contact
Simon & Schuster Special Sales at 1-866-506-1949 or business@simonandschuster.com.
The Simon & Schuster Speakers Bureau can bring authors to your live event. For more information or to book an event contact the Simon & Schuster Speakers Bureau at 1-866-248-3049 or visit our website at www.simonspeakers.com.
Book designed by Tiara Iandiorio
The text of this book was set in Sabon LT Std.
Manufactured in the United States of America 1221 FFG
10 9 8 7 6 5 4 3 2 1
Library of Congress Control Number 2021942071
ISBN 978-1-5344-7921-0 (hc)
ISBN 978-1-5344-7923-4 (ebook)

FOR COURTNEY AND
GRAYSON

MARCH 5, 2022

CONGRATULATIONS ON
MAKING OUR FAMILY BIGGER
AND BETTER. I LOVE YOU
MORE THAN WORDS CAN
EVER EXPRESS.

Billionaires' Row

IT WAS DARK, AND AS PARIS LOOKED OUT at the traffic, he caught a glimpse of his own reflection in the window. There was nothing remarkable about his face. No feature or quirk someone would notice or remember. He'd been born in Rwanda, grew up in Paris, lived in Scotland, and was now in London. And in each of those locations, he'd learned to blend in and disappear. This was an important quality because Paris wasn't just a schoolboy. He was also a spy. Blending in was essential.

Unlike spies in movies, whose modes of transportation ranged from jet packs and mini-submarines to bullet-proof Aston Martins tricked out with rocket launchers, he was headed to his latest mission on a city bus. The number seventy to South Kensington to be precise. That was the problem with being undercover *and* underage—you always needed somebody else to give you a ride.

"This is pathetic," he said, turning to Kat, who was sitting next to him. "Absolutely pathetic."

"What is?" she asked.

He looked around to make sure no one was listening and then leaned in to whisper, "We're about to break into one of the most expensive homes in London to steal a priceless work of art, and our getaway car is a bright red double-decker bus that does a max speed of five miles an hour."

Kat laughed, which only frustrated him.

"First of all, we're not *stealing* it, we're *returning* it," she answered in an equally hushed tone. "Or have you forgotten about the little treasure that's been sewn into the lining of your jacket? Second, once you've put it back, why would anyone bother to chase us? Logic dictates that our *getaway* vehicle is irrelevant."

He nodded reluctantly and admitted, "Okay . . . you may have a point there."

"Of course I do," she replied. "Your problem is that you think being a spy is like being in an action movie."

"It's not?"

"No. It's like eating in the lunch hall at school."

"How do you figure that?" Paris asked.

"You pretend you belong and hope nobody notices you while you figure things out," she said. "Not to mention there's a decent chance the food's been poisoned."

He chuckled and saw that they were nearing their stop at Notting Hill Gate. "Finally, this is us."

He stood up to leave, but she stayed put, blocking his way.

"I'm not moving until you say it," she said firmly.

Paris was the alpha, which meant he was in charge now that they were in the field. It also meant he was the one who was supposed to say the phrase that officially started the mission. It was as much a good-luck ritual as it was an operational command.

"Here?" he replied. "On the bus?"

"Don't knock the bus," she said. "James Bond was named after one just like this."

"What do you mean?"

"When Ian Fleming was writing the first Bond book, he lived out in Kent and had to ride the bus back and forth to London," she explained.

"And?" he replied, not getting the connection.

"The bus from Kent to Victoria was number double oh seven."

"You're joking," he said.

"No. That's where he got the name. And if the bus is good enough for Ian and James, it's good enough for you and me."

"Well, if you put it that way." He flashed a sly smile and said, "This operation is hot. We are a go."

Paris and Kat were part of the City Spies, an experimental team of five undercover agents, aged twelve to fifteen, who MI6 used when they had a mission in which adult agents would stand out. In this instance, they were about to crash the sweet sixteen party of a London socialite named Tabitha Banks.

The British Secret Intelligence Service wasn't really interested in the birthday girl, but they were fascinated by her father. Reginald Banks was a multibillionaire whose business dealings sometimes involved nefarious underworld characters and shadowy figures from foreign intelligence agencies. MI6 desperately needed to get an agent into his home, and this party offered a rare opportunity to access the highly secure mansion located on Kensington Palace Gardens, one of the most exclusive neighborhoods in the world.

"Testing comms, one, two, three," Paris said as they walked away from the bus stop. "Can you hear me?"

He was using a covert communication device that looked like an everyday earbud to speak with team members monitoring the situation from a nearby safe house.

"Roger that, we hear you loud and clear," replied Mother, the MI6 agent in charge of the team.

"How about me?" asked Kat, testing her comms device.

"Perfect," Mother replied. "We are ready to rock and roll. We've got Brooklyn on the computer, and Sydney is . . ." There was a pause as Mother turned to Sydney. "What exactly are you doing?"

She gave him a look as if the answer were obvious. "I'm standing by just in case," she replied.

"We have Sydney standing by . . . just in case," Mother continued. "Although, technically, she's pacing more than standing."

"Relax, Syd," Paris said confidently. "We've got this."

"She's not pacing because she's worried about the mission," Brooklyn pointed out. "She's pacing because she's jealous that she's not the one doing it."

This brought a round of laughs, and Sydney didn't even bother to disagree. She always wanted to be the alpha and hated it when she missed out on the action.

"Just remember that I'm here if you need me," she offered. "Ready and willing."

"Good to know," said Paris.

"We've almost reached the guard gate at the end of the street," Kat said. "Any last words of wisdom?"

"Yes," answered Mother, who cleared his throat and paused dramatically before saying, *"This mission is fraught, so don't get caught."*

He liked to use rhyming couplets, nicknamed Motherisms, to remind the team of important elements of spycraft. This one left Kat and Paris completely uninspired.

"Seriously?" Kat replied.

"Is that the best you've got?" asked Paris.

"Well, I could've pointed out that if you get caught, it will not only involve the Metropolitan Police, but quite likely the prime minister, the head of MI6, the foreign secretary, the French ambassador, and the president of Nepal," said Mother. "But I didn't want to overwhelm you, and it's exceedingly difficult to make all that rhyme."

"Fair points all," said Paris.

"Oh, there is one more thing, Paris," interjected Brooklyn.

"What's that?" he replied.

"Try to remember that your microphone is very sensitive," she said.

"Okay, but why am I remembering that?"

"Because it will blow out our headsets if you squeal too loudly when KB5 take the stage," she said, eliciting more laughter.

"You are so very funny," Paris replied. "Trust me, if I scream, it will be because I'm in musical agony. Although, calling what they do *music* is an offense to everyone from Beethoven to the Beatles."

KB5 was a British boy band whose heartthrob members had their pictures plastered on bedroom walls around the globe. Despite Paris's opinion of their musical ability, they regularly performed in sold-out arenas bursting with screaming fans. Tonight, however, they were playing a private concert for Tabitha's birthday. This was an advantage of having Reginald Banks for a father. Not only was he one of the richest people in the

United Kingdom, but he also created KB5 and owned the record label that produced their albums.

"I like their music," Sydney offered. "It's not too late if you want to swap roles."

"I would gladly do so," said Paris, "if only Australia had built their embassy on Kensington Palace Gardens."

Nicknamed Billionaires' Row, Kensington Palace Gardens was home to business tycoons, royal family members, foreign embassies, and the residences of several ambassadors. It was a half-mile long and protected at both ends by guard gates with armed police officers. For any outsiders who still didn't get the hint, there were even signs that read NO PHOTOGRAPHY.

Sir Reg, as he was known in the tabloids, couldn't just hold a concert in his backyard without the approval of his very powerful and extremely private neighbors. So, he'd come up with a brilliant solution and opened up the celebration to all the young people who lived on the street. Since no parent wanted to face the wrath of a furious teen or tween who'd missed out on the party of the decade, permission was granted.

Invitations were also extended to the children of embassy workers, which is when MI6 saw an opportunity.

As good fortune would have it, Kensington Palace Gardens was home to the ambassador of France and the embassy of Nepal, Paris and Kat's home countries. Some favors were called in and their names were added to the guest list.

For Paris, this meant swapping identities yet again, something he'd done countless times during his five years with MI6. As he approached the guardhouse, he flipped a mental switch and became someone else, like an actor stepping onto the stage in a West End play. Until the curtain fell on this little drama, he'd be Antoine Tremblay, the fifteen-year-old son of the second secretary for cultural affairs.

"Which embassy?" asked a guard.

"France," replied Paris.

The guard motioned him to a row of tables marked with flags representing the different countries. Here, the young guests were screened to make sure no overzealous KB5 fans were able to sneak into the party. Paris went to the table with the French tricolor and smiled at the man dressed in a sharp black suit.

"Invitation and identification," said the man.

Paris handed him two flawless forgeries: an official-looking invitation to the party, complete with a security hologram, and a French diplomatic ID for Antoine Tremblay.

"*Bonsoir, Antoine,*" the man said, slipping into French to test him. "*Ça va?*"

"*Oui, ça va bien,*" Paris replied naturally.

The guard checked his name off a list on a clipboard.

"*Comment vous aimez KB Cinq?*" asked the guard to see if he was excited about seeing KB5.

One of the keys to being undercover was not lying when it wasn't necessary. The more honest you were about specific things, the more believable you were overall. So rather than pretending to be excited about a boy band he detested, Paris answered truthfully. "*Disons, j'aime beaucoup mieux le gâteau d'anniversaire.*" Let's just say I'm more excited about the birthday cake.

The man laughed and handed him a red wristband. "Put this on now and don't take it off until you leave for the night."

"*Merci beaucoup,*" replied Paris.

At a nearby table, Kat answered similar questions in a mix of Nepali and English.

Unlike the other kids who eagerly hurried toward the party, Paris and Kat took their time as they walked down the street. They'd been trained to study the landscape surrounding any mission and make mental notes of key details like the locations of security cameras and the fact that one of the streetlights was out. They looked for escape routes and potential hiding places. They also marveled at the mansions.

"Wow!" Paris said when they reached the one belonging to Sir Reg. "It looks even bigger than I imagined. The pictures don't do it justice."

"No kidding," said Kat. "You're going to need GPS just to find your way around in there."

The two of them had studied everything they could about the house, including photographs, blueprints, and video from a BBC show about London's finest estates. The building was three stories tall and a showcase of Italian Renaissance architecture with thirty-eight rooms, including an indoor swimming pool, home cinema, and gymnasium.

It was also home to museum-quality art. There was a large Picasso that hung in the entryway, a pair of Van Gogh sketches in the living room, a Rodin statue in the garden, and an ornate Fabergé egg, known as the *"Pearl of Russia,"* that sat on the mantel above the fireplace in Sir Reg's private office.

Or at least that's what he thought.

In reality, it was a high-quality fake that contained a tiny hidden microphone British Intelligence had used to eavesdrop on his business meetings for nearly three years. The actual Fabergé egg—worth nearly five million pounds—was currently nestled inside a secret pocket sewn into Paris's jacket.

The *Pearl of Russia* was one of fifty jeweled eggs handcrafted over a period of three decades for Tsars Alexander III and Nicholas II. Each year they'd given them as Easter presents to their wives and mothers. Paris's assignment was to sneak the real egg back into the office and replace it before the fake was exposed. This was necessary because Sir Reg had recently announced that he was loaning it to a museum in Moscow, where it would no doubt be examined by experts who would uncover the microphone. MI6 couldn't let that happen.

"We've arrived," Paris announced to the others in the safe house.

"How are the access points?" asked Mother.

"The walkway gate is manned by staff directing everyone to go around the house to the party in back," answered Paris. "But the gate for the driveway is wide open. The tour bus and equipment trucks for KB5 have blocked it so it can't shut."

"What about the house?" asked Mother.

"Two guards at each door," said Kat. "Judging by the holster bulges underneath their jackets, I'd say they're all armed."

"If there was only one per door, you might be able to pull off a diversion and distract the guard long enough to slip in," said Mother. "But with two, the main floor is a no-go. That means you'll need to enter the house through the alternate route."

Paris and Kat both turned their attention to the roof.

"Looks like someone's going to be playing Santa Claus," said Kat.

Paris gave her a raised eyebrow and replied, "Ho, ho, ho."

Operation Kris Kringle

PARIS WAS THE ONE WHO'D THOUGHT OF using the chimney.

A month earlier, they were trying to figure out how to get into the office when they came across a magazine profile of Reginald Banks. In one of the photos, the *Pearl of Russia* was visible in the background, sitting on the mantel of a large stone fireplace.

"Look how big that fireplace is," Paris said. "It's huge. That means there should be an equally huge chimney that connects from the roof to the office. Why don't I just slide down like Father Christmas?"

"Not in a million years" was Mother's emphatic response. "Chimneys are way too dangerous. Eight million things could go wrong and most of them involve your untimely death." Then he thought about it for a moment and smiled. "Although, the roof is a promising lead."

And so Operation Kris Kringle was born.

Rather than having Paris use the chimney, it was decided he would take advantage of the rooftop helipad that also had been featured in the magazine article. Next to it was a door that led into the house. To access the door without setting off any alarms, the team needed to hack into the home's state-of-the-art security system—no easy task. Then, once he reached the office, Paris would only be able to enter if he could convince the biometric screening device that he was Reginald Banks. That meant before Paris climbed up to the roof, he had to find Sir Reg and steal his identity. Or at least a copy of his thumbprint.

"Where are you, Reg?" Paris whispered to himself as he scanned the faces of the partygoers. There were at least two hundred people already there, and the celebration was in full swing. A DJ on the stage was mixing multilingual pop songs to create a nonstop international groove while tented catering stations offered fusion cuisine blending cultures such as Korean beef tacos, Siberian pasta, Chinese barbecue pulled pork sliders, and Thai curry mac and cheese.

The music and food were all in keeping with the party's theme, "Around the World." Not coincidentally, this was also the name of KB5's soon-to-be-released album. Although he'd never admit it publicly, part of the reason Sir Reg invited the children of the embassy workers was so his publicity team could get pictures showing how popular KB5 was with fans across the globe.

One of the keys to his financial success was that he saw business opportunities in everything, even his own daughter's birthday.

"There he is," Kat said, nodding toward a man with flowing reddish-blond hair and a scruffy mustache and beard. His outfit—black jeans, T-shirt, and limited-edition sneakers—looked casual but cost a fortune. He greeted guests and happily posed for pictures, flashing the same media-savvy smile that could be found in countless newspapers and magazines.

"He looks more like a bass player than a billionaire," said Paris.

"I think that's the goal," said Kat. "Maybe you can get a selfie with him."

"That's brilliant," he replied. "If Reg takes the picture, then I'll have his thumbprint on my phone."

"Remember that little rhyme about not getting caught?" Mother interjected. "I think posing for a photograph with the person we're spying on would count as pushing our luck."

Paris and Kat both laughed. "We're just messing with you," he said. "I know the drill. Blend in and disappear. Make sure no one notices me. That's my specialty. I'll have his thumbprint in no time and remain completely anonymous while I'm doing it."

"That's nice and all," Brooklyn chimed in. "But it won't matter if I can't access the internal video security system."

"Give us a second, will you?" Kat replied, peeved. "We just got here."

"Sorry," Brooklyn apologized. "I don't mean to be pushy. It's just that I need as much time as I can get on this one. It's been a struggle."

"I understand," said Kat. "I'm on it."

Brooklyn was an amazing hacker, but after a week of relentless effort, she hadn't been able to access Sir Reg's system. According to her, it had "a ridiculously intense firewall with hyperparanoid levels of encryption." Since she couldn't hack it from the outside, she was hoping she could from within. To do that, she needed to trick KB5's stage crew into giving her a hand.

"All right," Kat said. "I'm in a good position to see the mixing board. It's set up in the middle of the lawn, facing the stage. I'll get in close and send you some pictures."

"Thank you," Brooklyn replied. "Try to get one that shows the manufacturer's logo so I can pull up the specs."

The mixing board was the centerpiece to the plan. It was a large electronic console filled with rows of buttons, knobs, sliders, and dials that controlled everything from the volume levels of the musicians and singers to the sound quality of the different instruments.

The key was that it was always set up in the audience, so the person operating it could properly hear how the band sounded in the crowd. This meant that Kat could get close to it. Hopefully, close enough to attach a tiny transmitter that connected to Brooklyn's computer. This was important because the mixer was also linked to the rest of the equipment by Wi-Fi. If it used the same network as the home security system, Brooklyn thought she might be able to piggyback on it and sneak in through a back door.

A man, dressed all in black, operated the board and was known as the "front-of-house mixer." It was his job to make sure KB5 sounded perfect. He was adjusting some dials when Kat covertly snapped three photos and texted them to the team in the safe house.

"Got 'em," Brooklyn said as she pulled the images up on her computer. "Perfect shot of the logo, Kat. That's a Digico Quantum Seven," she said as she did a quick search and pulled up a diagram of the console. "There is a USB port on the left-hand side."

"I guess that means it's time to turn on the charm," Kat said wryly.

This was part joke and part self-realization. Kat much preferred solving math problems to talking to people. Especially strangers. But she had to distract the sound engineer long enough for her to plug the transmitter into the USB port. The fact that he was wearing a thick set of noise-canceling headphones didn't help. He didn't even hear her the first two times she tried to get his attention. Finally, she tentatively tapped him on the shoulder.

He turned to see her, pulled the headset off one ear, and said, "Yes?"

This was her one chance to talk fast and engage him

in conversation. It was where she needed to be charming and interesting. The best she could do was "Hi."

Her voice was so soft it could barely be heard over the music the DJ was playing. Back in the safe house, Brooklyn and Sydney shared a worried look.

"Hi," he said curtly. As much as Kat hated social interactions, sound engineers hated having their work interrupted by fans of the band even more. "If you're looking for the inside scoop on KB5, I can't really help you. The lads are nice, but I don't hang out with them or know any juicy gossip."

"No . . . I'm . . . not really . . ." She paused and let out a frustrated sigh as all seemed lost. Then, out of nowhere, "Do you like the Quantum Seven?" she asked, referring to the mixing board.

The man gave her a curious look. "You're interested in audio mixers?"

"A lot more than I am in boy bands," she replied.

He gave her a raised eyebrow and asked, "What is it you like about it?"

"What don't I like?" she said, stalling.

Back in the safe house, Brooklyn quickly read off some statistics. "Huge channel count. Awesome processing power."

"The channel count is huge," Kat said, trying to sound like she knew what that meant. "And it has awesome processing power."

"Not only that," the man said enthusiastically, "but the clarity of the vocals is incredible, no matter the frequency range."

He started to rave about the equipment, and she listened and nodded while he did. When he gestured to the right side of the console, she deftly plugged Brooklyn's transmitter into the USB port.

"Way to go, Kat!" Brooklyn said when the signal reached her at the safe house. Within moments she pulled up the Wi-Fi and located the devices that were on it. Among them was the home security system. "I am in and you are free to get out of there."

"That was brilliant!" Sydney added proudly.

Kat lingered for a moment and listened to the man a little more before saying, "Thanks. I better let you get back to work."

Meanwhile, Brooklyn's fingers danced across the keyboard in a flurry as she started accessing the security system.

While she was hacking, Paris was stalking. He carefully followed Sir Reg around the party, studying the billionaire as he greeted people and posed for pictures.

"That's odd," Paris said.

"What is?" asked Mother.

"Three times now, Sir Reg has accepted presents for his daughter."

"What's odd about that?" asked Sydney. "It's her birthday party, isn't it?"

"It is," Paris replied. "But he can't carry them because he's shaking hands, so he has to pass them to an assistant who's following him around. And she keeps carrying them, even though there's a giant table where everyone else is putting gifts. Why not put them there?"

Inside the safe house, Mother tried to picture the scene. "These are being given to him by kids at the party?"

"No, adults," said Paris. "I think they're all staffers from the embassies."

"Why are there staffers there?" asked Mother. "I thought only their children were invited."

"Yes," Paris answered. "But alongside the tables of food, there are also tables set up with displays about the embassies in the neighborhood. It's all part of the 'Around the World' theme."

"Which countries?" asked Mother, his curiosity growing.

"Which countries have tables?" asked Paris.

"No," answered Mother. "Which countries gave him presents?"

Paris ran through them in his head and looked back at the displays. "Russia . . . and India . . . for sure," he answered. "And I think the other one was either Saudi Arabia or Romania."

As he was talking, Paris saw Sir Reg whisper something to his assistant, who nodded and took the presents away.

"And now the presents are on the move," he continued. "Instead of putting them on the table, the woman's carrying them into the house."

Mother thought about this for a moment. "If they're gifts from the embassies, he might not want his daughter to open them in front of the other guests," he said. "You always run the risk of one country being insulted or embarrassed if their present isn't as nice as another's."

"The good news is that Reg has stopped walking around for a moment," said Paris. "That means it's time for me to get to work."

Reg got a drink and joined Tabitha and some others standing around a table in a roped-off VIP section near the stage. To enter this area, guests needed a blue wristband, not red like the one Paris had. But that wasn't a problem. He simply slipped into one of the half dozen photo booths that had been set up for the party. Here guests could have their pictures taken in front of international backgrounds featuring landmarks like the Eiffel Tower or the Golden Gate Bridge.

Paris didn't want a picture; he just needed privacy for a quick change. It was a tight fit, but he'd practiced in a closet back at their HQ on the FARM. He held on to his cuffs and pulled his jacket up over his head so that when he pulled his arms out, it turned inside out. An MI6 tailor had made it reversible so now he had a perfect match for the ones worn by the catering staff. When he slipped it on, his cover instantly changed from guest to busboy. Another mental switch was flipped. It was time for a new character to take the stage.

He grabbed an empty tray from a dessert table featuring French pastries and started cleaning up after people. All the while, he kept a close eye on the VIP section, and when he saw Sir Reg finish his drink and place it on a table, Paris swept right in and picked it up.

"Got it," he told the others once he'd walked away. "There's a big fat thumbprint right on his glass. Perfect to lift and copy."

"What about the selfie?" joked Sydney. "Did you get that too?"

"No," answered Paris. "I was totally invisible. At a party like this, who's going to notice a busboy?"

Paris was right about that. With all the excitement, no one in the VIP section had even registered his existence. He simply blended into the background, nothing memorable about him. But as to total invisibility, that wasn't completely true.

What he hadn't realized was that all the photo booths had been set to take pictures automatically. One was snapped of him while he was doing his quick change. He didn't see the flash because his arms and jacket blocked his view.

In the picture, his face was mostly obscured, but it was still a visual record that he was at the party. And it sat in a tray at the photo booth, waiting for a time when someone might suddenly find him important enough to care about.

The *Pearl of Russia*

WHILE THEY WERE PLANNING THE MISSION, Mother handed Paris a photograph of the side of Reginald Banks's mansion and asked, "Can you climb this?"

"Easily," Paris answered as he studied the picture. "With the bricks, the chimney, the drainpipe, and the trellis, there are a lot of hand- and footholds. It'll be no problem to get up to the roof."

"That's good," Mother replied. "But do you think you can do it in twenty-one seconds?"

"Hmm," Paris said, thinking it over. "That's not a lot of time."

"Unfortunately, it's all you're going to get," answered Mother.

"Why's that?"

"Because that's how long it takes to sing 'Happy Birthday.' At least when I timed myself. Hopefully, KB5 doesn't sing it any faster. If they do, that would be bad."

"You've lost me," Paris said. "What do the two have to do with each other?"

"To get permission to hold the concert at his house, Reginald Banks had to give his neighbors and the Westminster council a schedule detailing, among other things, any lighting and noise variations," Mother explained. "They take this very seriously. At a celebration for the London Olympics, Bruce Springsteen and Paul McCartney held a concert right next door in Hyde Park, and when they went past their curfew, the council pulled the plug, literally. Their mics went dead while they were onstage performing. If they'll do that to the Boss and a Beatle, then . . ."

Paris waved his hands to stop him. "Still lost," he

said. "Let's get to the part where this has something to do with me climbing up the side of the house?"

"Right, right," Mother said as he handed him the rundown of the concert. "I've highlighted the key item."

Paris started reading aloud from the schedule. "'KB5 will sing "Happy Birthday" to Tabitha onstage. While they do, all the lights will be turned off except for a spotlight on them as they perform.'"

"That means no one can see you for twenty-one seconds," Mother said. "Is that enough time?"

Paris studied the picture and thought about it carefully before answering, "Yes."

"Are you sure?"

"Positive," Paris said confidently.

He truly was confident when he said it, but a few weeks later, as the moment was rapidly approaching, that certainty began to fade. In person, the house seemed taller and the challenge more forbidding. He didn't want to think about what would happen if the lights came back on while he was still dangling off the wall. Luckily, he didn't have much time to worry.

"Showtime," Brooklyn said from her seat in the safe house. "The cake's in place and KB5 are making their way to the stage." She knew this because in addition to hacking into the security system, she'd also tapped into the radio frequency the crew was using for their walkie-talkies.

Still dressed as a busboy, Paris was at the side of the house, loading dirty dishes onto a rack in a catering truck. He'd already used special tape to lift Sir Reg's print off a glass and scan it into a nifty little gadget designed by MI6. The device, a miniature 3-D printer, produced a rubbery cap that duplicated the print and fit directly onto Paris's thumb.

"If I can have everyone's attention," Sir Reg said as he took a microphone at the center of the stage, his daughter standing alongside him. "It's a pleasure to welcome you to our home as we celebrate this very special event—my lovely Tabitha's sixteenth birthday." He paused for a moment while the guests clapped. "Normally, this is when Tab's mum, my ex-wife, sings to her. But since she's currently performing an exclusive engagement in Las Vegas, I found someone else to handle the duties."

Right on cue, KB5 came onstage, pushing a giant birthday cake. The guests squealed in delight, and Sir Reg had to stop talking for a moment because it was too loud for him to be heard. The five band members smiled, waved, and flashed their signature pouty looks as they posed with Tabitha next to the cake. She basked in the glory while lights pulsed throughout the crowd as hundreds of phones snapped photos.

With all eyes on the stage, Paris moved over to the wall and studied it, trying to map out in his mind an image of the quickest and most secure route to the roof. Kat stood close by, acting as a lookout. When she was sure that no one was near, she said, "All clear."

Paris reached up to grab hold of a brick, and he put his foot on the edge of a planter so that he was ready to spring into action, like a sprinter getting into position before a race.

On the stage, Sir Reg prompted the crowd. "So, if you'll join us . . ."

Everything went dark, and a spotlight focused on KB5 as they began to sing. Paris started climbing and got off to a great start. He quickly cleared the first floor but ran into a problem when he jammed his thumb on a second-story windowsill.

"Oww," he groaned, recoiling as pain radiated through his hand.

"You okay?" asked Mother.

Paris didn't answer. Instead, he gritted his teeth

and continued clambering up the wall. By the time he reached the third floor, he'd lost the mental image and could no longer envision the path he'd planned to take. This meant he'd have to feel his way from here on out. Meanwhile, the song reached its final line.

"I might not make it in time," he admitted as he strained to reach the trellis.

In the safe house, Mother and Sydney held their breath while Brooklyn pulled up the concert's lighting grid on her computer. She'd accessed it earlier, just in case there came a time to take control and cause a blackout.

"If we need to, I can cut everything," she said.

"Don't unless I tell you," said Paris.

Luckily, one of the boys in the band started to ham it up for the audience, and the song stretched to nearly thirty seconds. Paris managed to grab on to the trellis, and although it slid down a few inches, it held. When the lights came back on and Tabitha went to cut the cake, there was no sign of him on the wall.

Kat nervously checked to make sure he hadn't fallen to the ground.

"Everything okay?" Mother asked quietly.

There was an extended delay before Paris responded

with a weak but relieved "Well, that was close." He was flat on his back, lying on the roof. There were some scrapes on his hands and face, but he was safe and out of sight. "Give me a second to catch my breath."

"Okay, but just a second," Brooklyn said, taking charge.

For this phase of the mission, she was in the driver's seat. There were three computer monitors set up in front of her, and on them she could see all the elements of the home's security system. These included the closed-circuit camera feeds, which allowed her to keep track of activity inside the mansion.

"Right now there's no one on the top two floors, so you should be good to go," she told Paris. "I've unlocked the door to the helipad and turned off the alarm."

"All right," Paris said with a pained grunt as he pulled his jammed thumb back into place. He flexed it a couple times to test it. "Ready to go."

From the back lawn he could hear the start of KB5's concert, their music drowning out any noise he made as he stealthily moved across the roof. "Never thought I'd be happy to hear them," he said.

"You know you love it," Sydney joked.

"Tell me before you open the door," Brooklyn said. "I have to freeze the cameras."

"Roger that," answered Paris.

There was only a sliver of moon, which had helped when Paris needed darkness but now made it difficult for him to find his way on the roof. The helipad was slightly elevated, and once he reached it, he was able to follow the edge around to the door. It opened onto a flight of stairs that descended into the house.

"All clear," he said as he reached for the doorknob. "I'm ready."

"Remember, once I hit freeze, I'm totally blind," Brooklyn reminded him. "The longer you take, the more dangerous it becomes."

"Yeah, I kind of put that together," he said, trying to make light of the concern.

"Okay, in three-two-one," Brooklyn replied as she pressed a button that froze all the camera feeds from the top floor. "Good luck."

Since the hallways and rooms were empty at the moment, they would continue to appear that way on the monitors in the guardhouse even as Paris moved through them.

He quietly opened the door and went down the stairs into what Sir Reg had referred to as his "toy room" during the BBC tour of the home. Electric guitars autographed by rock stars were mounted on the wall, a snooker table sat in the center of the room, and there was a cabinet with antique chess sets.

The love of chess was a passion Paris shared with the billionaire, who was a grandmaster and such a fan of the game that he'd named his company Caïssa, after the Greek mythological character known as "the goddess of chess." Even the black and white tiles on the floor looked like a massive chessboard.

Paris had memorized the layout of the house and knew exactly where to go. He cracked the door open and peeked out to make sure no one was there. Then, he rushed down the hall, moving on his toes and the balls of his feet just as he'd learned in the dance classes Mother insisted the team take in order to learn body control and graceful movement.

He passed three rooms before he reached the office and the door with the biometric scanner. His thumb had started to swell from when he jammed it, and it throbbed as he forced the rubber cap over it. It was painful, but it worked, and the door unlocked with a click.

"I'm in the office," Paris whispered into his comms device, prompting sighs of relief from everyone in the safe house.

There were no cameras or windows in this room. There wasn't even a computer. Those invited snooping eyes and ears, and Reg wanted to make sure no one knew his business. He was paranoid about getting spied upon, but not so much that it occurred to him to have his Fabergé egg reexamined after purchasing it at auction. He'd been so delighted to acquire the *Pearl of Russia* that he rushed right in and placed it on his mantel.

It was the perfect addition to an office designed to intimidate and impress anybody who came to negotiate. Along with works of art, there was a wall covered floor to ceiling with photographs of Reg with world leaders and celebrities, and another that featured framed magazine covers, honors, and recognitions he'd received.

Paris ignored them and moved straight to the massive fireplace, so large that it took up almost an entire wall. He pulled the authentic *Pearl of Russia* out of the secret pocket in his jacket and was about to put it in its rightful place when something caught his eye.

"The presents," he said.

"What?" asked Brooklyn.

"The presents that the embassy people handed to Sir Reg. Now they're sitting on his desk."

Brooklyn let out an exasperated sigh and said, "Would you forget about those presents and hurry up?"

"Okay, okay," he said. "I'm doing it."

He returned his focus to the eggs and swapped them putting the fake one into his pocket. While he was doing that, Kat chimed in from the party.

"Just so you guys know, right after they cut the cake, Sir Reg went back to the house," she said. "You see him, right?"

Brooklyn scanned the feeds on the monitors.

"No," she said. "I don't see him anywhere. Are you sure he went inside?"

"Positive," Kat replied.

It took a second until it dawned on Brooklyn. "The cameras are frozen," she said in a panic.

She hit a button and the third-floor security feed came back to life. That's where they saw Reg striding down the hall, heading straight for the office.

"The egg's been switched and I'm leaving the office," Paris informed them.

"No!" Brooklyn, Sydney, and Mother all answered in unison.

"Why?" asked Paris. "What's wrong?"

"Reg is coming your way," answered Brooklyn. "He'll be there in seconds."

"What do I do?" Paris asked desperately.

In the safe house, they could only watch the screen as Reginald Banks put his thumb on the scanner, opened the door to his office, and walked inside.

Apple Jack

EVERYONE IN THE SAFE HOUSE WAS IN full panic mode as Sir Reg stepped into the office. Since the room wasn't part of the security feed, they couldn't see what was happening, but one thing gave them hope: They didn't hear any confrontation. There wasn't the clatter and crash of a scuffle. Sir Reg didn't shout, "Who are you?" or "What are you doing here?" All that came over the comms was the sound of Paris taking shallow, nervous breaths.

"I know you can't talk," Mother whispered. "But if

you're safe at the moment, tap your microphone two times to let us know you're okay."

They listened intently as two soft thumps came over the speaker.

"That's good," Mother said in a calming tone. "We'll stop talking so you can focus on the situation, but if you need us to get involved, just say . . ."

He tried to think of a safety word when Sydney blurted out, "Apple Jack." It was a code from a recent mission and the first thing that came to mind.

"Perfect," Mother said. "If you need us, just say, 'Apple Jack.'"

Paris responded with two more taps on his microphone to signify that he understood.

Inside the office, Reginald Banks was completely unaware that there was an intruder. He was in an excellent mood because the party was going perfectly, his daughter was thrilled, and he'd received three presents so exciting he couldn't wait to open them. His impatience had reached the point that he'd slipped out of the concert to take a quick peek.

Less than six feet away, Paris tried to remain motionless inside the fireplace. There was just enough room for him to hide if he hunched over and pressed his back against the side of the firebox. He wasn't completely invisible, but it was the best he could do.

It helped that Sir Reg's attention was focused on the presents. He beamed as he opened the first one, a box that contained a top secret dossier from the FSB, the Russian equivalent of MI6 and the CIA. He flipped through the pages, delighted by what was inside. The other two packages also held intelligence files, one from the RAW—India's Research and Analysis Wing— and the other from the GIP—Saudi Arabia's General Intelligence Presidency.

Getting his hands on three sets of "eyes only/no copy" files was proof that Sir Reg wielded enormous power. Double agents on his secret payroll had smuggled them out of their nations' most secure intelligence facilities and through their embassies in London. Tabitha's celebration had provided the perfect cover so that they could visit his house and hand them over without attracting attention. After all, who would question three gift-wrapped packages among so many at his daughter's birthday?

"*Happy birthday to me,*" he sang to himself, gleefully drawing out the notes as he placed the files in a stack on his desk.

It took everything Paris had to stay quiet and still.

The stench of smoke made his eyes water, and he had to breathe through his mouth to keep from sneezing. Finally, after what seemed an eternity, he heard Reg get up and leave. Once the door shut, Paris whispered into the comms, "He's gone." Then he hacked out a few coughs and got out of the fireplace.

"Looks like he's heading back to the party," Brooklyn said as she watched Reg going down the stairs on the monitors.

"What was he doing up there?" asked Sydney.

"I couldn't see from inside the fireplace," answered Paris. "But, judging by the discarded wrapping paper on his desk, it looks like he came up to open those presents."

"Seriously?" asked Sydney. "He skipped out of the party to open his daughter's presents when she wasn't even around?"

"If these are for her, they're the worst birthday presents ever," he responded. "They're just files." He looked down at the top one and his eyes opened wide with surprise. "Strike that. They're not *just* files. They're intelligence files."

"How do you know that?" asked Mother.

"The first one has a couple stamps on the folder," he

answered. "One is for the FSB, and I'm pretty sure the other is Russian for 'top secret.'"

"Can you tell what it's about?" Mother wondered.

Paris flipped through the file. "I can't read any of it, but it's a dossier of some sort with multiple photographs of the same person."

"What about the others?" asked Mother.

"File number two is from Saudi Arabian secret intelligence," he said. "It also has pictures of the same man."

"Any idea who he is?" asked Sydney.

"Let's see if India's Research and Analysis Wing can answer that," Paris answered. "They were kind enough to write their file in English. Here we go. His name is Park Jin-sun, and he's a nuclear scientist from North Korea."

"That's troubling," Mother said. "What could Sir Reg be up to?"

"I don't know," said Brooklyn, "but I do know that he's left the house. Time to go, Paris. I'll freeze the cameras."

"Wait," said Paris. "Shouldn't I take pictures of these before I leave?"

Mother was torn. He was worried about Paris's safety, but he was also concerned as to why Reginald Banks would have top secret files about a North Korean scientist.

"Yes," he said. "But do it quickly."

Paris grabbed his phone and started flipping through the pages, taking photos of each one. Meanwhile, Mother, Sydney, and Brooklyn were glued to the monitors, making sure no one was headed toward the office again.

"Okay, done," Paris said when he slipped his phone into his pocket and replaced the files exactly as he'd found them. "Am I clear to make it to the balcony?"

Brooklyn scanned all the monitors one more time, double-checking to make sure she didn't make another mistake. "Yes," she said. "You're good to go. I'm freezing the cameras now."

Paris scurried down the hall and quietly made his way down two flights of stairs and through a guest bedroom onto a balcony. It was at the side of the house, but toward the front and away from the party. He could hear the music playing and crowd singing along as he slinked over the railing and dropped down to the ground beneath him.

He landed awkwardly and fell, but he was behind a catering truck so nobody saw. "Made it," he said, relieved. "Mission accomplished."

"Nicely done!" said Mother.

"Who's the man?" Brooklyn asked, holding up her hand.

"Paris is the man," Sydney responded, giving her a high five.

Paris headed back toward the party and joked, "I'm in such a good mood, I might even enjoy KB5 while I'm eating some of that Thai curry mac and cheese. it smelled incredi—"

He stopped midsentence when someone grabbed him by the shoulder and said, "Not so fast."

It was a man's voice, deep and threatening. Paris was expecting a security guard, but instead turned to see a very angry caterer. Paris was still dressed as a busboy, so this man obviously thought he worked for him.

"Did I do something wrong?" Paris asked innocently. "I was just putting dirty dishes back into the truck."

"Well, the dishes aren't all that's dirty," said the caterer. "Your uniform's filthy."

Paris looked down and realized his jacket was covered in soot from the fireplace.

"We run a luxury catering company and serve an elite, high-end clientele," the man continued. "I can't have you looking like this."

"Of course not, sir," Paris said. "I'm sorry. It must've just happened. It's dark behind the truck, and I tripped over something and fell to the ground. I was right there."

He pointed toward the truck, and as he did, the sleeve of his jacket pulled back to reveal his red wristband. The manager eyed this suspiciously, trying to figure out why a busboy had something that was only for invited guests. He looked back at Paris's face and realized he'd never seen him before.

"Who are you?" asked the manager.

Paris instantly imagined a worst-case scenario that involved security detaining him. First, they'd discover the fake Fabergé egg, then the phony identification in his wallet, and finally the photos on his phone. In just three steps, the situation could escalate from a busboy getting reprimanded by his boss to a crisis involving MI6 and three foreign intelligence agencies.

He looked at the man and answered, "Apple Jack."

"I'm sorry, what?"

"Apple Jack!" Paris answered forcefully.

"Don't worry, Paris," Brooklyn said, reacting to the signal. "Help is on its way!"

Brooklyn had already hacked into the concert's

technical software, which meant she could control everything from the audio board to the lighting grid or the music cues.

On the stage, KB5 was performing one of their biggest hits, a love song called "Break My Heart in Two." Roman, widely considered the band's adorable, brooding sensitive one, was singing lead, while the others harmonized and danced behind him in perfect choreography.

Girl, it ain't no mystery
Why our love is history
'Cause your favorite thing to do
Is break my heart in two

Normally, this was when there'd be four drumbeats and each of the background singers would raise two fingers in the air. Instead, the music from a different song started playing, strobe lights began to flash, and a fog machine went into overdrive.

The band had no idea what to do, so they froze and simply stood there shrouded in the rapidly growing smoky haze as the crowd tried to make sense of the scene.

Following on her computer screen, Brooklyn cackled with glee and said, "Why don't we get the attention of the borough council?" She turned the volume all the way up and clicked a button marked PYROTECHNICS.

Three loud booms filled the air, and plumes of gold and silver sparks shot up in spirals from the front of the stage. The party quickly went from confusion to pandemonium, and the caterer was distracted enough that Paris was able to make a run for it.

"You're a superstar, Brook," he said. "I'm heading for the street." He sprinted toward the driveway because he remembered that the band's bus and equipment truck had blocked the gate so it couldn't close. He'd already reached the sidewalk when a call went out over the walkie-talkie.

"We have a suspicious character, black male teenager, dressed as a busboy wearing a green jacket," said the voice. "He's heading toward the street. Detain him."

Brooklyn was still tapped into the walkie-talkies, so she gave Paris a heads-up. "A description of you just went out."

"Turn your jacket inside out again," Mother advised. "Change the color."

"Got it," Paris said as he headed away from the mansion. He was moving rapidly but made sure not to run so that he wouldn't attract any attention. Earlier, he'd studied the placement of the security cameras, so he knew when to turn his face away from them. When he reached the area where the streetlight was out, he quickly reversed his jacket so now it was white instead of green.

Back at the party, Kat was watching how Reg's staff reacted. She saw the head of security dispatch two women to chase after Paris.

"Here comes trouble," she said. "There are two women, late twenties, and identical twins. I noticed them earlier. They're part of the security team, and they're sprinting toward the street. They're coming after you, Paris."

"I see them on the security feed," said Brooklyn. "They look very athletic and very determined. Dressed in black from head to toe."

"Get a screengrab of them and text it to me," Sydney said as she rushed to the door. Before anyone could say anything, she was gone.

Paris couldn't believe how quiet and dark it was on the Kensington Palace Gardens. Brooklyn's pyrotechnic diversion was now over, and the concert had ground to a stop. Everything looked peaceful and perfect, which was exactly the opposite of how he felt.

Forty yards behind him, Sasha and Anastasia Sorokin rushed out from the mansion onto the street. The twins were former ballet dancers who were now part of the Banks family's personal security detail. Tabitha liked them because they looked less menacing than most bodyguards and didn't scare away her friends. Reg liked them because, despite their appearance, they were experts in Krav Maga, a fighting system developed by the Israeli military that combined aikido, boxing, wrestling, judo, and karate. Uncertain which way Paris went, they split up and headed in opposite directions.

"If you think someone's going to get to you," Mother said, "sprint to the French ambassador's residence."

"Why?" asked Paris.

"From a legal standpoint, the second you step foot on the property, you're on French soil," he explained. "Sir Reg's people can't touch you, and neither can the police. You'll be safe."

"Yes, but won't it cause problems with the French once they find out I claimed to be the son of their second secretary for cultural affairs?" Paris responded.

"They're good allies, and I'm sure French intelligence will be interested in what you've found," he said. "We'll minimize the damage."

Paris looked back over his shoulder. It was dark, and he couldn't see very far, but then again neither could anyone looking for him. At the moment, everything seemed clear.

"I think I can make it to the end of the street," he replied. "My only concern is the guardhouse."

"All they have is a vague description of a busboy in a different-colored jacket," said Mother. "And you've got a diplomatic ID. They cannot arrest you."

"Yeah," said Paris. "But the ID's fake."

"Made by the best forgers at MI6," he said, trying to build Paris's confidence. "The only thing that can trip you up is if you look and act suspicious."

"Got it," Paris replied.

Paris had been trained extensively in the art of acting like he belonged. If he tried to scurry in the shadows, that would attract attention. Instead, he walked confidently with his head held high as he approached the guardhouse. He didn't look away, but he didn't make eye contact, either. He was almost to the corner when one of the guards called to him.

"Hey, you, wait a second."

Paris's heart was racing, but he kept calm and turned to face the guard. It was the man who'd checked him in earlier. The one he'd joked with about KB5.

"So, which was better?" asked the man. "The band or the birthday cake?"

"The cake," Paris said with a wide smile. "It wasn't even close."

The man laughed and said, "Have a good night."

"You too," Paris said as he turned and headed toward the hustle and bustle of Notting Hill.

Sydney was standing right there on the sidewalk. She'd run from the safe house and was still catching her breath. When Paris made eye contact with her, she subtly shook her head. "You don't know me," she whispered as Paris walked past her and down the street.

Less than a minute later, Anastasia Sorokin came through the gate, scanning the faces on the street for any sign of Paris. Sydney recognized her from the screengrab that Brooklyn had texted her. She wanted to make sure she didn't follow Paris.

"Hey," Anastasia said, noticing Sydney. "Have you seen anyone suspicious come through here in the last few minutes?"

Sydney played the part perfectly. "A boy just came running out of there."

"What did he look like?"

"Sixteen, seventeen years old, and he was wearing a green jacket," said Sydney. "Like the ones waiters wear at fancy restaurants."

Sorokin's eyes opened wide. "Which way did he go?"

"He ran right into the tube station," she said, pointing at an entrance for the London Underground.

"Thank you," said the woman, who hurried toward the station.

Meanwhile, Paris was a few blocks in the opposite direction, boarding a double decker bus. He took his seat on the top tier and saw his reflection in the window. He looked tired but relieved and perhaps a bit gleeful—a thrilling and successful mission.

"Hey, Kat?" he said into the comms as the bus pulled into traffic. "Remember when you said that being a spy wasn't like being in an action movie?"

"Yes," replied Kat, who'd now left the party and was walking down the street.

"You don't know what you're talking about."

The Volcano

REGINALD BANKS WASN'T ONE TO SCREAM or yell. He didn't need to be. If he was angry, it was more than obvious to whomever he was speaking because his cheeks would turn red, the veins on his forehead would pop out, and his voice would get lower, slower, and much more menacing. He was like a volcano that rumbled but rarely erupted.

That's how it was as he addressed four members of his staff in the aftermath of Tabitha's birthday. What had started as a perfect evening had gone terribly wrong, and he wanted answers. "Can any of you explain what happened?" he asked. "Or should I just fire you all?"

He was in his office, and standing across the desk from him were his personal assistant, his home manager, his security chief, and the stage director for the concert. None of them wanted to be the first to speak, but after an awkward pause, his personal assistant broke the silence.

"With regard to which occurrence?" she asked.

"Oh, that's right," Reg responded sarcastically. "Tonight was such a colossal succession of embarrassments that I have to be more specific so we can address them one at a time. Why don't we start off with someone telling me why a barrage of fireworks went off in the middle of a love song? You know, the reason my daughter's sobbing in her bedroom and the Kensington and Chelsea Borough Council has already called a dozen times."

All eyes turned to the stage director, a burly man named Nigel, who'd overseen KB5's last two concert tours.

"I'm afraid we don't know why," he said. "We've used the same software for more than two hundred concerts, and nothing like that's ever happened. Although, Trevor thinks it may have something to do with this." He held up Brooklyn's tiny transmitter.

"Who's Trevor?" demanded Reg.

"The front-of-house mixer," answered Nigel. "He found this plugged into the USB port on his console." He handed the device to Reg. "He's never seen it before and has no idea where it came from."

Reg examined it and asked, "What is it?"

"I don't know," answered Nigel.

"Do you?" Reg asked the security chief.

"No," the man admitted. "Although I do know some people who should be able to tell me."

"Then show it to them and find out," Reg said as he handed him the device.

"Of course, sir."

"Now, what do we know about this busboy?" asked Reg.

"The caterer insists he wasn't one of their employees," answered the house manager, a woman in her midforties with short black hair, an angular face, and perfect posture. "They assembled their staff afterward and everyone was accounted for, as was every uniform."

"So, what's the explanation?" asked Reg. "Some zealous KB5 fan got his hands on a uniform so that he could sneak in and see the band up close?"

"That would've been my first guess," answered the

house manager. "Except the caterer said the boy was wearing a wristband that would have allowed him into the party anyway. So why go to all the trouble of masquerading as a busboy?" She paused for a moment as she reached into the inner pocket of her jacket. "Then there's this."

She pulled out a small photograph and handed it to him.

"I believe this is the young man changing into the uniform after he'd already crashed the celebration," she said.

"Where was this taken?" he asked.

"In one of the photo booths that were set up on the back lawn," she replied.

"You're saying that he didn't dress up as a busboy so that he could sneak into the party," Reg said, "but that he snuck into the party so that he could dress up as a busboy?"

"It appears so."

Reg's mood was changing from anger to concern. Rather than a series of inept mistakes, this appeared to be part of something bigger, perhaps something sinister, that he couldn't quite piece together. He carefully studied the photo, looking for clues in it. There weren't many, as Paris's face was almost entirely obscured while he turned the jacket inside out.

"Do we think the boy and the fireworks are related?" asked Reg. "Or are they two separate events that happened to coincide?"

"At this point it's impossible to know for sure," said the security chief. "But the fireworks did go off at the exact moment the busboy was confronted by the caterer. I'm not a big fan of coincidence, so I would lean toward related."

"And you said the twins chased him?"

"Yes," answered the man. "Anastasia pursued him all the way to the Notting Hill Gate tube station, but she couldn't find him in the crowd."

"Maybe we can help with that," said Reg. "There's CCTV for the entire London Underground."

"We're quietly working the back channels as we speak," said the security chief. "We should have access to that footage tomorrow."

"Good," said Reg. "I want the caterer and Anastasia both to look at them." He turned his attention back to the photo, studying Paris for any possible hint to his identity. "I want them to figure out who this boy is."

"Speaking of CCTV," the security chief said reluctantly. "There is another development that's rather troubling."

"Even more troubling than all this?" asked Reg, his cheeks quickly turning a dark shade of crimson. "Dare I ask?"

The man handed his phone to Reg.

"This is a security feed from tonight," he said. "Here in the house."

Reg looked down at the screen and saw an image of the third-floor hallway.

"An empty hallway?" said Reg. "Why is this troubling?"

"Press play."

Reg tapped the screen, and the video began to play. At first, it was just an image of the hall, but then, out of nowhere, Sir Reg materialized in the middle of the screen as he approached his office door and opened it.

"What just happened?" he demanded. "How did I just appear like that?"

The security chief nervously cleared his throat and said, "It seems as though the cameras were hacked."

Reg looked up from the screen, his eyes filled with rage. He could no longer contain his anger. The volcano was about to blow.

Skreich

KINLOCH, SCOTLAND—ONE MONTH LATER

A SCREAM FILLED THE AIR.

It was Brooklyn, and it brought a satisfied smile to her face. She closed her eyes, took a deep breath, and did it again. This time it was so loud she could feel it in her arms and legs. After that, she did it twice more.

She wasn't the only one. Most of the students at Kinloch Abbey had stepped out onto the quad to flex their vocal cords. It was an annual ritual designed to release stress on the final day of exams. Although few of her classmates matched Brooklyn's volume and intensity.

"That. Felt. Good," she said to Kat, who was standing with her. "Really, really good."

"It looked like it did," Kat responded. "Each time."

"I love this tradition. What do they call it again?"

"Skreich," answered Kat. "It's Scots for 'scream.' I think it has something to do with a Robert Burns poem."

"Ugh," Brooklyn said with a sour expression. "I don't ever want to hear that name again. My brain is bursting with Robert Burns."

Burns was the most famous poet in Scottish history and a big part of the English exam Brooklyn was about to take. She'd been cramming so hard for the test that his poetry was now a giant jumble in her head.

"Well, in a few hours you can forget all about him," Kat replied. "At least until the end of summer."

This brought a smile to Brooklyn's face. "I'll *skreich* to that."

She couldn't wait for summer to begin. For the first time in her life, school had become a struggle, and she needed the break. She'd been playing catch-up ever since she arrived from New York in the middle of the year.

She'd gone from an overcrowded and underfunded school in the heart of Crown Heights to a postcard-perfect campus sprawled across one hundred fifty acres in the Scottish Highlands. Everything about it was a culture shock. Her old school had bars on the windows while this one had a moat around the castle ruins. She'd had to learn British history from scratch and figure out how to use the metric system in science and math. Color was now spelled "colour," biscuits meant "cookies," and seventh grade was called S1. It was enough to make her head spin.

On top of all this, she had to adjust to life as a spy. Afternoons and weekends were spent learning new skills, like how to build an explosive device out of a toaster; and she was repeatedly pulled out of school to go on missions. All these things had been good for MI6 and the United Kingdom, but none gave her the necessary skills to analyze a poem written about a mouse in 1785. (Or rather, "analyse" with an *s*, because the Brits had to spell some words differently, just to make her life even more confusing.)

That's exactly what she was asked to do an hour and a half after the skreich as she took her English final. She stared at the highlighted section of the poem and shook her head in frustration.

The best-laid schemes o' Mice an' Men
Gang aft agley

"How can I possibly write an essay about something when I don't even understand what the words mean?" she asked herself. Or, at least, she intended to ask herself. In actuality, she blurted it out loud.

"I'm sorry, Ms. White," she said to the teacher. "I meant to think that, not say it."

"It's quite all right, Christina," the woman said, calling Brooklyn by the cover name MI6 had created for her at school. "I understand the frustration."

They were able to have this conversation because they were the only two people left in the room. The rest of the class had already finished the exam and gone off to start summer vacation. Brooklyn took this as yet another sign that she still had a great deal of catching up to do. Perhaps sensing this, the teacher offered some encouragement.

"I know it may not seem like it at the moment," she said. "But you've done a great job in this class. I've been impressed by your work."

Brooklyn swallowed a laugh. "This test should fix that."

"I doubt it," Ms. White replied. "You need to give yourself a break. You entered one of Scotland's most academically challenging schools in the middle of the year. The curriculum is rigorous and completely alien to anything with which you were accustomed. You're experiencing growing pains. That doesn't mean they don't hurt and aren't difficult, but you'll get past them."

"I hope you're right," Brooklyn said. "I mean, I have a plan and I study, and I think I've got it down, and then, when I take the test, everything goes haywire."

The teacher flashed a sly smile and said, "So you're saying that your best-laid schemes *gang aft agley.*"

Brooklyn gave her a wide-eyed look when she realized she was referencing the line in the poem. "That's it," she said, frustrated as she now remembered studying it. "It's about your plans going wrong and the unpredictability of life." She shook her head. "How'd I forget that?"

Ms. White nodded to the clock and said, "Luckily you remembered while you've still got four and a half minutes remaining."

Over the next four minutes and twenty-seven seconds, Brooklyn wrote as much as she could about the meaning of the poem. When she was done, she put her pencil down and said, "You're a goddess, Ms. White. You belong right up there on Mount Olympus."

"I usually think of myself more as a lesser deity or a sprite," she said, "but who am I to argue with someone such as yourself. Have a lovely summer, Christina."

"You too," Brooklyn responded as she handed in her exam. "Thank you for everything. Despite what this test might indicate, I really did learn a lot in your class."

Brooklyn exited the building and was pleasantly surprised to see her fellow City Spies waiting for her on a pair of benches. They stood up and offered good-natured applause, congratulating her on finishing her first year at Kinloch. She reciprocated by taking an exaggerated bow.

"How was the test?" asked Kat.

"I *think* I passed," answered Brooklyn. "But just barely."

"Just barely passing is still passing," Rio said. "I know that from experience."

"I'm starving," Brooklyn announced. "Who wants to get some pizza?"

"This will have to hold you over for now," Sydney said, pulling an apple from her backpack and tossing it to her. "We have to go to the chapel and watch Kat win an award."

"Oh, that's right," Brooklyn said as she bit into the fruit. "I forgot about the prize-giving ceremony. Hooray, Kat!"

"It's not definite that I'm going to win," Kat said modestly. "There are quite a few excellent maths students at this school."

Paris laughed. "There are three things about this world that I know to be true," he said as they started walking across the campus. "Brazil will always have an exceptional football team. You can never count on a sunny day in Scotland. And Kat will win the Isaac Newton medal for mathematics every year she's at Kinloch."

"You should've seen it the first time," Sydney said to Brooklyn. "There were all these posh boys about to head off to Oxford and Cambridge who were just certain they were going to win. They were so smug and full of themselves, but whose name was called? Our Kat's! An eleven-year-old girl from Nepal. I thought they were going to pass out." Sydney cackled at the memory.

"You know, if Brooklyn's really hungry, then maybe we should just go get pizza instead," Kat offered. "I don't have to actually be there to receive the medal. I can pick it up later."

"You're going," Paris said firmly. "We all are."

"I agree," said Rio. "And you know I *never* pass up pizza."

"Why would you miss it?" Brooklyn asked Kat.

"The winner's supposed to say a little something,"

said Sydney. "And you know how Kat is in front of a crowd."

"The first time she won it, the speech was just two words," said Paris. "'Thank you.' Then, last year, she trimmed that down to one: 'Thanks.' This year I'm expecting nothing more than a nod and a wave. Perhaps some interpretive dance and mime."

"I just don't see what public speaking and mathematics have to do with each other," Kat protested. "I'm more than happy to let my numbers speak for themselves."

"Then don't say anything," suggested Brooklyn. "Just take the award and let out a skreich. After all, this is the day for it."

The chapel was a centerpiece of the campus. Hundreds of years old, the stone building hosted school assemblies as well as weekly religious services. Normally, students sat by grade with their classmates, but at the prize-giving ceremony, they were allowed to sit with whomever they wanted, an indication the school year was over and things were looser.

The team sat together, ready to share their enthusiasm when Kat's name was called. They considered it confirmation of her impending victory that Mother and Monty had snuck into the visitors' section on the upper floor. They'd obviously gotten a heads-up from the school.

"For a pair of covert agents, you'd expect them to be better at hiding," joked Rio.

"They're not spies right now," Sydney said, smiling. "Today, they're just family. Goofy with pride, just like the other parents."

Paris turned to Brooklyn. "Prepare to pose for pictures afterward."

No one was surprised when Kat won the Newton medal, not even the posh boys about to head off to Oxford and Cambridge. By now, everyone at Kinloch knew that her math skills were otherworldly. She did shock the rest of the team, however, when she gave what was, by her standards, a long-winded acceptance speech:

"Thank you all very much. I'm honored."

"Seven words," Paris said to the others, holding up as many fingers to punctuate the point. "Seven!"

If Paris was surprised by Kat's speech, he was downright gobsmacked to hear his own name called not once but twice, later in the ceremony. First, he was recognized as the Scottish interscholastic chess champion. He'd won the tournament several months earlier but had no idea they were going to mention it now. Then he was awarded the Burns medal.

This was a shocker.

So much so that he didn't even move when they called his name. He sat there clapping, expecting someone else to stand up until Sydney turned to him and said, "That's you! *You're* the winner!"

Ms. White was presenting the award on behalf of the English department, and she spoke about it as Paris made his belated and somewhat stunned walk down the aisle.

"The Robert Burns medal is not solely about academic achievement," she said. "It also comes with a responsibility. It is given every year to a returning student who excels at writing with the expectation that that student will serve in the role as Kinloch Abbey's poet laureate. He will craft poetry in response to world events and campus happenings and will recite them for all of us next year at assemblies such as this. I cannot think of a more deserving recipient."

Paris still had a dazed look on his face when he reached her and she handed him the medal.

"Congratulations," she said.

He looked at it, still disbelieving, and said, "Wow." The honesty of his reaction drew a laugh from the crowd, and he was suddenly self-conscious. "Thank you," he added meekly before returning to his seat.

This brought more laughs, and Ms. White added, "He's no doubt saving all his best words for the poetry."

After the ceremony, Paris was still stunned when they were standing outside and he was getting congratulatory handshakes from schoolmates. Kat, however, was teasing him mercilessly.

"Three words," she said. "You give me grief about my acceptance speeches and when the time comes for you to give one, all you've got is three words. And one of them was 'wow.' I don't know if that should even count. It's just an interjection."

"I still can't believe I won it," Paris said.

"Yeah," added Brooklyn, "just when I thought I'd gotten Robert Burns out of my life."

Moments later, a joyful Mother and Monty arrived on the scene and were all hugs and high fives. They took some pictures of Kat and Paris with their medals in front of the chapel and then a few group shots of everybody.

"I believe this calls for some serious celebrating," Monty said. "As well as an abundance of baked goods."

"I like the sound of that," said Paris. "Maybe I'll write a poem about pineapple upside-down cake."

"Let me guess," said Kat. "The first line will just be, 'Wow!'"

"We'll pick up the ingredients on the way home," Monty replied. "I'm so proud of all of you."

As everyone headed to the parking lot, Mother pulled Brooklyn aside.

"Actually, you and I are going to take the train and catch up with them later," he said.

"Why?" asked Brooklyn.

"I'm not exactly sure," Mother answered. "But before the ceremony, the headmaster said he'd like to speak to us."

"*Us* as in you and me?" asked Brooklyn.

"Yes."

She slumped in defeat. Despite their many differences, one thing was true of her school in New York and this one in Scotland: getting called to the office was rarely a good sign.

She felt like skreiching all over again.

The Best-Laid Schemes

LONG BEFORE HE BECAME HEADMASTER at Kinloch Abbey, Dr. Christopher Graham was an army intelligence officer with the Royal Scots. His work there had been so impressive that, when he left the military, the Secret Intelligence Service sent a senior agent named Gertrude Shepherd to recruit him for MI6. He politely declined, saying that his heart was in education, but promised that he would always help in any way that he could.

Years later, that agent returned to take him up on

his offer. Shepherd, a legendary spy known throughout the service simply as Tru, was Mother's supervisor and one of only a handful of people who knew the details of Operation City Spies. She needed a school that could provide an elite education for, as she put it, "some very special children."

Graham didn't know what these students did for MI6, but he knew enough not to ask any questions and to make sure their teachers didn't either. That's why he chose his words carefully when Mother and Brooklyn sat down in his office.

"Thank you both for coming in on such short notice," he said. "Can I get you some tea or biscuits?"

"None for me, thank you," said Mother.

They both looked at Brooklyn, who just shook her head, a forlorn expression on her face.

"Okay, then let's get started," Graham said. "I appreciate that we have a special arrangement with regard to you, the children, and our mutual friends in London. I assure you that I do not want to interfere with that in any way. But, as headmaster of this school, my highest priorities must always be the health and welfare of our students and the success of their academic lives."

"Those are my priorities too," said Mother. "What did you want to discuss?"

The headmaster looked at Brooklyn, but she avoided eye contact and looked down at the floor instead.

"I'm concerned about Christina," he said, calling her by the only name he'd ever known for her. "She joined us midyear, which is always a challenge, and she's missed a considerable amount of class time since then. As a result, her grades have suffered, and I thought that since you're her guardian—"

"Father," corrected Mother.

"What's that?"

"I'm her *father*," Mother answered proudly. "I adopted Christina and the others a few months ago."

The headmaster smiled broadly. "That's wonderful news. Congratulations to you all."

"Thank you," said Mother. "It was a big—"

"How bad are they?" Brooklyn asked, interrupting. "My grades, I mean. Did I fail?"

"No, you didn't," he said. "But, here at Kinloch, we set the bar quite a bit higher than pass or fail. Your teachers feel as though you're not performing to your full ability."

Mother put a reassuring hand on Brooklyn's knee as he asked, "Is this across the board with all her classes?"

"Her computing teacher says she's extraordinary," answered Graham. "But, other than that, she could use help in all her core subjects. I think there have been flourishes of great potential mixed in with a fair amount of scrambling and struggle." He turned to Brooklyn, "Would you say that's accurate?"

She nodded reluctantly. "Yes, but I try really hard."

"Of course you do," he said. "There's no question about your effort."

"It's just that everything's so new," she explained. "I didn't take any algebra back in New York. History here is all about kings and queens and the Middle Ages. And I'd never even heard of Robert Burns before. Now, I'm expected to recite his poetry in Scots dialect. It's a lot."

"It's more than a lot," said Graham. "It's overwhelming. But, unfortunately, these elements are the building blocks of a Kinloch education. They're essential."

"And, even though I try hard, I can't seem to learn them," she said. "So, what does that mean? Are you kicking me out of school?"

Graham gave her a surprised look. "Quite the contrary," he said. "We'd like you to move in. At least for a month."

"What?" asked Brooklyn.

"We have an intensive summer program called Kinloch Academy," he explained. "It helps students strengthen their scholastic foundation."

"That's just a fancy name for summer school," Brooklyn said, getting agitated. "Summer school is for people who fail."

"No one's saying that," Mother said reassuringly. "No one at all."

"I'm twelve years old," she replied, her frustration building. "Do you know how many schools I've attended? Kinloch's number ten. And believe me, the other nine were nothing like this. There weren't Newton medals or school poet laureates. So I'm sorry that it's taking me a while to memorize which kings were Plantagenets and which ones were Tudors."

"Christina, you have every reason to be frustrated," said Graham. "But do you realize how impressive it is that you've done as well as you have? Can you imagine how you'll thrive if you aren't always in a state of having to catch up? I'm confident this would alleviate that frustration. You can soar here."

"Does she have to move in order to participate?" asked Mother.

"I'm afraid so," answered Graham. "The program's intensive and immersive. In addition to daytime classes, there are evening lectures and discussion groups as well as several overnight trips. It wouldn't work as a day student."

"I don't want to do it," Brooklyn said to Mother. "We're just getting used to living together. We just became a family. This would make me an outsider all over again."

Mother thought for a moment and looked to the headmaster. "Is it mandatory?" he asked. "Does she need to attend in order to return to Kinloch next year?"

"No," Graham responded. "It's not mandatory."

"Great, then that settles it," Brooklyn said under her breath.

"But when Tru came to me," Graham continued, leaning forward to emphasize his point, "she said that she was sending Kinloch some very special children and that we were to provide them with an elite education." He looked at Brooklyn. "There's no doubt that Christina is very special; I'm just trying to keep our end of the bargain."

"I appreciate that," said Mother. "We both do. Can we think about it overnight and give you our answer tomorrow?"

"Of course," said Graham.

"I don't need to think abo—" Brooklyn started to mutter, but Mother gave her a withering look, and she stopped. "Sorry."

"Thank you, Dr. Graham," Mother said.

"Thank you," the headmaster replied. "And congratulations again on the adoptions. That's wonderful news."

Brooklyn stayed in a funk and didn't say a word for the entire walk to Kinloch station, but as they waited for the train to Aisling, she mumbled, "Kat and Paris both win medals and look at loser me."

"I don't know what you see," said Mother, "but when I look at you, I see someone who's absolutely amazing."

"But you think I should go for the extra schooling, don't you?"

He nodded. "I do."

"That's a month away from home," she said. "I mean, I finally have a home, a real home, and that would mean spending a month away."

"The beauty of a real home is that it's still there for you if you go away for a bit. That's one of its best features."

"And a month without any spy training."

"That's not a worry," he said. "You won't lose a step. You're a natural."

"Too bad I'm not a natural at this," she said. They heard the train approaching, and Brooklyn let out a deep sigh. "Okay, I'll do it. You convinced me."

"I did?" he asked, perplexed. "But I hadn't even given you my big speech yet. I was still working it out in my head."

"I don't need it," she replied.

"Then how did I convince you?" he asked.

The train was almost there, and when she looked up at him, he could see that her eyes were glassy, on the verge of tears. "Earlier, when you told Dr. Graham that you were my father, not my guardian. I've never felt that way before. Looked after. Taken care of. I trust you. If you think I should do it, then I should do it."

Mother put his arm around her shoulder and gave it a fatherly squeeze as they stepped onto the train.

Land of the Midnight Sun

MURMANSK OBLAST, RUSSIA

IT WAS JUST AFTER TWO IN THE MORNING as the old supply truck rattled along a mostly forgotten roadway, its asphalt scarred from years of neglect. Despite the hour, there was still a haze of daylight this far north of the Arctic Circle as the truck made its once weekly journey to deliver fresh produce to the remote outpost known as "Kola-27."

This had once been home to a thriving military base, an essential link in the Soviet Union's nuclear line of defense. Rather than a proper name, it was given only a region and a number because it was what was referred to as a "closed city," so secret its location couldn't be listed on maps and planes were forbidden from flying over it. Technically, it had been against the law to even speak of it in public.

Now, Kola-27 was a ghost town with abandoned buildings and empty streets where all that thrived were the weeds that had overgrown the sidewalks and parks. A city without people in a land without sunsets.

All that remained was a small detachment of soldiers left to look after the remnants of the base. They provided maintenance for the radar system, operated a communication center, and guarded the storage facility that still held nuclear weapons for the Northern Fleet. With no city left to support them, the essentials of living had to be shipped in or delivered, which was why the truck had driven all the way from Murmansk nearly three hours away. It stopped at a checkpoint on the edge of the base where a lone guard manned the gate.

"You're late," chided the soldier as the driver rolled down his window.

"I know," grumbled the driver. "It's this truck. It's ancient. It broke down about fifty kilometers away. I had to fix it on the side of the road."

"You should've called," said the guard. "We have a schedule."

"I did call," said the driver. "Or at least I tried to. But I couldn't get any service out in the middle of nowhere."

The guard nodded. "I know how that is," he said. "Unfortunately, everyone's gone to bed. There's no one to let you into the mess hall."

"*You* could let me," suggested the driver.

"No," the guard scoffed. "I can't leave my post."

The driver considered this for a moment. "Understood," he said. "I'll go back to Murmansk. They'll send another truck in four or five days. You'll just go without fruit and vegetables until then." He reached down to shift gears and put the vehicle into reverse, but the soldier stopped him.

"Wait a second," he said. He went back into his guardhouse momentarily and returned with a set of keys. "You know where everything goes?"

"Of course," said the man.

"You can unload it yourself," the guard said, handing him the keys. "Bring these back when you're done."

The driver nodded and, once the soldier lifted the gate, drove onto the base. He tried to appear frustrated about having to do all the work by himself but secretly was overjoyed. Everything had gone according to plan.

That's why he'd waited until the middle of the night when there wouldn't be any help. He knew that the guard couldn't leave his post, but also that he wouldn't want his fellow soldiers to be without fresh produce. The driver had forced the soldier into an impossible situation and been rewarded with a treasure—a full set of keys. This meant that while he unloaded a week's worth of fruits and vegetables into the mess hall, the three Umbra operatives hiding in the back of his truck had total access to the base.

A few hours later, the soldiers awoke and arrived for breakfast. They were pleased to discover the food exactly where it was supposed to be. It wasn't until later in the week that anyone realized three of the nuclear warheads were missing.

Tru Calling

AISLING, SCOTLAND

PARIS WAS ONLY HALF-AWAKE AS HE walked down the stairs and was greeted by an unmistakable and completely irresistible aroma.

"Is that bacon?" he said, perking up, equally confused and delighted.

The smell was mystifying because bacon was at the top of Monty's so-called "No Fry" list, which meant it was banned from the house. She could *maybe* be talked into it for a holiday or special occasion, but a random Tuesday in June? Never.

This required further investigation, and as Paris stepped into the kitchen, his surprise turned to astonishment when he saw who was at the stove.

"Tru?" he said, confused. "What are you doing here?"

Standing nearly six feet tall, with a stylish bob of silver-gray hair, Gertrude Shepherd cut a dashing figure. Always impeccably dressed, her tailored black pants and shirt were what you might expect of a high-ranking member of MI6's senior directorate. Less predictable was the cotton-candy pink KEEP CALM AND BAKE ON apron she wore over them as she made eggs, bacon, sausage, beans, and fried bread.

"What does it look like I'm doing?" she asked.

"Cooking breakfast," he said, still trying to make sense of the scene.

"Good for you, Paris. Nice to see your spy training hasn't gone to waste. Now, be a dear and stir these while I tend the eggs."

Paris took a wooden spoon and began to stir the pot of baked beans. "Does Monty know you're making bacon and sausages?" he asked. "Because those are on her banned list."

"There are many privileges that come with my position at MI6," Tru said. "In addition to the security clearances, intelligence briefings, and consultations with the prime minister, I also get to eat what I want. Besides, don't forget that I outrank Monty. She has phenomenal skills when it comes to cryptography but is sorely lacking in her appreciation for the importance of a full English breakfast."

"Maybe that's because I'm Scottish and not English," Monty said, entering the room with perfect timing. "Or perhaps because I fully appreciate what a plate full of fried bacon, fried eggs, fried sausage, and fried bread does to one's arteries. Tell me, do you also fry the orange juice that you drink with it?"

"No," Tru said. "But we would if we could. Lovely to see you, Monty."

"Lovely to see you, too. Welcome back to the FARM."

The FARM was the Foundation for Atmospheric Research and Monitoring. As far as the general public was concerned, it was a weather station that occupied a centuries-old manor house overlooking the North Sea. What they didn't know was that the sprawling three-story home was also a covert spy base owned and operated by the British Secret Intelligence Service.

Originally, it had been a listening post that eavesdropped on the Soviet Union. Now, it was a cryptography center, ideal because the supercomputers used to predict weather patterns were identical to those necessary for high-level code-breaking.

The FARM was also home to the City Spies. That addition was Tru's idea.

For her, there were three factors that made it the perfect fit. The first was its location in northern Scotland, which put it far from the prying eyes of MI6 headquarters. The second was its proximity to an elite school with a headmaster who understood the world of espionage and knew how to keep government secrets. But most importantly, the FARM already had Monty, who was, according to Tru, "an excellent spy, an amazing cryptographer, and an even better person."

Breakfast was a hit with everyone, including Monty who told Tru, "It may not be healthy, but it sure is delicious. If you ever get tired of being a spymaster, you'd make an excellent fry cook."

"What do you think I did every weekend at university?" Tru replied. "My fashion sense far exceeded any allowance my parents were willing to provide. Back then, I had a saying, 'Looking good means cooking good.'"

Once the food was eaten and the dishes were cleaned, everyone headed down to the basement where there was a concealed room known as a "priest hole." Hundreds of years earlier, priest holes were built in castles and manor homes as hiding spots for people who were persecuted for their religious beliefs. At the FARM, MI6 had converted the priest hole into a high-tech, high-security situation room that housed cutting-edge equipment like the supercomputer Brooklyn had nicknamed Beny.

"So, what's up?" Sydney asked Tru once they'd all taken their seats around the sleek black conference table. "What brings you all the way from London to make our breakfast?"

"Paris does," Tru answered. "Or at least the files he found in Reginald Banks's office. We've spent the last month following leads from them."

Paris couldn't help but smile.

"Unfortunately, they've taken us to some troublesome conclusions." Tru pressed a button and a picture appeared on a wall monitor. It was a photograph of a Korean man in his early forties with thick black hair and horn-rimmed glasses. He had a serious expression, but it was offset by kind eyes and the hint of a smile on his lips.

"Meet Park Jin-sun," Tru said.

"He's the scientist in the files," said Paris.

"Correct," said Tru. "He's also a rising star in the North Korean nuclear weapons program. He's of great interest to several countries, including our own, and we think that Sir Reg wants to flip him."

"What does that mean?" Brooklyn asked.

"It means he's trying to get Park to abandon his comrades in North Korea and bring all of his top secret knowledge about their nuclear weapons, missiles, and bombs to work for someone else."

"Like who?" asked Rio. "One of those countries?"

"I'm afraid it's much worse than that," she said. "It appears Reg is working for Umbra."

Umbra was a global syndicate made up of criminals, terrorists, mercenaries, and rogue intelligence agents. They were driven by profit, not politics, and run by a shadowy figure known only as "Le Fantôme." The organization's involvement deepened everyone's level of concern.

"We've long suspected that he has had business dealings with them," said Tru. "That's why we bugged the Fabergé egg in his office. But up until now, it's been limited to money laundering and influence peddling. This is a serious, and extremely dangerous, escalation in their relationship."

"How confident are you that that's his plan?" asked Mother.

"We're MI6," said Tru. "We are always confident, even when we shouldn't be."

"How would he even get a chance to flip him?" Mother wondered. "North Korea doesn't let their top scientists go anywhere they can be tempted to change sides."

"Normally, no," said Tru. "But they're making a pair of exceptions for Park."

She pressed the button and changed the photo on the monitor to one of Park with a teenage boy. They were sitting on a bench, and both were smiling for the camera.

"Here he is with his son," said Tru.

"Why does he look familiar?" Paris asked. "I feel like I've seen him before."

"Of course you have," said Sydney. "You went through the files."

"No," said Paris. "He wasn't in there."

"Then where else would you see a kid who lives in North Korea?" asked Rio.

Paris's eyes opened wide when he realized the answer. "It's Park Dae-jung!" he exclaimed in a eureka moment. "The scientist's son is Park Dae-jung."

"Very good, Paris," said Tru. "Very good indeed."

Everyone else at the table was completely confused.

"Okay," said Kat. "Who's Park Dae-jung?"

"He's a chess prodigy," said Paris.

"And you know this how?" asked Brooklyn.

"Because I'm a member of multiple online chess discussion groups," he said. "He's one of the biggest mysteries in the game right now."

"What's so mysterious about him?" asked Monty.

"There's no question that he's good. I mean, he's a legitimate prodigy," Paris answered. "But it's hard to say how good he is because there isn't really a chess culture in North Korea. There aren't any big tournaments or high-level opponents for him there. Technically, he isn't even a grandmaster, although he's certainly good enough to be one."

"If he's good enough, then why isn't he?" asked Brooklyn.

"Because you have to do well in tournaments against competitors from at least three different chess federations," Paris explained. "You need to beat international competition."

"Which is a problem for the North Korean government," said Tru. "They want to show him off because his chess prowess brings glory to the country, but to do that they need to let him leave North Korea. So, they're allowing him to play in Russia and China, their two most trusted allies."

Mother smiled as he saw where this was headed. "And his father travels with him."

"He insists on it," answered Tru. "Park's wife died eight years ago, and he's extremely protective of his son. He won't let him go anywhere unless he goes with him. Which brings us back to Reg and how he plans to pull this off."

She pressed the button, and a video of Reginald Banks playing chess appeared on the screen. It was footage of him in college playing four separate games at once, walking from table to table, making quick, decisive moves.

"Chess is the only thing Sir Reg loves almost as much as he loves money," Tru said. "He's obsessed with it. This summer he's sponsoring the Around the World Chess Invitational, a series of youth events to be played in different countries in conjunction with the concert tour for his band, KB5. This includes tournaments in Moscow and Beijing."

"And will Dae-jung be playing in both of them?" asked Paris.

"Yes," said Tru, who smiled before adding, "and so will you."

"I will?" he answered, surprised.

"Operation Checkmate," Tru said. "It involves missions on two continents, deep undercover work, and a code so baffling that my team at Vauxhall Cross has declared it unbreakable. This is the biggest, most challenging, most complex mission the City Spies have undertaken." She scanned their faces around the table and said, "That is, if you're up for it."

And just like that, everybody's excitement meter went into overdrive.

"Oh, yeah," Paris said, brimming with confidence. "We're up for it."

Operation Checkmate

ALL THE CITY SPIES WERE EXCITED ABOUT the mission, but each was excited in their own way. Paris was ecstatic because it seemed like he'd automatically have the main role since he'd be playing in the tournaments alongside Park Dae-jung. This, of course, instantly made Sydney jealous because she always wanted to be the alpha. Still, she was thrilled about going to Moscow and Beijing and confident that she'd play a big part. Kat was hooked the moment Tru said there was an unbreakable code, and Rio had his fingers crossed that with a mission this big he'd be given real responsibility for a change.

Then there was Brooklyn.

She was perhaps the most excited of all. She'd already played a key role in the team's two most recent missions, and this was going to be bigger still. Better yet, this was her ticket out of summer school. Rather than sitting in a classroom studying algebra, she'd be racing across two continents on an adventure. The morning had taken a decided turn for the better.

"This operation has separate missions to Moscow and Beijing," Tru said. "You'll need to approach it on multiple fronts, which I'll discuss in just a moment. And, it has two very straightforward objectives. The first and most important is to make sure that Park Jin-sun does not join forces with Umbra. We simply cannot let that happen."

"And the second?" asked Monty.

Tru flashed the smile of a greedy politician. "Make sure he joins up with us instead. That way we don't have to worry about Umbra taking another run at him, and we'll have valuable insight into the capabilities of North Korea's nuclear program."

"You want us to flip him to the UK?" asked Mother.

"We think he's ripe for the picking," Tru responded.

"What makes you say that?"

"First of all, he's not militant. He attended the Moscow Engineering Physics Institute, and his time there indicated that he wanted to study nuclear physics for use in energy, not weapons. The North Korean government didn't give him that choice, which he may resent and could explain why, unlike most of the other scientists in the program, he's not an officer in the army. Second, his wife died from tuberculosis, a huge problem in North Korea because of the low quality of their health care. It's widely accepted that he blames the government's ineffectiveness for her death. And the third reason, Dae-jung. Park wants a better life for his son, which he'd be certain to have if they defected to the West."

"How do you know all this?" asked Brooklyn.

"Those files are very thorough," she said. "As are the ones MI6 has put together. We targeted Park as a possible flip years ago because he's such a strong candidate. The North Koreans know this too, which is why they keep such a close eye on him. To be honest, we never thought we'd get near enough to have a chance. This would be a huge coup."

"You said there were multiple different fronts that we'd have to approach," said Monty. "What are they?"

"The first is the chess tournament," said Tru. "Paris qualified by virtue of his victory in the Scottish inter-scholastic. We've already entered him, but, as it stands now, he won't be playing in the same group as Dae-jung."

"Why not?" asked Rio.

"I'm sure my Elo rating's not high enough," said Paris.

"That's exactly right," said Tru.

"What's an Elo rating?" asked Brooklyn.

"It's the way the World Chess Federation rates a player's skill level," he explained. "At an elite tournament, Dae-jung would play in a group of the highest-ranked entrants. I'm good but not that good."

"Don't worry," said Tru. "We're going to fix that number right away."

"How?" asked Paris. "It's not like you can just hack into the federation's computers and change it."

"I bet I could," Brooklyn said confidently.

"Okay, yes, you could," said Paris. "But it wouldn't matter because it would be obvious whenever anyone pulled up my record. It's too easy to check. The only way I can raise it is by playing in a bunch of events and beating higher-ranked opponents."

"Four," said Tru.

"Four what?" asked Paris.

"Events," she answered. "We have mathematicians down at MI6 headquarters in Vauxhall Cross. They're not as sharp as Kat, but they're still pretty good with numbers, and they assure me that if you enter the right four tournaments over the next three weeks and win them all, then your rating will improve just enough to put you in the highest group."

"*Win them all?*" said Paris. "That's easier said than done."

"If spy work were easy, everyone would do it," she responded. "But don't worry, we've gotten you an excellent coach to help raise your game. His name is Barnaby Fitch."

"The five-time Scottish champion?" Paris asked.

"By all accounts he's a superb teacher."

"Who also happens to be in prison," Paris responded, incredulous.

"What?" gasped Monty.

"As luck would have it, he received an early parole just last week," Tru said with a wink. "And believe me when I say that he's very motivated to help you play well."

"Why do I feel like *luck* had nothing to do with it," Mother said.

"You got him released from prison?" Paris asked.

"He's the best," she said. "And the best is what we need."

"Why was he in pri—" Monty started to ask.

"Don't worry," Tru said, anticipating the question. "Strictly white-collar crime. Paris is completely safe as long as they don't start trading stocks and bonds." She turned her attention back to Paris. "He's going to teach you and train you and drill you mercilessly. And you're going to win those four tournaments."

"I'll try my best," he said.

"Do or do not," said Tru. "There is no try."

Paris laughed. "Did you seriously just quote Yoda to me?"

"Why not?" Tru smiled. "Jedis and spies have a lot in common, don't you think?"

"Except I don't think the Force is going to help me win those tournaments," Paris replied.

"You don't need it," she said. "You'll win. I know it in my bones. And when you do, you'll get moved into the top group alongside Dae-jung. In Moscow, you'll befriend him, and Mother will get to know his father. It's a completely natural setting, the perfect position to keep an eye out for anyone from Umbra, and an ideal situation for Mother to start recruiting Park for MI6. It's a win-win situation."

"Actually, it's more like a win-win-win-win situation," Mother joked.

"What's the second front?" asked Monty. "And does it also include a fortunate parolee, or is there a jailbreak involved?"

"No one behind bars on this one," Tru said. "It's all about Sydney."

Sydney's eyes opened wide with anticipation. She already liked the sound of it.

"Tell me, dear," Tru continued. "Are you familiar with a website called *All Roads Lead to Audrey*?"

"Are you kidding?" said Sydney. "I'm obsessed with it. I read it every day."

"I've never heard of it," said Paris

"That's because it's the opposite of an online chess discussion group," joked Sydney. "It's a teen lifestyle site that focuses on fashion, health, trends, politics—everything. It's run by a woman named Francesca Lloyd. She's young and amazing, a fashion icon and an activist. She's a hero of mine."

"Lovely girl, Frankie," said Tru.

"Wait," Sydney said, suddenly geeking out. "You know her? You call her *Frankie*?"

"She used to work for me at MI6," said Tru. "That's why she's so good at finding out all those secrets."

"How does this relate to the mission?" asked Mother.

"Sir Reg is devastated about the events that occurred at his daughter's birthday party." Tru gave Brooklyn a wink. "I believe there was an unexpected fireworks display."

Everyone laughed.

"Anyway, in a bid to make it up to her, he's letting dear Tabitha travel along for part of the KB5 tour this summer so she can jet-set and hang out backstage at the concerts. He wants her to feel like a star, so *All Roads Lead to Audrey* is assigning a reporter who will travel with her to Russia in order to document it all for the website."

"No way," said Sydney, getting even more excited. "No way! Please tell me that I'm that reporter!"

"I know your birthday's not until next month," Tru said, smiling, "but consider this my present."

Sydney didn't say anything; she just stood up, raised her arms in triumph, and did a slow victory lap around the table.

"The third front's in Russia," Tru continued. She

pressed a button, and a new picture appeared on the monitor, "and involves these two."

"The twins," said Kat, recognizing the sisters from Tabitha's party.

"Their names are Anastasia and Sasha Sorokin. They trained at the Bolshoi Academy in Moscow and came to London looking to dance with the Royal Ballet. Injuries sidelined their performing careers, and they wound up doing some choreography for Reg's record label. This led to a much more lucrative position as part of the Banks family's personal protection team. One of them is with Tabitha Banks anytime she goes out in public."

"But the twins are here in the UK," said Paris. "And you said this front was in Russia."

Tru clicked the button again, and now the screen featured a photo of a man in his midthirties. He was a classic tough guy with muscled arms, a thick neck, and a face that looked like it had been in its share of fights.

"Nicholas Sorokin," she said.

"Is he their brother?" asked Sydney.

"Cousin. And not from the ballet side of the family. He's what's known in the underworld as a fixer. We think he's the most likely resource if Banks is looking for criminal support in Moscow."

"Why would he need criminal support?" asked Rio.

"Because the Russians are North Korea's allies," said Tru. "They are going to be looking after Park to make sure nothing happens to him. They're not just going to let him go with someone else. If he agrees to flip, he'll need to be smuggled out of the country. And if he refuses, Umbra may just kidnap him instead. Either way, Reg will likely need criminal help with strong local connections."

"Is Nicholas Sorokin part of Umbra?" asked Kat.

"We think so," said Tru, "but they don't exactly have employee records, so it's hard to be certain. That's why you, Rio, and Monty are going to go to Moscow ahead of the group to try to figure out what he's up to."

"We are?" said Rio, excited. "Just the three of us?"

"Yes," answered Tru. "He's suspicious and careful, but when he's not breaking the law, he works in a souvenir shop the family owns near Red Square. He won't suspect you three. He'll just assume that you're tourists."

"What makes you think he'll be their fixer?" asked Mother.

"His criminal past and his connection with the twins put him in Sir Reg's orbit," Tru said. "And then there's the code, which is the fourth front on which we need to pursue this operation."

"This is the code that you said was *unbreakable*," said Kat.

Tru smiled. "Actually, a team of MI6 cryptologists said it's unbreakable. I just told you that to light a fire under you."

"Consider it lit," said Kat. "I want a crack at it."

"So do I," said Monty.

"Well, here you go," Tru responded. She pressed a button, and a series of vintage-style postcard images filled the screen. There were twelve of them, and they were brightly colored renditions of famous locations throughout Russia, including Moscow's Red Square and the Winter Palace in St. Petersburg.

"Every morning at 9:05 London time, a social media account posts one of these images. There's no pattern as to which, but it's always one of these twelve. Then, every day five minutes later, an IP address in Moscow accesses the picture and looks at it. We've traced the social media account to a group connected with Reg's record label, and we've traced the IP address to a souvenir shop near Red Square."

"Let me guess," said Sydney. "It's the shop the Sorokin family owns."

"That's right," Tru answered. "And here's where the

code comes in. The pictures are always identical except for this one of St. Basil's Cathedral."

The screen filled with eight images of St. Basil's. It was one of the most famous buildings in Russia and had nine so-called "onion domes," each with a different pair of patterned colors.

"These all look the same to me," said Rio.

"But they're not," Kat interjected. "The colors change on one of the domes."

"Sharp eye," said Tru. "And on the days when that picture's posted, Nicholas makes a flurry of calls, many to numbers belonging to people with known associations to Umbra."

Kat stood up and approached the monitor so that she could study it more closely. "Do you have all the posts that have been put up on this account?"

"Of course," said Tru.

"In chronological order?" asked Kat.

"All in a file for you to study."

"When was the last time the picture of St. Basil's was posted?" asked Mother.

"Four days ago," said Tru. "And here's what has us particularly worried. The following day, three nuclear warheads were stolen from a storage facility at Kola-27, a Russian military base near Murmansk. We don't know if the two events are related or not, but the thought that Umbra could be making a move to acquire nuclear materials and flip a nuclear scientist is terrifying."

Everyone was stunned by this development, and a quiet came over the room. Finally, Brooklyn broke the silence.

"What about me?" she asked. "Paris is going to be playing in the tournaments. Sydney is going undercover with *All Roads Lead to Audrey*, and Rio and Kat are headed to Moscow to spy on Nicholas Sorokin. What am I going to do?"

"I'm afraid you're going to be sitting this one out," Tru said. "You can certainly help try to break the code, and I expect you'll be part of the mission for Beijing, but you're not going into the field for Moscow."

Brooklyn couldn't believe it. "You're leaving me here?"

"Yes, dear," said Tru.

"It sounds like a pretty important mission."

"It is," said Tru.

"So, what then? I'm *not* important?" Brooklyn tried to control her frustration.

"You're very important," Tru said. "But we decided it's more important for you to stay at Kinloch."

"*We?*" Brooklyn said, suspicious. "I've never known you to put anything ahead of a mission."

"I insisted," said Mother. "Tru wanted you to go, but I wouldn't budge."

For Brooklyn, this felt like a betrayal. Missing a month of summer vacation was bad enough. But missing a mission like this was unthinkable.

"Right," said Brooklyn. "Because whether or not I understood the quadratic equation was such a vital part of how I saved the day in Paris and on the *Sylvia Earle*."

"I know you're disappointed but—" Mother started to say, but Brooklyn cut him off.

"My disappointment was thinking there were finally some adults in my life who wouldn't let me down."

She got up and bolted from the room.

Sydney stood to follow her.

"Don't," Mother said. "I'll go."

"I don't know if that's the best idea," said Sydney. "I've never seen her as mad at anyone as she is at you right now."

"I know," said Mother. "But it should still be me."

"Why?" asked Sydney.

"Because I'm her father."

Colors

BROOKLYN WAS IN FULL SELF-PITY MODE as she lay on her bed and stared at the ceiling. Mother and Sydney had each come in attempting to lift her spirits, and both had failed. No matter what they said or how Brooklyn tried to look at it, she could only see that she was about to miss out on something incredible. Everyone else was leaving on an adventure, and she was heading back to Kinloch to study algebra and poetry. It didn't seem fair.

There was a knock at the door, and she suspected

that it was either Paris ready to try his understanding big brother approach or Monty willing to listen to her vent. She didn't have the heart for either.

"Go away," Brooklyn called out.

Despite the plea, the door opened and into the room stepped Kat. This was a surprise. Kat was awesome, yes, but even she would tell you that she was socially awkward. Interactions involving sensitive feelings and mushy emotions were never something she sought out.

"I appreciate it, Kat," Brooklyn said, "but I really don't want someone to cheer me up right now."

"Good," Kat replied, "because that's not why I'm here."

"It isn't?" asked Brooklyn.

"No," said Kat. "Why would I need to cheer you up?"

Brooklyn gave her an "are you serious?" look. "Because you're all about to go on an amazing mission, and I'm going to miss it."

"Yes, but Tru told you that down in the priest hole nearly an hour ago," Kat said. "Are you still upset about it?"

"Of course I am," said Brooklyn.

"Oh, I see. Does that mean you were upset when you and Sydney went undercover for a week on the *Sylvia Earle* and *I* stayed home?"

This caught Brooklyn off guard. "Um . . . not exactly . . . but you wouldn't have liked it on the ship. You would've had to share a cabin with a group of girls."

"Were you upset when we had a mission in Paris and you were given the lead role, even though you had the least experience?"

"Well, that was only because it involved computers and—"

"Or were you upset when we all went to London to break into Reginald Banks's house but Rio stayed home with Monty?"

Brooklyn squirmed. "No . . . but . . . those were all . . . *different*."

"Of course they were," said Kat. "They were different because *you* weren't the one left behind. We're like a theater company. Every play has distinct roles. Sometimes you're the star. Sometimes you're a supporting role. And sometimes . . ."

"You work in the box office selling tickets," Brooklyn said, seeing this reasoning.

"Exactly," said Kat. "So, this time, you're the box office. Who knows, in Beijing you may be the lead again."

"Okay," Brooklyn said as she let out a deep sigh. "You may have several points there."

"Good," Kat said. "Now, the reason for my visit. Do you want to use your computer skills to help prove to the cryptographers at MI6 that no code is unbreakable? Or do you want to lie on your bed and feel sorry for yourself? It's totally up to you."

"I want to help," Brooklyn reluctantly admitted.

"Excellent," Kat said. "Then come down to the priest hole and let's put Beny to work."

"Okay." Brooklyn nodded and smiled. "Just let me freshen up. I'll be right down."

Kat started to leave, but Brooklyn gently took her by the arm and said, "Thank you."

Kat turned to look at her. "Did I cheer you up?"

Brooklyn chuckled. "Yes. In your own special Kat way, you did."

Kat smiled proudly. "I told them I could do it."

A few minutes later, Brooklyn entered the priest hole to find Kat sitting at a table with Monty and Rio as they looked up at a monitor showing the pictures of St. Basil's Cathedral.

"Join us," Monty said. "We've been reading about the church to see if it gives us anything."

"Okay," said Brooklyn. "Get me up to speed."

"There are nine domes for the church's nine chapels,"

said Rio. "They're called onion domes because of their shapes, and each one has a pattern with two colors." He pointed at one. "This is the one that always changes colors in the social media posts. And, get this, it's the dome for the chapel of St. Nicholas."

"Nicholas," Brooklyn said, seeing the connection. "Just like the twins' cousin."

"Exactly," said Rio.

"Are the colors ever the same as the actual church?" Brooklyn asked.

"No," said Monty. "It should be red and white, like it is here." She clicked open a photograph of St. Basil's that hadn't been altered to look like a postcard.

"Is this the order in which they were posted?" asked Brooklyn.

"Yes," answered Kat. "The one on the far right was the one posted four days ago that may be connected to the theft of the nuclear warheads."

"Green and purple," said Brooklyn, looking at it. "So, that's the code. One of the Sorokin twins posts a picture on social media, and it's really a postcard to their cousin Nicholas with the message 'green and purple.'"

"You are now fully caught up," said Rio. "And if you're like the rest of us, fully stumped."

"This is not *stumped*, this is *thinking*," Kat said. "Code-breaking isn't a race; it's a puzzle."

"Maybe it has something to do with what colors normally symbolize," said Brooklyn. "On a traffic light, green means *go*. Maybe it means the plan's a go, like we say, 'This operation is hot, we are a go.'"

"It could be simple like that," said Kat. "But here's what puzzles me."

She stood up and pointed at another picture. "Here it is green too."

"Which could mean a different mission was a go," said Rio.

"But it's a different shade of green," she responded. "And it's an even different shade of green over here," she said, pointing at another one of the shots. "Three greens, but three different greens. Why go to the trouble of making different shades? And, if you look at them all, there are also different shades of red in four of them, and five different blues."

"So the code is different depending on the shade?" asked Brooklyn.

"We can't be sure," said Kat. "But everything else about this is very precise. The post goes up every day at the exact same time. Nicholas Sorokin checks it every day at the exact same time. If they are precise about everything, then they are likely being precise about the color, too."

"Luckily, we have a supercomputer than can help sort through all this," Brooklyn said. "Let's get him fired up."

She stood and headed for the workstation she used to operate Beny, her mood greatly improved by her involvement in the mission. As she did, the others traded looks and smiles, happy to have her back in the fold.

"I saw that," Brooklyn said, pointing at the reflection in a monitor next to the workstation. "And I know that Monty has more than enough computer skills to do this type of search."

There was a pause as they were all busted, but Brooklyn wasn't upset. She just said, "Thanks for including me."

"You're welcome," mumbled the others in return.

"Now, let's show everyone at Vauxhall Cross what real cryptography is all about."

The Scotch Gambit

EDINBURGH, SCOTLAND

PARIS KNEW HE WAS CUTTING IT CLOSE, but he still thought he had enough time until he heard the bells from the clock tower. He'd wanted to make a good first impression, and arriving late wasn't the way to do it. He let out a frustrated growl and sprinted the last two blocks to Number One Alva Street, a stone building with a blue door and a plaque that read EDINBURGH CHESS CLUB. He took a deep breath to calm his heart rate, tugged at his shirt to straighten out any wrinkles, and rang the buzzer.

"Hello," crackled a voice over the intercom.

"Hello," Paris answered, still catching his breath. "I'm here to meet Barnaby Fitch."

"He's in the members lounge," replied the voice. "First floor, to the left."

The door buzzed open, and Paris stepped into the second-oldest chess club in the world. He entered the room marked MEMBERS LOUNGE, which had dark wood paneling adorned with photographs of grandmasters and plaques displaying the names of club champions dating back to 1822. Sitting at a table in the center of the room was a small man who looked nothing like a hardened criminal. Barnaby Fitch had a friendly face, was bald on top with a pink scalp, and had little tufts of white hair on the sides. His eyes were a piercing shade of blue and stared right at Paris.

"Good morning, sir," Paris said. "I'm sorry I'm late."

"You're not late," Fitch replied, checking his watch. "You still have thirty-four seconds."

"But I heard the bells—"

"Of a clock that's purposely set three minutes fast," Fitch explained.

"What?"

"It's one of the quirks of Edinburgh," he explained.

"The clock in the tower above the Balmoral Hotel is always set three minutes fast to hurry people on their way to catch a train at Waverley station. Apparently it also works for young men on their way for chess instruction."

Paris couldn't believe that in all the times they'd been to Edinburgh, Mother had never mentioned this tidbit. No doubt it was because he was always exhorting them to "pick up the pace and not be late."

"Let that be lesson number one," said Fitch. "Always stay on top of the situation. That applies to the pieces on the board and the eccentricities of where you are playing. Now, I understand you need some intensive training to get tournament-ready so that you can improve your rating."

"Yes, sir," Paris replied.

"How many points in how much time?" asked Fitch.

"One hundred seventy-five points in just over three weeks."

"That's quite the challenge," Fitch said. "Let's say we play first so that I can see what I'm working with."

A board was already set up for a game on the table in front of Fitch. Paris sat down opposite him.

"By the way, I saw you win the interscholastic tournament," Fitch said. "Congratulations."

This caught Paris by surprise. "But . . . how could you . . . ?"

"What? Watch you play chess while I was locked up in Saughton Prison?" Fitch asked.

"Yes," Paris said tentatively, worried he'd broached a taboo subject.

"Chess Scotland streams the tournaments it sponsors," he explained. "I had an abundance of free time, so I watched them all. As for my incarceration, there's no reason to be shy about it. I did what I did, and I got what I deserved. Lucky for me, you have friends in powerful places." He paused for a moment and added, "Just like it was lucky for you that boy from Glasgow fumbled his endgame."

"Wait, what?" asked Paris.

"In the final of the interscholastic," Fitch said. "He had you beat. At one point, he was only eleven moves away from mate, but he missed it."

"Oh," Paris said, stung by the revelation. "I didn't realize. I guess I am lucky, then."

"Look at me," said Fitch. "Let this be lesson number two. Just because luck played a role doesn't mean talent didn't too. You're quite skilled, but you can't get mopey just because I point out facts about your game. We don't have time for that. Understood?"

Paris nodded. "Understood."

"Okay, so let's play. But I warn you, I'm not going to be sloppy like that Glaswegian."

"Good," said Paris. "I don't want you to take it easy on me."

Barnaby laughed. "No need to worry about that."

The first game was over before Paris even settled in, and the second and third passed in a blur. Paris thought he had Fitch on the run momentarily in game number four but was completely obliterated in the fifth. He'd never lost so much so fast at anything, much less chess, which he'd loved for as long as he could remember. He felt as if all the grandmasters in the photos on the wall were laughing at him.

"That was brutal," Paris said, surveying the damage. "I guess I really was lucky to win the interscholastic. Do you honestly think you can help me? Or am I a lost cause?"

"That depends," said Fitch. "Complete this sentence for me. 'What I know for certain about chess is . . .'"

Paris thought for a moment and answered, "That there are sixty-four squares, thirty-two pieces, and much for me to learn."

Barnaby smiled broadly and chuckled. "That's quite good," he said. "If that's what you truly think, then I can help a great deal." He cleared most of the board and arranged one of each piece in a line across the middle. "Which one are you?"

"What do you mean?" asked Paris.

"Pawn, rook, knight, bishop, queen, king," the teacher answered. "When you play, which one do you imagine you are?"

This was an easy decision for Paris. "The queen," he answered without any hesitation. "She's the most powerful piece on the board."

"Good," said Fitch. "That means in your heart you're aggressive, not cautious. You need to play that way. Your style should match your personality. From what I've seen, you keep switching between the two, and that's a recipe for disaster. If you're not true to your soul, you can't unleash your creative potential. Chess is not a game or a science; it is an art. If you are Van Gogh, you need to paint like him. Understand?"

Paris nodded. "Absolutely."

"Now you get the benefit of my checkered past."

"What do you mean?"

"I am the five-time Scottish champion," said Fitch.

"But, as we discussed, I also did five years in Saughton. It was what I knew from chess that helped me get by in prison. And one of the most important things to know is the difference between tactics and strategy."

"Well, then, I'm in trouble," Paris said. "Because I thought those were the same thing."

"They're related, but they're distinctly different," Fitch said. "Tactics are what you do when there's something to do. Strategy is what to do when there's nothing to do."

"I don't understand," said Paris.

"Say you want to capture a specific piece," said Fitch. "If you look at the board, you know that there are a series of moves you can do to take that piece. That's *tactical*. It's immediate and it's focused."

"Okay," said Paris. "I get that."

"But sometimes you look at the board, and there are no tactical options worth pursuing," Fitch continued. "You're concerned not about taking a specific piece, but with winning the game. That's *strategic*."

"Okay, that makes sense," said Paris, getting it.

"One eye on the present and one eye on the future," Fitch said, summing it up. "That's how you make it on the board and that's how you make it in life."

They spent the next hour and a half going through Fitch's core beliefs about chess, and Paris was struck by the fact that so many of them aligned perfectly with spycraft. The techniques of deception and observation that helped take pieces on the board translated directly to those that helped outwit opponents in the field.

At one point, Fitch said, "Now, tell me, do you know what correspondence chess is?"

"Not really," said Paris.

"Back in the olden days, when these blokes were still breathing," Fitch said, pointing at some of the pictures on the wall, "there was no computer chess over the Internet. If you wanted to play someone who wasn't sitting across a board from you, you played correspondence chess by mail. You'd write down your move, drop it in the post, and wait for your opponent to mail his move back."

"Must've taken forever," said Paris.

"It did," said Fitch. "And in 1824, the early members of this very club challenged a more established one in London to a series of correspondence games to determine British supremacy. They took four years to play, and do you know who won?"

"Since you're telling me, I'm guessing the Scots," said Paris.

"You got that right," Fitch said with pride. "And here's the good part. You're not alone. There's hardly anybody outside these four walls who knows anything about it."

"Why's that good?" asked Paris.

"Because that means hardly anyone knows how they won," said Fitch. "I'm going to teach you their secret weapon. It's a series of aggressive opening moves that should catch your opponent completely off guard, just like it did the Londoners."

"What's it called?" asked Paris.

"The Scotch gambit."

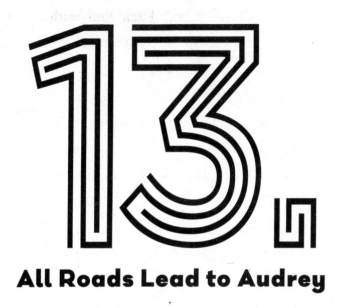

All Roads Lead to Audrey

LONDON, ENGLAND

IT WASN'T LIKE SYDNEY TO BE STARSTRUCK, but she could barely contain her excitement when she met Francesca Lloyd, the founder, editor-in-chief, and CEO of *All Roads Lead to Audrey*. Unlike many teen lifestyle websites, *Audrey* was fun without being fluffy, informative but not gossipy. It dealt with real issues, treated its readers with intelligence and respect, and encouraged young people to embrace their true selves.

Despite still being in her twenties, Lloyd was already a leading voice in fashion and social activism, as well as a passionate advocate for British youth. Add the fact that she was also a former MI6 agent, and for Sydney it was like meeting her future self.

"You must be Eleanor," Lloyd said, greeting Sydney by her cover name. "It's so nice to meet you."

"The pleasure's mine, Ms. Lloyd," replied Sydney.

"Please," said the woman with a friendly smile, "call me Frankie."

Sydney beamed. "Okay . . . *Frankie*, call me Ellie."

"Perfect," said Lloyd. "Frankie and Ellie, just like old friends."

The meeting took place at *Audrey*'s headquarters, a Victorian warehouse in East London that had been converted into a modern open-air workspace with hard timber floors and exposed brick walls featuring large black-and-white photos of Audrey Hepburn, the Hollywood legend and style icon who inspired the website's name.

"This place is amazing," Sydney said as they walked from the reception area to Frankie's office. "I love it."

"So do I," replied Lloyd. "For decades it was a textile factory run by three sisters, so it's always been home to strong women with a passion for fashion."

When they entered the office, Frankie shut the door so they could talk privately. "I've been dying to meet you," the editor said as they sat down in a pair of comfy, overstuffed chairs. "This is so exciting."

"I think you've got that backward," said Sydney. "I'm the one who's dying to meet you. You're literally a hero of mine."

"My guess is that the feeling will soon be mutual," said Frankie.

Sydney was flummoxed. "Why?"

"Why?" said Frankie. "I get a call from Tru Shepherd, legendary MI6 spymaster and one of *my* personal heroes, and she say says I am to put you on assignment to follow Tabitha Banks around Russia, no questions asked. How could I not be excited?" She studied Sydney for a moment. "Can I ask how old you are?"

"I turn fifteen next month," answered Sydney.

Frankie shook her head. "Fascinating. Is there anything you can tell me about the purpose behind all this?"

"No, not really," Sydney answered. "You know how Tru is."

"Pity," Frankie said. "Okay then, let's get to work. In a couple hours, Tabitha's coming in with a publicist, and I want you up to speed."

They proceeded to talk about the history of the website, which began as Lloyd's personal blog. She shared her thoughts about what stories were right and wrong for *Audrey*.

"I don't want the story that you'd tell your parents, and I don't want the story that you'd tell your friends at school," she said. "I want the story that you call up your best mate to tell, even though you're just about to see her, because you can't wait to share it. It's urgent. It's personal. It's exciting to you. Because if it's exciting to you, it will be exciting to our readers."

"Got it," said Sydney, savoring the moment.

"The key is to write about people, not things; feelings, not actions. A great piece doesn't tell us what someone does; it shows who they are."

"What do you mean?" asked Sydney.

"You're going to write about traveling to Russia, hanging out backstage with pop stars, attending fancy parties, and all variety of things that our readers can only dream about doing," Frankie said. "They're exciting, and you have to mention them, but they are just *things*. We can't connect with *things*. You need to make the people real; that's what will bring it all to life."

"That's what I love about the site," said Sydney. "But my worry is that I don't know how to do it."

"The trick is finding the engine," said Frankie.

"What engine?" asked Sydney.

"If the person were a car, then the engine is what makes them go," Frankie answered. "At heart, everyone has a problem that drives them. Something they're trying to prove to themselves or to the world. Something they're trying to fix from their past. It's the reason they choose their career. The reason they choose who to fall in love with. Even the reason they choose what to eat for lunch. And although most readers don't realize it, that's what they're looking to connect with. Because while virtually none of us have billionaire fathers who manage rock bands, we all have problems. Never forget that 'ordinary' is part of 'extraordinary'; you can't have one without the other."

"That's brilliant," said Sydney. "Did they teach you that at university?"

"No. I learned it at MI6. That's what human intelligence is. It's understanding other people. If you want someone to do something for you or to tell you a secret, then it's essential that you understand what makes them do anything. You need to identify their problem and then help solve it."

They continued talking until an assistant came to Frankie's office to tell her that Tabitha Banks had arrived for their meeting.

"But the publicist isn't the only one with her," the assistant continued. "She's brought a bit of an entourage, including Sir Reg himself."

"Interesting," Frankie said. "Why would Mr. Big bother to come all the way out to Shoreditch to meet little old me?"

"We've got to treat it like a story," said Sydney. "We've got to find his engine."

"Yes, we do," said Frankie, lighting up. She turned to the assistant. "We can't have the meeting in here; there's not enough space. Take them to the conference room and make sure there's plenty of snacks for everyone. You know how the posh love to be pampered."

When Frankie and Sydney entered the conference room, there were five people waiting for them: Sir Reg; Tabitha; a publicist from the record label; Tabitha's best friend, Violet; and Anastasia Sorokin, who was introduced as the director of the social media team.

Sydney shouldn't have been surprised that Sorokin was there; after all, Tru had said one of the twins was almost always with Tabitha. Her concern, though, was that if Anastasia was who she encountered chasing Paris the night of Tabitha's birthday party, she might recognize her and blow her cover.

"Thank you all for coming," Frankie said, starting the meeting. "Everyone here at *All Roads Lead to Audrey* is very excited about this opportunity. Our plan is a series of features following Tabitha around Moscow as she travels with KB5. We'll post new updates every day with great photos, and the primary focus will be on her, not the band."

"Why's that?" asked Reg.

"Our readers love the band, but they already know a lot about them. Tabitha's the one they only know a little bit about, but she's a person who we think they'll love too."

Sydney sat quietly and studied the others across the table. Tabitha and the publicist looked thrilled; her best friend a bit jealous; Sir Reg was disinterested; and Anastasia seemed to be looking at Sydney as if she recognized her.

"The series will consist of stories, photographs, and short videos," Frankie continued. "All of them will be posted on the site and on our social media platforms. We think there will be a great deal of engagement there. The series will be branded 'Around the World with Tabitha,' which will tie in nicely with the album."

"That sounds amazing," said Tabitha.

"To you, maybe," said Sir Reg. "But to me it sounds *intrusive*. We're often targeted by tabloids, and I need to protect our privacy."

"We're hardly a tabloid," Frankie replied firmly. "We take the principles of journalism seriously, but unfettered access is essential for a series like this."

"Exactly," said Reg. "So here's what I propose. No offense to the young lady here," he said, pointing at Sydney, "but rather than let a stranger into our private lives, Violet will write the stories. She's Tabitha's best mate and knows all about her. More importantly, we're already comfortable with her in our circle."

Sydney was worried, but Frankie played it cool.

"Does Violet have any writing experience?" asked Frankie.

"They're teenagers; how much experience can they have?" Reg asked. "She's a bright girl and a top student. Besides, I'm sure you've got some editors here who can fix up any shortcomings with, how did you say it, 'the principles of journalism'?"

Frankie considered this for a moment and said, "And if I say no?"

"Well, then, we'd have to say thanks but no thanks," said Sir Reg. "But I'm sure you're too smart a business-person to do that."

"Maybe you overestimate my intelligence," Frankie said. "Because the answer's no. Thanks for coming in."

It was an abrupt turn in the meeting. There was no negotiation, just a rejection. Tabitha looked devasted while Sir Reg simply looked stunned.

"*You* are saying no to *me*?" he asked.

"Yes, I am," Frankie replied.

"Just because I won't let her write the stories?"

"That's right," she said. "She's essential. No Ellie, no deal."

"Is she a relative or something?"

"Her mother and I happen to be longtime friends, but that's not pertinent," Frankie said. "Ellie's writing these features because she's ideal for the assignment."

"You realize I can go to any other website or maga-zine and offer them the same deal," Reg said.

"Of course," said Frankie. "But I also know that sto-ries written by friends are worthless. You need someone with a fresh and honest perspective. Someone who's not in your inner circle." She turned to Violet. "No offense."

Tabitha gave her father a desperate look, but he didn't care. He turned his attention to Sydney. "What do you even know about my daughter?"

"You mean biographical information like her birth date and where she goes to school?" asked Sydney.

"No, not stuff you can look up on Wikipedia," he said.

"Actually, Tabitha doesn't have a Wikipedia page," she said. "But I do know those things about her. I also know that she keeps an EpiPen with her at all times because she has a severe nut allergy. I know that last year you managed to keep it out of the press when she got caught shoplifting a belt at Harrods." She moved her attention to Anastasia and went for broke. "I also know that although you introduced her as the director of social media, Anastasia and her twin sister are actually Tabitha's bodyguards."

Reg wasn't sure how to respond to all this, so Sydney just kept going.

"I even know that on the night of Tabitha's birthday party, it was either Anastasia or her sister who chased a boy down Kensington Palace Gardens and into the Notting Hill Gate tube station."

"That's why I know you," said Anastasia. "You were there."

"Yes, I was there," said Sydney.

"You crashed my birthday party?" said Tabitha.

"No," said Sydney. "We don't work that way. But I was down the street getting a feel for the people who were coming and going."

"Why?" Reg asked suspiciously.

"Because I sent her," said Frankie, jumping in. "It was all part of her research for this series. We're thorough that way."

"That's it, Tabs, we're leaving," Reg said angrily. "This doesn't smell right."

Tabitha's head was spinning, and she looked upset at the change of events. Her father might not have understood the importance, but for her, *All Roads Lead to Audrey* was the site she specifically wanted to make her a star.

"'Tabitha's Tears,'" said Sydney.

"I beg your pardon," said Reg.

"'Princess Pout,'" answered Sydney. "Or the worst, 'It's My Party and I'll Cry if I Want To.'"

"What are you implying?" he demanded, his anger rising.

"I'm not implying anything," answered Sydney. "I'm quoting. The day after Tabitha's birthday, those were the headlines on all the other sites. The ones you're going to offer your story to instead of *Audrey*. They ran that brutally unfair picture of her, devasted by what had happened, and they mocked her pain. They treated her like a punch line. That's who you're turning to. Do you know what story we ran about the party?"

"No," said Reg.

"Tell him, Frankie," said Sydney.

Frankie smiled. "We ran nothing," she said. "We don't celebrate people's misfortune. It's very un-Audrey-like." She pointed toward a close-up of Audrey Hepburn with her chin on her hand as she smiled at the camera. "She was all about class and respect and integrity. That's what we pride ourselves on. And that's why we don't change our standards no matter how much we may want a story."

"Just like we didn't run the story about Tabitha shoplifting," Sydney added. "That would've been a scoop. No one else had it. But it was none of our business and not something our readers need to know."

"How do you even know about it?" Reg demanded.

"We're not going to say because we don't tell our secrets—we keep them," Sydney answered. "Just like Audrey would've."

Thirty minutes later, Reg, Tabitha, and their entourage were all smiles as they left, having agreed to all of Frankie's conditions, including the fact that Sydney would be the one writing the stories. Once they were gone, Frankie turned to her.

"Okay, amazed," she said. "I'm utterly amazed."

Sydney smiled.

"How'd you pull that off?" asked Frankie.

"I did what you said," answered Sydney. "I looked for his engine."

"Which was what?"

"He wanted to protect his daughter," she said. "He threw the party, and it went terribly wrong, so this was going to be his way to make it up to her. I just had to make sure he knew we were the best ones to protect her reputation."

"And all that information about her? Like the shoplifting? I never heard about that, and I hear everything."

Sydney smiled wryly. "Let's just say MI6 does a lot of research before undertaking a mission."

"Mission?" Frankie asked, her eyes lighting up. "Would that be the same mission that brought you here today?"

"No comment."

"Brilliant," she said, bursting with excited energy. "You see that desk over there?" She pointed at an empty desk in the office bullpen. "It's yours, and it's close to my office so I can keep an eye on you."

"But I'm writing the stories in Russia," said Sydney.

"Not for now, for later," said Frankie. "When you're done with school and MI6, I want you back here working for me. You've always got a place at *Audrey*."

Sydney could barely contain her glee.

Pygmalion

KINLOCH ABBEY, SCOTLAND

ON A SCALE OF ONE TO TEN, BROOKLYN'S
jealousy was currently at eleven and a half. While Paris
was reveling in chess-geek heaven learning the intri-
cacies of the Scotch gambit, she was slogging through
a grammar book trying to figure out the differences
between conditional and subjunctive moods. And,
unlike Sydney, who was living the glamorous life
with a fashion icon in London, Brooklyn was in the
school lunchroom gnawing on a sandwich that had

been labeled roast beef but would be more accurately described as gristly mystery meat with wilted lettuce and tomato.

She sat alone and was so focused on her book that she didn't realize someone had approached the table.

"Hello."

Brooklyn looked up and was surprised to see Charlotte standing across from her, lunch tray in hand. She had been a member of the City Spies before Brooklyn arrived, and the relationship between them had been frosty at best.

"What do you want?" asked Brooklyn.

Charlotte held up her tray as if the answer was obvious. "I thought maybe I could sit here," she said. "If that's all right with you."

"Why?" asked Brooklyn.

"To eat lunch."

"Not why do you want to sit," said Brooklyn. "But why here with me?"

Charlotte exhaled. "I know we haven't gotten off to the best start," she said. "And, if I'm honest, that's completely my fault. But I thought maybe the two of us could try to get along."

She seemed sincere, but Brooklyn wasn't sold.

"We've got a lot in common, actually," Charlotte continued.

"Do we now?"

"We're both Americans," Charlotte offered. "And we're both amazing hackers."

"How do you know that?" asked Brooklyn.

"I know that I am because, well, I just am," said Charlotte. "And I know you are because, for one thing, you hacked me. That's not easy. The fact that I was furious about it doesn't mean I wasn't also impressed."

Brooklyn tried to hide her smile as she thought about it. "That was rather crafty on my part."

"And I also know that neither one of us wants to eat this lunch. So that's three things we have in common." Charlotte smiled. "We'd probably find more if we just talked a little bit."

"Yeah, okay," Brooklyn relented. "Have a seat."

"Thank you," Charlotte said as she sat down.

"Are you here for Kinloch Academy?" asked Brooklyn.

"Yes and no," said Charlotte. "There are about a dozen of us who live at the school year-round for one reason or another. We help out with the academy. I'm chipping in in the computer lab."

"I'm taking a computer art class," Brooklyn said. "But mostly I'm here to brush up on English, history, and algebra."

"It's hard when you move in midyear," said Charlotte. "Especially considering all the . . . *extracurricular* . . . activities that go on at the FARM."

"I'm willing to talk," said Brooklyn. "But not about that. Nothing about what's going on at the FARM or MI6 or any of that."

"That's fine," said Charlotte. "I'm glad to be done with all that stuff."

"Really?" asked Brooklyn, not buying it.

"Don't get me wrong," said Charlotte. "It was fun and exciting, but I wasn't always the best at drawing the line between good and bad behavior."

Although it was a secret to the others, Brooklyn knew that Charlotte had been kicked off the team because she tried to use the FARM's supercomputer to hack into several banks and steal money. If Mother hadn't caught her, she would've ended up arrested, and the team almost certainly would've been disbanded.

"How are you at drawing the line between conditional and subjunctive moods in grammar?" Brooklyn asked. "Because it's all a blur to me."

"Pretty good, actually," Charlotte said. "You want some help?"

Brooklyn nodded, and Charlotte moved to the other side of the table so they could look at the book together. As they reviewed the lesson, the mood between them relaxed.

"Thank you," Brooklyn said when they were done with it.

"No problem," Charlotte said. "So, here's a question for you. What do you miss most about America?"

Brooklyn thought for a moment. "The food," she answered. "There was such good food in New York, and here it's all kind of . . . *meh.*"

"I know what you mean," said Charlotte. "I do like the Indian food but can do without the rest. What I really miss is good old Southern food like barbecue or fried chicken and biscuits."

"You mean *actual* biscuits," joked Brooklyn. "I don't understand how that word means 'cookies' here. They don't know what they're missing."

"No, they don't," said Charlotte.

Brooklyn paused for a second and asked, "Did you

mean it when you said you didn't miss it? All the cloak-and-dagger spy stuff?"

"I thought we weren't talking about that," said Charlotte.

"Well, we can talk about it without really talking about it. If you know what I mean."

Charlotte nodded. "Sometimes I miss the excitement, I guess. It was fun being in on a secret." She paused for a moment before adding, "I miss being friends with every-one. I miss that terribly."

"They still go to school here," Brooklyn replied. "You could try to talk to them like you did to me."

"I don't know," Charlotte answered softly, lost in thought. "I didn't handle a lot of things well on my way out the door. I think those bridges are permanently burned."

"You never know," said Brooklyn.

Charlotte flashed a half-smile. "I tell you what else I really miss," she said, trying to change the mood. "That gorgeous Cray XC40 supercomputer capable of per-forming over five hundred trillion floating-point opera-tions per second."

"Beny!" Brooklyn answered with joy. "Isn't he the best?"

Officially, *he* belonged to the FARM as part of its weather research. Unofficially, it had been tricked out by MI6 and was the sixteenth-fastest computer in the United Kingdom.

"I was totally spoiled having access to him," said Charlotte. "Everything else feels like a toy or some antiquated OG computer from last century. Do not take him for granted."

"I won't," said Brooklyn. "I promise."

Brooklyn looked at the clock on the wall and realized that lunch was almost over.

"I better get going," she said. "I've got to do some reading for English. Thanks for your help."

"Happy to do it," said Charlotte. "Thanks for talking to me."

"Of course," Brooklyn said as she stood and picked up her tray. "We should try this again."

"I'd like that," Charlotte said. "What are you reading for English?"

"A play," said Brooklyn. "Pig something."

Charlotte chuckled. *"Pygmalion."*

"That's it."

"It's good," said Charlotte. "Henry Higgins and Eliza Doolittle. He's a professor and makes a bet that he can turn a lowly flower girl into a lady. You'll like it."

"I hope so."

"She's kind of like you and me."

"Who?" asked Brooklyn.

"Eliza Doolittle."

"How so?"

"Eliza is Henry Higgins's experiment, and we're Mother's," said Charlotte. "He found us downtrodden and turned us into something we weren't."

"I don't look at it that way," Brooklyn said defensively.

"I didn't mean anything by it," said Charlotte. "But there's a parallel if you're honest with yourself. And, as a friend, I'd recommend you remember that."

"Half a lunch doesn't make us friends," Brooklyn responded sharply. "And it certainly doesn't come between family."

"You're not a family," Charlotte responded. "You're a team of agents. Remember that, too."

"I don't know," said Brooklyn. "The adoption felt pretty official."

This took the wind out of Charlotte's sails. "Adoption?"

Brooklyn felt bad. She realized that in her rush to defend Mother, she'd not thought about how this news would affect Charlotte.

"He adopted you?" Charlotte asked, wounded.

Brooklyn nodded.

"Just you?"

"No," said Brooklyn. "All of us."

Matryoshka

MOSCOW, RUSSIA

"ISN'T THIS BEAUTIFUL?" MONTY ASKED Kat and Rio as she looked down the length of the concourse. It had a vaulted ceiling and was lined on both sides with marble arches, each one guarded by a pair of statues. "It looks like something you'd expect to see in a museum, not a metro."

It was their third day in Moscow, and they were still in awe of the city's famed subway stations. They'd passed through nearly a dozen so far, and each had its own special flair. This one was named Ploshchad Revolyutsii, or

Revolution Square, and was located in the city center, not far from the Kremlin and St. Basil's Cathedral.

Here it was traditional for Muscovites to touch the bronze statues for luck. Petting the rooster brought money; tapping the shoe of a girl helped one's love life; and rubbing the nose of a dog named Ingus improved grades on upcoming exams, which explained why his muzzle shined brightly even though the rest of the sculpture had long since tarnished with age. Despite the fact Rio had no tests on the horizon, he gave the dog a pat, willing to try anything that might bring good fortune in the upcoming school year.

"You know, scientifically speaking, there's no such thing as luck," Kat said. "Although germs are very real."

It was just over a week before Operation Checkmate was set to begin, and they'd come to the Russian capital for a three-day reconnaissance mission. This involved scouting all the locations that were crucial to the mission and spying on Nicholas Sorokin.

They'd studied the hotel where everyone was staying, as well as the museum that was hosting the chess tournament. And every day, just before noon, they visited the souvenir shop where Sorokin worked. They wanted to be there when the social media post went up so that they could make sure he was the one checking it online. They also wanted to see how he reacted in case that day's post was a picture of St. Basil's.

Gorky's Gifts was large with two separate entrances and a brightly lit glass storefront that stretched half a block. Sales counters ran the length of the rear wall, and shelves were filled with traditional keepsakes, including fur hats with earflaps known as "*ushankas*," handcrafted lacquer boxes that featured paintings of Russian landscapes, and most popular of all, wooden nesting dolls.

The dolls came in themed sets that pulled apart in the middle to reveal progressively smaller ones inside. To Rio, they were the perfect symbol of espionage—layers of secrets hiding one inside the other. He went to a counter and picked up one that featured dolls of famous Russian leaders throughout history, opening each as he worked his way toward the center.

"*Matryoshka*," said a salesclerk, a woman in her fifties with a round face and apple-red cheeks.

Rio gave her a confused look. "Not babushka?"

"Nyet," the woman said, shaking her head. This was a common mistake by Westerners who thought they were called "babushkas" from the Russian word for "grandmother."

She leaned forward and conspiratorially pointed out an older woman with white hair who was looking at a shelf of wooden toys. "Babushka." Then she held up a nesting doll and said, "Ma-troosh-ka," sounding out each syllable.

"Ma-mush-ka," he said, trying it.

"Ma-TROOSH-ka."

He scrunched up his face humorously and gave it another try. "Ta-toosh-ka?"

"Nyet," the woman said, laughing.

"Baba ghanoush-ka?"

Now she was laughing hard, and Rio flashed a grin before saying it perfectly. "*Matryoshka.*"

"*Molodyets,*" said the woman. Well done.

Monty marveled at the scene while she pretended to browse at a table with brightly colored boxes of chocolates. Rio was an amazing street magician who spent years dazzling tourists along the boardwalk at Copacabana Beach. But as skilled as he was with sleight of hand, *charm* was his greatest gift. She remembered how Mother described the first time he'd witnessed him in action. *"I saw him perform for a crowd and was mesmerized,"* he'd said. *"The tricks were incredible, but the real magic was how he connected with strangers. Even ones who didn't speak the same language."*

"It's almost time," Kat whispered to Monty. "It's 9:05 in London. Today's post should be going up right now."

They watched Nicholas Sorokin as he walked behind the counter as if he were in charge. If the pattern held, in five minutes he'd duck into the little office in the back corner to check the computer. The City Spies didn't dare look for the post here because they didn't want to leave any digital trail that connected them to the site and the Wi-Fi in the store. Instead, Mother was checking it back home. He was supposed to send Monty a message if it was a picture of St. Basil's.

"Any word?" Rio asked as he joined them at the chocolate table.

Just then, Monty's phone buzzed, signaling a text. It was Mother letting her know that a picture of St. Basil's had just been posted. As prearranged, the text was simply the two colors that had been changed on the onion dome. She held it out in her palm so that Kat and Rio could read it too.

Dark Green. Dark Blue.

Each of them could feel their heart rate quickening. They had only one chance to get this right. As soon as Sorokin saw the post, he'd react, and they had to be ready to jump into action. If he left on foot, they were going to tail him. If he rode off on his motorcycle, the plan was to hop into a nearby taxi whose driver was on a special contract with the British embassy.

They spread out to get three different vantage points and watched as Sorokin slipped into the office right on cue ten minutes after eleven. He logged onto the computer, and they could see the slightest hint of a reaction when he saw the post.

He's got it, Monty said to herself.

Sorokin clicked his mouse a few times, and after typing onto the keyboard, he wrote something down on a small piece of paper. Next he placed three quick phone calls, none lasting more than forty-five seconds, before going behind the sales counter and through a back door into an employees-only area.

"Could you make out what he was writing?" Rio asked Kat when they huddled back together. She had the closest vantage point.

"No," replied Kat.

"I wish we could see what he was doing back there," Monty said.

"There's no way to make it to the door without the salesclerks seeing," said Kat.

A smile came over Rio's face. "I'll take care of the clerks so one of you can slip through the door," he said.

"How are you going to do that?" Monty asked, concerned that a misstep might blow their cover.

"Trust me," he said confidently. "This is my specialty."

He walked back to the counter displaying the Matryoshka dolls, and the clerk gave him a "not again" look. He held up the one of the Russian leaders.

"*Matryoshka*," she said flatly, not wanting to repeat their routine.

"Nyet," said Rio. "*Magiya.*" Rio had looked up the word before the trip. It was Russian for "magic."

She rolled her eyes, but he was undaunted.

He pulled the top off each doll in the set until he got to the tiny one in the center. It was a small wooden Catherine the Great. Then he took three of the top halves and arranged them side by side like the cups in a cups-and-ball trick. Except, in that trick, the cups are supposed to be identical to make it hard to tell them apart. Not only were these different sizes, but they had different faces painted on them.

He held up the Catherine the Great for the salesclerk to inspect, and then he hid it under the top that had Mikhail Gorbachev's face on it. He shuffled them around on the counter and then stopped and looked up at her.

"Where is she?" he asked.

Unimpressed, the woman tapped Gorbachev's head; but when Rio lifted it, Catherine the Great was gone. The clerk let out a gasp. *"Oi kak ty eto sdelal?"*

This attracted the attention of nearby coworkers, and she waved for them to join her.

"Pokazhi yeshche raz," she said, and judging by her expression, Rio assumed this was something like "Show me again."

Rio repeated the trick, this time adding some flourishes with his hands and playing it up to his growing audience. The language barrier was no problem as they oohed and aahed when he showed them that Catherine the Great had disappeared again.

"Pokazhi yescho raz," the clerk said again, delighted. All six of the store's clerks were gathered now, and Rio positioned himself so that they were turned away from the rear door. No one was watching it.

"I'll go," Kat said impulsively to Monty. "I'm smaller and less noticeable."

Kat didn't wait for a response. Instead, she moved behind the counter and slipped unnoticed through the door into a long hallway.

Unlike the bright and open vibe of the shop, the hallway was cramped and industrial, tight spaces accompanied by the constant hum of fluorescent lights. There were several padlocked cages that held merchandise, a grimy employee locker area, and a row of four rooms. Either Sorokin was in one of them or he'd gotten away through a rear exit down the hall.

The first two rooms were offices, and the third was used for additional storage. The fourth was secure with a combination lock built into its handle. Kat used an app to translate the doorplate written in the Russian alphabet. It read карты, which meant "maps."

She could hear that someone was inside, but the only way to see who it was was to stand on her toes and peek through a tiny window. This is where she found Sorokin. He was hunched over a table, looking at a large map spread out over it. She stretched as tall as she could, trying to get a good look, and reflexively put her hand on the door to keep her balance.

The door jiggled just enough to make a noise and attract Sorokin's attention. He turned and spied Kat through the window.

He was not happy.

16

Yuri

KAT STEPPED BACK FROM THE DOOR AND tried to duck out of sight, but it was too late. Nicholas Sorokin had seen her, and there was nowhere to hide. For a moment she thought about sprinting back toward the shop, but that would only make her look more guilty.

"Chto zhe Vy zdes' delaete?" he roared as he flung open the door and confronted her.

Kat didn't understand Russian, but the fury was unmistakable. She tried to think of what to say but stood there frozen.

"Vam zdes nelzia! Vydi otsiuda!" he continued, a spray of spittle flying from his mouth.

She finally remembered a Russian word that might help. *"Tualet?"* Toilet. She bounced on the balls of her feet like she had to go and was holding it in. *"Tualet?"*

This calmed him slightly. *"Nyetu,"* he responded, and pointed back down the hall to the store. *"Nazad. Vam zdes' nelzia."*

"Okay, fine," she said. "I'll hold it."

As she turned to leave, she got a quick glimpse into the room. In addition to several maps that were spread out on the table, there were shelves teeming with them, rolled up in tubes. She hurried back down the hall through the door. Rio still had the salesclerks captivated, and none of them noticed Kat when she slipped back into the store and approached Monty.

"Did you see him?" Monty asked

"Yes, but he also saw me, and he's furious," Kat said, still trying to calm her nerves. "He was looking at a map."

"Of what?"

"I couldn't get a good enough look to tell."

Just then, Sorokin came back through the door carrying a purple motorcycle helmet. Already angry about Kat's intrusion, his mood worsened when he saw that none of the salesclerks were doing what they were supposed to be doing. He yelled at them, and they all scurried back to their workstations.

"Nice job," Monty told Rio when he rejoined them.

"Thanks," he said. "Do we know anything?"

"Not much," said Kat. "Just that he checked a map."

"If we follow him, maybe we'll find out what he was looking up," Monty said.

Sorokin left the store and got on his motorcycle. He was already revving the engine when Monty, Rio, and Kat came out the other exit and headed toward a taxi parked on the corner.

Like many Moscow taxis, the car had seen better days and its once bright yellow paint had faded. The light on the roof indicated it was currently out of service and the driver, a balding man with a bushy mustache, was halfway through lunch, chomping on a large sandwich while he sat behind the wheel.

None of this deterred Monty, who got into the passenger seat as Kat and Rio slid into the back.

The driver started to rant in Russian, but Monty simply said, "Russia is to hockey what England is to football."

This was the secret code that had been given to the driver by his contact at the embassy, but it was obvious he didn't anticipate hearing it from a woman with two kids.

"I know. Not what you expected," Monty replied. "But we don't really have time to discuss gender equity across cultures, because I need you to follow that motorcycle and it's getting away."

The driver flashed a broad smile and stuffed the sandwich into a bag between them. "My name's Yuri," he said with a thick accent. "Hold tight."

Yuri stomped on the gas, and the car zipped out across three lanes of traffic, eliciting protest horns and raised fists in the process. Up ahead, Sorokin was maneuvering between cars where there was barely enough space for his motorcycle. Yuri did the same, even though his taxi was much too wide. Cars had to swerve out of the way to avoid him.

Despite the pinball nature of the drive, Yuri talked to them as he would on a normal taxi ride. "Are you enjoy Moscow? Good visit?" he asked, as though they were out for a leisurely ride.

"What?" asked Rio, not making sense of it.

Just then a car cut in front of Yuri, and he had to slam on the brakes. He laid on the horn and yelled at the other driver before resuming the conversation.

"Subway's beautiful, no?" he asked.

"Yes," Monty said uncertainly. "Lovely."

They were driving along Kutuzovsky Prospekt, which ran five lanes in each direction and whose traffic was nerve-racking under the best of circumstances. With Yuri behind the wheel, it was petrifying. Each of the passengers held on tight. They could see Sorokin's purple helmet up ahead, but despite Yuri's best efforts, the motorcycle began to pull away.

Sorokin changed roads a few times, and Yuri managed to stay with him for nearly fifteen minutes before the motorcycle disappeared from sight. The taxi simply could not keep up.

"You can slow down," Monty said. "He's gone."

"No, no," said Yuri. "We keep looking."

"I think we need a break," said Monty.

"Yes, please," Kat moaned queasily. She had her window rolled all the way down, trying to get as much fresh air as possible.

Reluctantly, Yuri slowed the taxi to a manageable pace, and they continued along the road. It felt like a lost opportunity until a few minutes later when Rio piped up from the backseat.

"Motorcycle."

He leaned forward and pointed through the windshield to where the motorcycle was parked, Sorokin's distinctive purple helmet sitting on the back.

"Nice," Monty said. "I don't see him, so let's be careful," she said to the driver. "We can't let him spot us."

"I know way around," Yuri said confidently as he continued through a few intersections before looping back. They approached the motorcycle from a different direction and parked a block away.

"Where is he?" asked Rio.

"I don't see him," Monty replied.

They looked for a while, but there was no sign of him, just the motorcycle on the side of the road next to a small park and across the street from a complex of buildings that sat behind a tall iron fence.

"What building is that?" asked Kat.

"How you say . . . *posol'stvo?*" the driver answered, trying to think of the right word. "Embassy?"

"It's an embassy?" Rio said. "For which country?"

Monty looked up at the flag in front of the building and instantly realized the connection. "Interesting," she said. "It's the embassy of North Korea."

"Why is that interesting?" asked Yuri, fully invested in the excitement of the moment.

"I'm sorry, but I can't tell you that," said Monty.

Yuri smiled. "The fact that you can't tell me is even more interesting."

They waited for about fifteen minutes until Sorokin suddenly appeared walking out of a small, wooded area alongside two other men.

"Where'd they come from?" Kat asked, surprised.

"I have no idea," said Rio. "Were they in those trees the whole time?"

"Maybe," Monty said. "They could've been studying the embassy from there."

They were still trying to figure it out when Sorokin hopped on his motorcycle, and the others got into a black sports car. The car quickly pulled away, but Sorokin stayed a moment and studied the embassy before putting on his helmet and starting up the motorcycle.

"We still follow?" asked Yuri.

Monty thought it through quickly. After receiving the message, he'd come here to meet others. She felt like the location was the key factor.

"No," she said. "Let him go. I want to look in that park."

Sorokin sped off, and they waited a few minutes to make sure no one else emerged from the woods before getting out of the taxi. Curious, Yuri started to get out too, but Monty stopped him.

"It will be too suspicious," she said. "Pull away and pick us up on the other side of the park in fifteen minutes."

"*Da*," said Yuri. "Be safe."

Monty nodded and then started walking toward the park with Kat and Rio.

The park was directly across the street from the embassy and had a fountain in the middle. There were benches, a small playground, and three wooded areas. Luckily it had rained the night before, so they were able to find three sets of shoe prints in the damp dirt where Sorokin and his friends had emerged.

The prints went about fifteen meters into the woods before stopping.

"This must be where they were," Monty said, turning to look back across the street. "You can see the embassy, but it's not a particularly good vantage point."

"That's not what they were doing," said Kat.

"What do you mean?" asked Rio.

"Check out this shape." She pointed to the indentation

of a circle in the dirt mixed among all the shoe prints.

"What made that?" asked Rio.

"This," Kat said as she brushed away some leaves to reveal a nearby manhole cover. "They went underground."

The Birthday Party

THE TRAIN WASN'T CROWDED, SO BROOKLYN had the row to herself and placed Sydney's present on the seat next to her. The small box was gift-wrapped, and she was worried that if she put it in her backpack, it might crinkle the ribbon and bow. Inside was a silver chain with a turquoise dolphin that she'd picked out because Sydney loved the ocean. It was simple and inexpensive, but the sentiment was priceless. Brooklyn couldn't remember the last time she'd purchased a birthday present for anyone.

Although she'd begrudgingly come to accept that summer school was actually helping her the way Dr. Graham suggested it would, she desperately wanted to be home. Even if it was just for a few hours. Charlotte had planted a seed of doubt in her mind—*"You're not a family. You're a team of agents"*—and Brooklyn needed to see everyone again to make sure things really were what she thought they were.

First, though, she had to convince Graham to let her leave campus. "Birthdays are a huge deal for the family," she'd told the headmaster. "Especially considering it's the first one since the adoption."

She felt a little bad about throwing in that last line. It was pure manipulation, but it worked. After also assuring him that she was ahead on all her assignments and that this would be a one-time-only request, he relented.

"Tell Eleanor happy birthday from me," he said. "And make sure you're back before lights-out at ten."

"Yes, sir," she promised.

As part of the fun, she wanted it to be a surprise, so she didn't tell anyone she was coming. She even borrowed a page out of Rio's misdirection handbook when she'd sent Sydney a text that morning, wishing her a happy birthday and expressing how sorry she was to miss celebrating it together.

She was so excited by the time the train pulled into Aisling that she almost forgot to pick up the present from the other seat. Since it was almost dinnertime, she went straight to the kitchen when she arrived at the FARM. There she found Paris deep in thought as he studied the contents of the open refrigerator.

"Are you looking for something in particular, or just trying to cool your face?" she asked.

"Brooklyn!" he said happily when he looked up and saw her. "Don't tell me they kicked you out."

"No," she answered. "School's actually going well, thank you very much. I just managed to escape for a few hours."

"Look who's here," Rio said, entering the kitchen. "What brings you home?"

"What do you think?" Brooklyn said. "I'm here for the big event. Where's the cake?"

"There's cake?" Rio said, suddenly excited.

"What cake?" asked Paris.

"For Sydney's birthday," said Brooklyn.

"Oh, that's right," said Paris. "I totally forgot that's today."

"You forgot Sydney's birthday?" Brooklyn asked, shaking her head. "She won't be happy about that."

"It's not too late. I can still text her," Paris said.

"Why not just tell her face-to-face?" Brooklyn asked.

"Because she's in London."

"What?" Brooklyn was completely caught off guard.

"She's celebrating the big day with her new BFF," Rio said as he cut right in front of Paris and grabbed some string cheese from the fridge.

"*What* BFF?"

"Tabitha Banks," Rio answered. He rolled his eyes comically and added, "They're like besties now."

"What are you talking about?" Brooklyn asked.

"She's fully undercover for this mission," Paris explained. "They've hung out a couple times, and it slipped that her birthday was coming up. Tabitha invited her to celebrate together London-style."

"And she accepted?" Brooklyn continued. "She picked her over us?"

"She probably figured one present from Tabitha Banks was worth far more than anything we might give her," Rio said.

Suddenly, the gift that had meant so much to Brooklyn seemed small and insignificant.

"It's all part of the mission," said Paris. "The closer she gets to Tabitha, the better she can spy on her and Sir Reg. It's kind of funny when you think about it, considering this whole thing started off with Tabitha's birthday."

Paris finally decided and pulled an apple out of the fridge and took a bite.

"Why are you all eating right before dinner?"

"This is dinner," said Paris as he chewed. "Monty and Mother won't be home until late, and Kat's downstairs, obsessed with cracking the St. Basil's code."

"We're going to fire up some frozen pizzas soon," said Rio. "You want one?"

Brooklyn had trouble processing the situation. She had a vision for the evening, and the reality was nothing like it.

"Is something wrong?" asked Paris, concerned.

Brooklyn couldn't find the right words. Finally, she just said, "Not *something* . . . everything."

"What do you mean?" Paris asked.

"Why didn't anyone tell me?" Brooklyn asked.

"Tell you what?" asked Rio.

"That there's no dinner tonight," she said. "That Sydney's not even home for her birthday. That she has a new BFF. Any of it. It's all news to me."

"Relax," said Rio. "We didn't know you were going to be here."

"I texted Sydney this morning and she didn't say a word." Brooklyn took a deep breath. "I told Dr. Graham that this birthday was a big deal for the whole family, so now I'm a liar too."

"Why'd you tell him that?" asked Rio.

"I don't have a lot of experience being in a family," Brooklyn snapped. "But I thought one of the things they did was celebrate their birthdays together."

"Maybe that's what most families do," said Rio. "But we're not like most families."

The London Birthday

TABITHA BANKS COULD NOT CONCEAL her delight when she looked at herself in a trifold of full-length mirrors. "Am I right?" she squealed, more like a declaration than a question.

"You are so right," Sydney agreed, peeking over Tabitha's shoulder to get a good view. "So very, very right."

Sydney's fifteenth birthday was one she'd never forget. Despite Francesca Lloyd's warnings not to be "blinded by the glitter of luxury," nothing could've prepared her for the dazzling display of opulence that Tabitha unleashed. They were currently getting pampered in a VIP-only fitting room at a boutique on New Bond Street, the most expensive shopping street in Europe.

Sydney loved fashion and thought Tabitha had a tremendous sense of style. The outfit she was trying on—ankle boots, leather pants, retro T-shirt, and denim jacket—looked amazing. Of course, it helped that Sir Reg had given her an unlimited budget and that the store had provided her with a private shopper who was bringing in clothes by the armful.

For Sydney, the day had provided a glimpse into a world about which she could have only imagined. Her own outfit, which she also thought looked amazing, was from a wardrobe painstakingly built by scouring the discount racks at vintage and charity shops throughout Edinburgh. Combined, the five most expensive articles of clothing Sydney had ever owned cost less than the boots Tabitha was trying on.

"Let me take some pictures," Sydney said, grabbing her camera, a top-of-the-line model she was using to shoot photos and video for *All Roads Lead to Audrey.* "Move over here away from the window so you're not backlit."

Sydney had quickly fallen in love with the camera work. One of the website's photographers had given her a crash course on how to take professional-looking images, stressing the importance of using natural light and interesting framing. She found herself taking pictures with it everywhere she went. She'd also received additional training from an MI6 tech about how to activate the secret recording device that had been installed in the camera's body. So far she hadn't had an occasion to try that.

Tabitha posed, Sydney snapped, and everyone was happy. Everyone, that is, except for Anastasia. Or was it Sasha? Sydney still had trouble telling them apart. It didn't really matter which twin it was because neither was happy when she was around. Like all good security professionals, they were suspicious of outsiders, and Sydney knew that they were keeping a close eye on her, scrutinizing her every move.

Originally, the plan was for Sydney to accompany Tabitha one afternoon while she shopped for clothes to wear on the Russia trip, but, when Tabitha found out about Sydney's birthday, the day was rescheduled so that Tabitha could take her out for a celebratory dinner afterward.

"What size shoe do you wear?" Tabitha asked as Sydney crouched down low to get a creative camera angle.

"Why?"

"Because I saw the way you looked at those Italian sandals," said Tabitha.

"What? The gladiators with the hand-sewn stitching, snakeskin straps, and studs?" said Sydney. "I barely even noticed them."

"You should definitely try them on," said Tabitha. She turned to the personal shopper, who nodded and ran off to get them.

"I didn't even tell her my size," Sydney said.

"You didn't have to," said Tabitha. "This is what she does for a living. I guarantee she brings back a perfect fit."

Now Sydney was a little embarrassed. She moved in closer so that Anastasia couldn't hear her. "I really appreciate you including me. But I shouldn't try on those shoes. I can't afford them. I mean, I'm not even close to being able to afford them."

"All you're doing is trying them on," Tabitha said. "You don't have to buy them. Besides, half the time these places give me clothes for free."

"They do?" Sydney asked, incredulous. "Why?"

"Because I'm going to post about them on social media, and you're going to write about them on *All Roads Lead to Audrey*," Tabitha answered. "And, of course, because they want to kiss up to my father because of who he is."

"Wow, I never imagined," Sydney said. "If you get them for free, then why . . ." She stopped herself when she realized she was about to overstep her bounds.

"What?" asked Tabitha.

"Nothing."

"If I get clothes for free then why did I shoplift a belt from Harrods?" she asked, finishing the thought for her.

Sydney nodded. "Yeah."

Tabitha shrugged. "I don't know," she said. "My therapist thinks it was some kind of desperate cry for attention. It was right around the time my parents were getting divorced."

The personal shopper came back in the room with three shoeboxes. "I think this should be the right fit," she said, holding up one of them. "But I brought half a size up and half a size down just in case."

As Tabitha predicted, the sandals fit perfectly. They also looked amazing.

Sydney stood up and walked over to admire them in the mirror.

"How do they feel?" asked Tabitha.

"Like heaven," Sydney admitted.

"They look fantastic," said Tabitha.

"It's like they were made for you," said the personal shopper.

Even Anastasia (or Sasha) piped in, "Perfect."

Sydney did a couple turns as she looked at them and smiled. "One day," she said.

"No," Tabitha responded. "Today."

"What?"

"Happy birthday. They're yours."

Sydney gave her a look. "No. I can't accept them!"

"Why not? It's your birthday."

"No, I mean, I really can't accept them," said Sydney. "It's against the editorial policy at *All Roads Lead to Audrey*. I can't accept anything of value from a company that will be featured on the website. It destroys our credibility."

"It's not a gift from the store," said Tabitha. "It's a gift from me. My money. I'm going to pay full price, no Sir Reg discount. You put up with me trying on clothes like a diva all through your birthday. You more than deserve it." Then she added. "You can accept a present from a friend, can't you?"

The word "friend" caught Sydney off guard. Did Tabitha really think of her that way? And if she did, was it wrong of Sydney to spy on her? Or maybe she was just buttering her up because she wanted to look good in *All Roads Lead to Audrey*. Sydney had to force such thoughts out of her mind and focus on the mission. The mission depended on her gaining Tabitha's trust.

"They do look amazing," Sydney said, admiring the shoes in the mirror again.

The Briefing

PARIS HAD WON FOUR TOURNAMENTS IN three weeks, but he'd lost a few games along the way and worried he hadn't done enough to raise his rating. He needed it to be above 2450 in order to qualify for the top group in Moscow and wouldn't know if he'd made it until Chess Scotland posted its monthly grading update on their website.

"Come on," he said impatiently as he clicked the refresh button yet again.

"Anything?" Mother asked.

"No," Paris grumbled.

"Relax," Mother said. "You won four straight tournaments, which is amazing. There's nothing more you could've done."

The team was in the priest hole taking care of final preparations for the mission. Mother was fine-tuning the ops plan, Kat and Monty were still trying to decipher the St. Basil's code, and Rio was studying maps of Moscow.

"Anyone know where this came from?" Sydney asked as she entered the room carrying a gift-wrapped box. "There's no tag on it."

"It's from Brooklyn," Rio said. "She dropped it off on your birthday."

"She came to the FARM?" Sydney asked, surprised. "I thought she was supposed to stay at school."

"She convinced Dr. Graham that we were throwing a party for you," Paris said. "She seemed kind of disappointed when she found out we weren't."

Monty and Mother shared a concerned look. They knew she'd stopped by but hadn't heard this detail.

"What did you tell her?" asked Sydney.

"That you'd dumped us for Tabitha Banks," Rio said.

"Perfect," Sydney said, annoyed. "And you never thought to mention this to me?"

"I'm not your secretary," said Rio. "Besides, I put the present in your room."

She gave him a look. "Actually, you left it on a table in the hall."

"True," Rio said, "but, I quote, 'Don't go in my room unless I give you permission.' The hall table was as close as I'm allowed to get."

"In his defense, you're pretty adamant about that rule," Paris said.

"Boys are so thick," she said, frustrated. "She came by to surprise me with a present, and now she thinks I'm a total toff because I never thanked her."

"Come to think of it, she wasn't thrilled to find out you were palling around with Tabitha on your birthday, either," Paris said. "Apparently, you'd not mentioned that in any of your texts."

"No, I hadn't," Sydney said pointedly. "I didn't want her to feel jealous about missing out."

"I guess that backfired," said Rio. "Just text her thanks and blame the rest on me like you do everything else."

"I'm not going to text her two days later," she said. "Especially after she went to the trouble of coming here." She turned to Monty and Mother. "Can I go up to

Kinloch and thank her in person? Maybe try to explain the situation with Tabitha?"

"Of course," Monty said.

"But first we have to do a briefing," Mother added. "We need to make sure we've got everything covered."

"Okay, thanks," Sydney said.

Paris hit refresh again, and his eyes opened wide when he saw the update. "Boom!" he said as he jumped up from his seat and raised his hands in triumph. "I made it."

"Nicely done," Mother said. "What's your new rating?"

"Twenty-four sixty-six!" said Paris, now moving his shoulders in a victory shimmy. "That means I'm in the top group with Park Dae-jung."

"And it means we're ready to go over the mission," Mother said. "Come on, let's gather round and run through the checklist."

Everyone sat at the conference table.

"First things first," Mother continued. "How are we with the St. Basil's code?"

"Frustrated," said Monty.

"*Very* frustrated," added Kat.

"We know that Nicholas Sorokin is the one receiving the messages because we saw it happen," said Monty.

"And we know that somehow dark green and dark blue are code for the North Korean embassy."

"Or the underground tunnel near the embassy," added Rio.

Monty clicked a button, and some photos of the embassy appeared on the screen as well as pictures of the wooded area in the park and the manhole cover.

"We also think the code involves a map," said Kat. "But the colors could refer to the map, the name, anything, really."

"Maybe Tru was right," Paris said. "Maybe it's unbreakable."

"It's not unbreakable," Kat said defensively. "We just don't have enough samples to see the pattern."

"Here's one good thing," Sydney said. "Once we hit Moscow, I'm going to be with Tabitha twenty-four seven, and the Sorokin sisters go wherever she goes. I should be able to see if they're the ones sending the posts."

"That could help," said Monty.

"Speaking of Tabitha," said Mother, "how's that going?"

"Pretty good, actually," she answered. "I thought I'd hate her, but I don't. Yes, she's completely spoiled, but she's not a bad person."

"You're just saying that because she gave you those shoes," Paris joked.

"You mean those very expensive shoes," Rio interjected.

"I was worried that if I turned them down, it might seem out of character and blow my cover," Sydney said defensively.

"They're quite nice," Monty said. "Don't know that you need any excuse for that."

"What's the latest on Jin-sun and Dae-jung?" asked Kat.

"To get them to the UK, we have three major obstacles," he answered. "And that's if they want to come with us, which is no guarantee."

"What are the obstacles?" asked Kat.

"First, it's security," Mother answered. "The North Korean government is going to have both father and son under constant protection. My guess is it'll be the RGB, which is North Korean intelligence, or the Ministry of State Security, which is their secret police. Either way, we'll have to communicate with Jin-sun right under their noses. And if the time comes for an extraction, then we're going to have to get Jin-sun and Dae-jung away from them."

"What's obstacle number two?" asked Sydney.

"The Russians," said Mother. "As we know, they're North Korea's allies, and they will not just let us take the Park family with us."

"So we don't let them know," said Rio.

"That's easier said than done," Mother answered. "We will be under constant surveillance in Moscow. Everyone is. There are cameras, listening devices, plainclothes police officers, and military guards everywhere. We have to assume that everything we do is being watched and recorded. We'll have to be like Houdini to make them disappear."

"Good thing we have a magician on the team," Paris said with a wink to Rio.

"And if we do get them away from the North Koreans and Russians, how do we get them out of the country?" asked Monty.

"That's the third obstacle," said Mother. "Luckily, Tru will be in charge of that."

"She's going to be in Moscow?" asked Paris.

"She's already there," said Mother. "She went for a conference on cybersecurity and will be based out of the British embassy. If I get her word that Park is willing to flip, she's going to run the team that's smuggling him and Dae-jung out. She's still ironing out the kinks in the plan, but my guess is they'll hide inside a secret compartment in a vehicle that drives across the border."

"Let's hope neither one of them is claustrophobic," said Monty.

"And none of that takes into consideration the biggest obstacle of all," Mother said. "We're going to try to flip him at the same time Sir Reg is doing the same."

"If it's hard for us," said Paris, "that means it's hard for Sir Reg and Umbra, too."

"Yes, but our plan relies on Park's willingness to participate," Mother said. "They might not be worried about such niceties. They could just kidnap him and take advantage of the crime and corruption that runs rampant through the country."

"When do you think they'd do that?" Kat asked.

"It could be while we're at the hotel, during the tournament, or even at the KB5 concert," Mother said.

"What makes you think he's going to the concert?" asked Rio.

"The concert is tied into the tournament," Paris said. "That's where Sir Reg is presenting the awards, and Dae-jung winning one is about as much of a lock as Kat winning the Newton medal at school."

"So basically, you're saying we have to cover everywhere all the time," Monty said.

"Yes," Mother said. "You, Kat, and Rio are going to keep a close eye on Sorokin. Meanwhile, Paris and I will be with the Parks, and Sydney's going to be with Tabitha and Sir Reg. It's going to take the entire team."

"Except for Brooklyn," Paris added. "Good thing we don't have any hacking needs on this one."

"How do we communicate if we see something?" asked Kat. "Our covers will be totally unrelated. It's not like we can meet up to compare notes."

"Francesca Lloyd helped us out there," said Sydney. "Don't forget that before she ran *All Roads Lead to Audrey*, she worked for Tru at MI6."

"What did she come up with?" asked Paris.

"I'm supposed to submit material three or four times a day to go on the *Audrey* website," Sydney explained. "That includes photos, videos, and stories. I upload all that to a special portal for her to get in London. But she's set it up so that you can access it too."

"That's genius," said Monty. "It won't look suspicious to them, but you can put in messages to us."

"And you can send messages back that I will see," said Sydney.

"We also have this," said Mother as he held up a smartphone SIM card for them to see. "Our friends at Vauxhall Cross came up with it. Normal SIM cards won't work in Russia, and you have to assume that they're monitoring all calls and messages. But this has some deep encryption that should keep us out of trouble. It comes with an app that sends instant messages that are truly instant."

"What do you mean by that?" asked Sydney.

"They disappear after fifteen seconds and leave no digital trace," he said.

They continued going over details for another thirty minutes, and when they were done, Sydney took the train to Kinloch. She loved the dolphin necklace and wanted to thank Brooklyn. She also missed her friend and wanted to spend a little time with her before leaving on the mission.

Sydney arrived on campus just after dinner as all the students were headed to the auditorium to hear a lecture by a visiting author. She spotted Brooklyn walking across the quad and sped up to catch her before she went back inside. But just before reaching her, Sydney recognized the girl who Brooklyn was walking with.

It was Charlotte.

And they weren't just walking. They were talking and laughing like old friends. Charlotte, who had abandoned the team and turned her back on all of them.

For Sydney it felt like a complete betrayal. She stopped cold and watched them walk away.

Gorky Park

SHEREMETYEVO INTERNATIONAL AIRPORT—MOSCOW, RUSSIA

IT DIDN'T MATTER WHICH AIRPORT HE WAS at, or whether he was traveling on a mission or vacation, Paris always felt uneasy at passport control. Maybe that was because he owned seven passports, each with a different name and identity. That meant there were seven distinct biographies he had to keep straight in his head. One wrong answer could ruin everything.

This anxiety was only magnified when he and Mother arrived in Moscow, where the vibe was anything but welcoming. The walls were colorless, the air stifling,

188

and the line felt like a herd with no apparent order or organization. It took them more than an hour to work their way to the front, where an immigration official in a glassed-off booth signaled them forward.

"Passport, visa," she said, like a recording that repeated the same phrases all day long.

They slid their papers through an opening in the glass, and she held up the passports to compare the photos to their faces.

"Where are you staying?" she asked in a thick Russian accent.

"The National hotel," Mother answered.

"It's near Red Square," Paris added, trying to be helpful.

"I know where National hotel is," she said sharply. "How long is your stay?"

"Four days," Mother said.

She gave Paris a raised eyebrow to see if he was going to add anything, but he didn't.

"Purpose of visit?"

"Chess," Paris answered.

This surprised her. "What you say?"

"Chess," he repeated. "I'm playing in the Around the World Chess Invitational."

"I have heard of this," she said. She didn't smile, but for the first time during the encounter, she wasn't frowning. She actually seemed . . . *interested.* "Are you good player?"

"He's very good," Mother said proudly. "He's already won four tournaments this month."

She eyed Paris critically. "Maybe I should keep you out of country so you don't beat any Russian players."

Paris went to protest, but then the woman let out a loud laugh, stamped their visas, and handed back their paperwork. "*Udachi tebe,*" she said. "That means 'good luck.'"

"Thank you."

They left, and once they were out of her earshot, Mother commented, "Well, that tells you something."

"What?" asked Paris.

"Do you know how hard it is to get any emotion, much less a laugh, out of a Moscow passport officer?" Mother asked. "It's unheard of. But they love chess in this country. They respect it and the people who play it well."

When they reached the baggage carousel, they saw a blond woman wearing a blue polo featuring the logo of the chess tournament. She held up a sign that read LUCAS DOINEL, Paris's cover name.

"I'm Lucas Doinel," he said to her.

"Excellent," she said. "Welcome to Moscow. My

name's Marina. We are running a bit behind schedule, so we need to hurry. Get your bags and we go."

"Hurry for what?" asked Paris.

"Publicity opportunity," answered the woman. "Gorky Park."

Domodedovo International Airport

Monty, Kat, and Rio arrived on a different flight at an airport on the opposite side of the city. It was standard procedure for the team to travel separately on missions in which their cover stories weren't linked. They operated in pods to make it impossible for anyone to connect them through the digital trail of receipts and reservations.

Because the trio had just been to Moscow a week earlier, they knew what to expect once they exited the terminal. The city was notorious for unlicensed cab drivers who aggressively jockeyed for business at airports and train stations, only to triple the charges upon arrival at the destination. It was not unheard of for some to try to get passengers by grabbing their suitcases before they had a chance to say no.

"Hold on to your bags and keep close," Monty reminded them moments before they were greeted by men shouting, "*Taksi. Taksi. Taksi.*"

The swarm was short-lived as one voice rose above the others and took control. "*S moyego puti*," the man bellowed. "*Oni so mnoy.*" Out of my way. They're with me.

Monty smiled when she looked up to see the bushy mustache and broad smile of Yuri, the driver who'd helped them chase Nicholas Sorokin. The British embassy had booked him for the day, and the crush of cabbies provided the perfect cover for them to connect without attracting any attention. If anyone were watching them, he'd look just like all the other aggressive cab drivers.

He took their bags and put them in the trunk and gave no indication that he recognized them until they were safe inside the cab.

"Hello, Yuri," said Rio.

"Hello, my good friends," Yuri replied warmly. "Welcome back to Moscow. I've been getting ready for you."

"Ready how?" Monty asked.

"We are looking for Mr. Motorcycle again?" Yuri asked.

Monty didn't know what to make of this, so she offered a cautious, "Maybe."

"Take you straight to him," he replied, tapping the smartphone mounted on his dash that he used as a GPS device. He swiped the screen to reveal a different map. It was green except for a red dot signaling Sorokin's present location.

"There he is," he said, pleased with himself. "Yuri put tracker on motorcycle, so we no have crazy chase."

Monty turned to look at the others in the back, and they shared a surprised and delighted look.

"Well, all right, Yuri!" Rio said.

Yuri grinned and said, "Just like James Bond, no?"

Vnukovo International Airport

Moscow had three major airports, and Sydney arrived at the third. Unlike the rest of the team, she didn't have to wait in line at passport control or face a gauntlet of dodgy cab drivers. This had nothing to do with where she landed and everything to do with who she landed with.

She was one of eight passengers who touched down just before noon on the *Caïssa II*, a private jet owned by Reginald Banks. Everything about the Gulfstream G650 was luxurious. It had a bedroom, a private office, and a deluxe entertainment center with a giant flatscreen.

Sydney and Tabitha spent most of the flight talking fashion while they ate snacks prepared by the family's personal chef and watched a yet-to-be-released movie that Sir Reg had financed. For security reasons, Sydney wasn't allowed to take any photographs inside the jet, but she planned to start shooting the moment they got off the plane. As soon as they landed, she pulled her camera out of her bag and started getting it ready.

"I want to cover every stage of the journey from start to finish," she said. "I was thinking we might shoot some video once we're inside the airport. Maybe interview you at the baggage carousel or as you walk through the terminal."

Tabitha chuckled.

"What?" asked Sydney, confused. "Did I say something wrong?"

"Not *wrong*, just *cute*," Tabitha said condescendingly. "We don't go *in* the airport."

"What do you mean?" asked Sydney. "We just landed in a new country. We have to show them our passports."

"Yes," Tabitha said. "But they come to us."

"Which is also something we do not take pictures of," said Sasha, who was sitting across the aisle, watching as always. "It's a special arrangement with the Russian government."

"Okay," Sydney said, embarrassed. "I'll put the camera away."

They were greeted by a pair of luxury SUVs, both

black with heavily tinted windows. Two valets instantly started loading their luggage into one, and a tall woman who looked more like a fashion model than an immigration official boarded the plane to check passports.

Sir Reg, who'd spent the entire flight in his office, joined them.

"I can't believe I missed the whole movie," he said humorously. "What'd you think?"

"I loved it," said Tabitha. "Although I still think you should've cast Idris."

"What about you?" he asked Sydney.

"I loved it too," she answered. "It's really good."

"I should hope so," Reg said with a playful smile. "I certainly paid enough for it."

"Thank you for letting me fly with you on the plane," Sydney said. "It was amazing."

"My pleasure," he answered. "If you think this was good, wait until the flight back."

"Why will it be different?" asked Sydney.

"Because we'll be flying with KB5," said Tabitha. "Which means we'll have to make our way through a mob of screaming fans just to get on board, and a nonstop party the entire flight home."

At 12:05, they were already in an SUV headed for the

hotel when Sydney saw Anastasia posting an image from her phone. Anastasia had turned away to block the view of the screen, but Sydney caught a quick glimpse of its reflection in the window.

It was a picture of St. Basil's cathedral.

Gorky Park

Stretching along the Moscow River, Gorky Park was the largest green space in the city and a popular destination for tourists and residents alike. Its main entrance was a massive colonnade nearly five stories tall that served as a portal to three hundred acres of gardens, fountains, walkways, recreation facilities, and waterfront beaches.

Just inside the colonnade, fifty small folding tables had been set up in rows as a publicity event for the chess tournament. The visual was a nod to the days when Moscow's parks were filled with people playing chess outdoors. Each table featured a game between two of the tournament's competitors, who were all going to make their first moves at the same time as a ceremonial beginning of the event. It was a picturesque setting, and the country's love of chess was evidenced by the large number of photographers and television crews who were on hand to document the ceremony.

Paris introduced himself to the tall girl with shoulder-length blond hair sitting across the table from him. "Hi, my name's Lucas."

"Antonia," she responded with a dimpled smile. "But call me Toni, like my friends."

"Nice to meet you," he answered. "I live in Scotland; how about you?"

"Würzburg, Germany," she answered.

Paris smiled at a memory, "In Bavaria, with the beautiful castle?"

"You've been there?" Antonia responded, surprised.

"Yes," he answered, although he couldn't really tell her why, since it was as part of a mission that was designed to capture a German engineer selling secrets to the Jordanian army. "On vacation with my family."

Mother stood off to the side with a crowd that included family members, tournament officials, and people who'd just been passing by and stopped to see what was going on. He kept scanning the faces of the competitors and their parents but saw no sign of Park or Dae-jung.

With all the competitors in place, another tournament

official in a blue polo came out with a microphone and addressed the media in Russian before turning to the players and signaling them to begin.

"*Nachinat'*," she said with a flourish, and the players all started their games.

Antonia was playing the white pieces, so she went first.

These games were only for the media event and didn't count as part of the tournament. This gave them a relaxed feel, which was evidenced by the smiles and conversation at many of the tables. Things would be much more serious and competitive when they played for real.

"Any sign of Park?" a voice whispered to Mother.

He turned and was surprised to see Monty had taken a position right next to him. They stood side by side so that if anyone noticed them, they appeared to be two strangers watching the event.

"None," he said. "I don't know what to make of it, but since this is just a photo op, it's not a big deal. I won't be worried unless he misses the opening ceremony tonight." He raised an eyebrow. "How did you know to come here? I didn't even know this was scheduled until they picked us up at the airport."

"My taxi brought me here for a different reason," she said.

"Which is what?" asked Mother.

"Look over there," she said, nodding toward a clump of people. "The tall guy in the red shirt with jeans and black boots."

"What about him?"

"That's Nicholas Sorokin."

Mother's eyes opened wide, and he studied the man. Unlike everyone around him, Sorokin wasn't looking at the chess players. He was scanning the faces of the people watching.

"So," Mother said. "Who's he looking for?"

21.

Rare Books

"INCREDIBLE," RIO SAID DREAMILY AFTER taking a bite of a meat-filled dumpling known as a "*pelmeni*." "I know you like patterns, Kat, so figure this one out. The three most delicious Russian foods all start with P: *pelmeni*, *pirozhki*, and *ponchiki*, which are those little doughnut holes. Think there's some meaning in that?"

"Definitely," said Kat, to Rio's surprise.

"You do?"

"Yes. I think it means you're obsessed with food and can never get enough."

Monty laughed at this. "She may be onto something."

"True," he responded as he savored another bite. "But you have to admit those doughnut holes are amazing."

Kat smiled. "Okay, you've got me there."

"Delicious," said Monty in agreement.

The three of them were sitting in a café across the street from Nicholas Sorokin's gift shop. After the photo op in the park, they followed him back here to see what he was up to, but so far it seemed as though he was just working, business as usual.

"Speaking of patterns, here's one I don't get," said Kat. "In the hallway behind the store, there was a locker area for employees, cages that held merchandise for the store, and offices."

"Right," said Monty.

"But there was also a room labeled 'maps'?" Kat said. "The others all make sense for the gift shop, but a whole room of nothing but maps? That doesn't make sense."

"Don't they sell maps?" Rio asked.

"Yes," said Kat. "But little souvenir ones for tourists. These looked detailed and were bigger than this table.

Why devote so much storage space to them?"

Monty stared at the shop for a moment and had an idea.

"What if they're not for *this* store?" Monty suggested. "The building fills the entire block, so maybe the storage area is also the storage area for whatever business is on the opposite side of the building."

Kat nodded as she considered this. "I hadn't thought of that. We should walk around and see what's over there."

"Let's," said Monty, liking the idea.

"You mean after I'm finished with these dumplings, right?" Rio said, looking up from his plate.

"You can eat," Monty said as she stood. "Stay here and keep an eye on Sorokin while we go."

"No, no, no. I don't want to miss anything." Rio scooped up the dumplings in his hands. "I can walk and eat. Besides, there's a shop over there that sells *plombir*."

"What's *plombir*?" asked Kat.

"A type of extra-rich ice cream," he answered. "It's a Russian specialty."

"You're going to eat more?" Kat asked in disbelief. "You haven't even finished the dumplings."

"Not yet," he mumbled, his mouth full as he chewed. "But I'll be done before we make it around the block."

"You're amazing," said Monty with a chuckle.

"Thank you," Rio answered proudly.

"I don't think she meant it as a compliment," Kat added.

"Hey, I just thought of something!" Rio said. "*Plombir* is another Russian food that starts with *P*. That means it's got to be delicious."

First, they crossed the street via an underground walkway known as a "*perekhod*." Then they tried to figure out the approximate distance from the souvenir shop to the corner so that when they were on the other side, they could determine what was directly behind it.

"It should be one of these three," Monty said when they reached a women's clothing boutique situated between a bookshop and a jewelry store.

"I think so too," said Kat.

Rio was midswallow as he finished the last dumpling and nodded. "Mm-hm."

"Of the three, the bookshop makes the most sense to have maps," Monty said. "Why don't I go in alone and you two wait out here?"

"Perfect, because the ice cream shop is right over there," Rio said, pointing just down the block. "We can wait for you there."

"We can?" asked Kat.

"My treat," Rio offered. "It's supposed to be incredible."

"Okay," Kat relented. She was a sucker for ice cream. "We'll wait for you there."

Monty went into Karamazov's, a rare books store with a cozy atmosphere. There were large wooden bookcases, soothing classical music, and busts of famous Russian authors such as Tolstoy, Pushkin, Chekov, and Dostoyevsky.

She was checking to see if there were any maps on display when a bookseller with wire-framed glasses and curly unkempt hair approached her. He looked like a professor, or maybe a poet.

"*Chem ya mogu vam pomoch?*" he asked.

Monty's wide-eyed reaction made it obvious that she didn't understand a word of what he said, although she assumed it was some variation of *May I help you?* "I'm sorry," she responded. "I don't suppose you speak English."

"As it happens, I do," said the man with a smile.

"Unlike many of our neighboring stores, we sell to an international clientele. Although, I'm afraid virtually all our books are in Russian, so I don't know if we would have anything you'd want."

This was where Monty decided to act like she knew more than she did.

"I'm not actually looking for any books," she said. "I was told you also sold maps."

The man was surprised by this and sized her up before answering.

"We have a few," he said cryptically.

"I'd like to see them," she responded.

He thought for a moment before answering, "Please, come with me."

He led her to a small reading room with an oak table and two chairs. An antique cabinet ran the length of one wall.

The man didn't speak again until he shut the door behind them. "In addition to our books, we have a special collection of papers, posters, and other miscellaneous objects," he said as he motioned for her to sit at the table. "This includes some antique maps."

He unlocked the cabinet and carefully pulled out an

oversize folder, which he placed in front of her. "Perhaps these are the maps you're thinking of," he said as he opened the folder to reveal them.

Monty tried to make sense of the scene. She knew these maps were smaller than the ones Kat had seen but couldn't understand the secretive attitude of the bookseller.

"No," she said. "The maps were described to me as being much bigger than this. The size of this table and larger."

"And may I ask who told you this?"

"You can ask," Monty said. "But I'm not going to tell you." She decided to go for broke and make up a cover story on the spot. "The buyer I represent is discreet. He doesn't share where he receives his information, just as he won't tell anyone else where he makes his purchases." Then she added, "And, if you have what he's looking for, the purchase he plans to make is significant."

He looked at her carefully before saying, "One moment, please."

He left the room and closed the door. Monty had no idea what she'd stumbled onto, but judging by his reaction, there was some black-market element to these maps. She assumed that there was a security camera somewhere watching her, so she made no move that might give her away. Instead, she projected confidence and calm as her mind raced through questions, trying to figure out what was going on and how the maps related to Sir Reg and the secret code.

The man had been gone for nearly five minutes before the door opened again.

Monty was surprised to see that it wasn't the bookseller returning.

It was Nicholas Sorokin.

Charm School

RIO HELD HIS ICE CREAM CONE IN ONE hand while he typed something on his phone with the other. He was sitting on a wooden bench next to Kat, and when she tried to take a look at the screen, he turned his body to block her view.

"Come on," she said. "You can show me. What's the score? Ninety? Ninety-two?"

"It's too soon to give a precise number," he said. "But it should be strong. I'm guessing mideighties."

"Guessing?" she said. "How can it be a guess when you make it up?"

"You know very well that I don't *make it up*," he replied, shooting her the side-eye. "I give grades that are part of a complex formula, and the *formula* determines the score. Besides, nothing will be firm until tonight, when I figure out the anticipation-to-satisfaction ratio and enter the numbers for aftertaste, digestion, and cravings for seconds."

The score they were discussing was the rating for the *plombir* ice cream in Rio's exhaustively detailed food journal. He evaluated all new foods on a scale from one to one hundred, taking into consideration criteria ranging from taste and texture to originality and presentation. Or, as Paris liked to say, "everything except whether or not it's good for you."

Rio took the journal so seriously that he refused to share the specifics of his formula with anyone and hoped one day to turn it into an app. Kat and Brooklyn had an ongoing bet to see who could be the first to figure it out, but so far neither had made any headway.

"Not that it matters, but I think the ice cream's delicious," said Kat.

"So do I," said Rio. "But there's much more to food than how good it tastes."

Kat licked her cone a few times and said, "Can I ask you a favor?"

"That depends. Is it about my formula?"

"No. It's about what you did the other day, when your magic trick distracted everyone so I could sneak in the back." She sighed, almost embarrassed. "Do you think you could show me how to do that?"

"Sure," he said. "It's just the cups-and-ball trick. Very basic. I can teach you that."

"I don't want to learn the cups-and-ball trick," she said. "I want to learn the trick of how you talk to people."

Rio had a confused look. "I don't know what you mean."

Kat thought for a moment, trying to figure out how to put it into words. "I'm not good with, you know, people," she said. "And I hate to admit it, but you're kind of charming. That's a word that will never be used to describe me. Normally, I couldn't care less, but I feel like it limits my effectiveness in the field. You couldn't even speak the same language they did, and you still had them wrapped around your finger."

Rio appreciated the compliment and knew that it was

rare for Kat to open up like this. He was touched that she would ask for his help with anything.

"I can't teach you to be like me, because you're not like me," he said. "At least, not in that way."

"So, I'm a hopeless case."

"No, that's not what I mean," he said. "The thing is, I think you already are charming."

She gave him a dubious look. "You know that's not true," she said. "I'm completely awkward in virtually all social situations."

"Yes," he said. "But *that's* your charm. The only trick you need is to be comfortable with it. You are who you are, Kat. Lean into it."

"So, when some girl at school asks me about my favorite band, I should say, 'I'm not really into bands, but I love left-and-right truncatable prime numbers'?"

Rio laughed. "Okay, maybe don't lean that far. But you could say, 'I don't really have a favorite band, what's yours?'"

"Why would I do that?" she demanded. "I have no interest in knowing her favorite band."

"Right," he said. "But she doesn't really want to know yours, either."

"Then why did she ask me?" Kat asked, baffled.

"Because she wants to talk to you," he answered. "She wants to get to know you, and the only way she can do that is by asking questions to find out what you like."

"But I like left-and-right truncatable prime numbers."

He laughed. "Okay, why do you like them?"

Kat's eyes lit up. "Because they're elegant and surprising and rare."

"Elegant, surprising, and rare," said Rio. "Three words that describe my sister Kat."

The sweetness of this statement caught her completely off guard and made her blush. "See what I mean?" she said. "Charming."

"I think I can help you figure out how to be you *and* be like that," he said. "But right now I'm a little concerned about Monty. She was only going to see if the bookstore sold maps. She should be back by now."

"You're right," Kat said as she finished her last bite of ice cream. "Let's go check on her."

As they headed to the store, Monty was still in the reading room with Nicholas Sorokin. Luckily, he hadn't recognized her, so she'd continued playing her role as someone looking to buy special maps for a wealthy client. Unfortunately, she didn't know why they were special, which made the conversation tricky.

"I would like to see some of the merchandise to make sure they are as they are advertised," Monty said.

"Of course," said Sorokin. "Pick any two cities in the world and I will bring them to you."

She had to pick quickly and carefully. She knew that he'd checked a map before going to the North Korean embassy and she wanted to see it, so she said, "Moscow." But she didn't know Moscow well enough that she could tell what made the map special, so she picked someplace familiar. "And London."

"I'll be right back," he said.

A few minutes later, he returned with two maps that he laid out on the table, one on top of the other. They were so big that they hung over all four sides. In addition to their large size, they were extremely detailed, more so than any she'd ever seen.

"They're beautiful," she said.

"Most accurate maps in the world," replied Sorokin, and although he was giving the sales pitch, she wondered if he might not be exaggerating by that much.

Not only were streets marked, but so were individual buildings. And while she couldn't translate the wording, she could tell they listed everything from elevations to the width of roads and length of bridges. She assumed they'd been created by the military, which might explain one Russian word she did recognize: секрет. Secret. It was written in the top right corner of each one.

"How many do you have?" she asked.

"Thousands and thousands," he answered. "Any place in the world, and since they've never been publicly available, it means your client would have something rare and special."

Monty thought they were fascinating, but she couldn't tell how they fit into the bigger picture. They seemed to be part of the St. Basil's code, but she couldn't imagine any connection between them and Sir Reg or Park Jin-sun.

"May I take pictures to show my client?" she asked.

"Two," he said. "If he wants to see more than that, he has to buy them."

Monty snapped a photograph of each map. They were too big for her to get them entirely in the frame, so she got as much as she could.

"How do I place an order once I've shown these to him?" she asked.

"You leave me out of that," he said. "You call Maksim, the one you already met. We'll go get his card."

They exited the reading room and went to the back

of the store, where Maksim was working behind the counter.

"Give her your business card so she can make an order," Sorokin instructed, like a boss, not a friend.

"Of course," said Maksim. He handed her the card and said, "You like what you saw?"

Monty nodded. "Very much."

"By the way, I think these two are looking for you." Maxim pointed toward the door where Kat and Rio were standing.

Sorokin looked too and recognized Kat, although it took him a moment to remember where he'd seen her.

Monty, sensing trouble, moved quickly and was halfway across the store before Sorokin roared, "Wait a minute! You two are together?"

"Run!" Monty said to Kat and Rio as she bolted for the door.

The instant they reached the sidewalk, Monty was on her phone calling Yuri.

"We have an emergency," she said.

She looked over her shoulder and saw that Sorokin was half a block behind them.

"Faster!" she told the others, and they found an extra gear and picked up their pace.

Despite the increase, Sorokin was gaining speed and had narrowed the gap by the time they turned the corner and saw Yuri's cab ahead of them.

"*Ostanovka!*" shouted Sorokin. "*Ostanovka!*"

All three of them jumped into the backseat of the taxi and quickly locked their doors.

"Go, go, go!" barked Monty.

"Who are we chasing?" Yuri asked.

"We're not," she said. "We're being chased. We need to get to the British embassy."

Just then Sorokin reached the car and pounded his fist against the window next to Monty. It was startling, but there was nothing he could do to stop them.

"Hold tight," Yuri said as he gunned the engine and began speeding away.

Rio turned around to look out the back window. He watched as an angry Sorokin rushed back to his motor-cycle and started pursuing them.

"Here he comes," he said. "He's on his motorcycle."

"Don't worry," the driver said. "Yuri will lose him."

He made an abrupt and sudden turn and pulled across multiple lanes to jump onto a different road. Sorokin had to work through traffic to follow.

Meanwhile, Monty called an MI6 emergency number.

"Waterloo Bridge?" she said when the phone was answered.

"Identify," came the voice.

"Windsor, Chelsea, Stratford," Monty answered.

"Temperature?"

She looked through the rear window and could see Sorokin closing on them.

"Very hot."

"ETA?"

"How soon will we be there?" Monty asked Yuri as he zipped between two cars and made another sudden turn.

"Fifteen minutes," he answered.

"One-five," Monty said in the call.

"Copy," said the voice, and then the call clicked off.

As he weaved through traffic, Yuri reached up and swiped his smartphone so that it showed Sorokin's tracker.

"We don't need to track him," Rio pointed out. "He's following us."

"Yes, but this way I can tell when I lose him."

Yuri laid on his horn as he cut through a busy

intersection and onto a bridge over the Moscow River.

"The embassy's that way," Monty said, panicked.

"First we go somewhere else," Yuri responded, accelerating.

"No!" Monty said. "We need to get to the embassy!"

"Trust Yuri," he said.

Monty didn't exactly trust Yuri's judgment, but there wasn't much she could do about it as he zipped through a maze of roads, turning corners so fast that Rio and Kat were holding on tight in the backseat.

"Where are we going?" Monty demanded.

"Here," said Yuri as he pulled onto a congested street. They were surrounded by hotels and next to a train station, which meant there were taxis everywhere. Yuri pulled in among them and slowed to a normal pace.

"Brilliant," Monty said. "Let's hope it works."

On the tracker they could see the motorcycle getting close to them.

"Get down," she told the kids. "He's looking for three in the backseat."

Rio and Kat laid low while Monty fought the urge to look out the window, where Sorokin might see her face. Instead, she kept her eyes on the tracker. At one point he was within ten meters of them, but he kept going. Yuri turned the next corner and went in the opposite direction.

"Now we go to embassy," Yuri said.

23.

The Tretyakov

"REMEMBER ME?" PARIS SAID IN A LOW voice, a mischievous grin on his face.

He was looking at the *Pearl of Russia*, the Fabergé egg that two months earlier had been nestled in his jacket as he scaled the wall of Sir Reg's London mansion. Now it was on display at Moscow's Tretyakov Gallery as part of an exhibit titled *Treasures of the Imperial Collection*.

He leaned forward to get a closer look and received an instant rebuke from a nearby woman.

"*Otstupit,*" she said firmly.

Paris turned to Mother and whispered, "Did she just call me stupid?"

"*Otstupit*," he said. "It means 'back away.' She's the guard."

Paris raised an eyebrow because she didn't look like a guard. She was in her midsixties and barely five feet tall. She had gray hair, sensible shoes, and wore a sweater over a long-sleeved shirt, even though it was the middle of summer.

"Really?" he asked.

"It's tradition in Russian art museums," Mother answered. "Rather than imposing guards in uniforms they have . . ."

"What? Grannies in cardigans?"

"Pretty much," Mother said with a smirk. "But don't be fooled. She's probably ex-KGB. If you get too close to the art, she'll go from babushka to ninja in no time flat."

"How do I say 'sorry' in Russian?"

"*Izvinite*," Mother answered.

Paris gave the woman an apologetic smile and said, "*Izvinite*."

The Tretyakov occupied several buildings, including one with a redbrick facade that looked like it belonged in a fairy tale. In addition to housing the world's largest collection of Russian art, it had been the site of the 2012 World Chess Championship between Viswanathan Anand and Boris Gelfand. This intersection of fine art and elite chess had proved irresistible to Reginald Banks. He not only loaned the museum his Fabergé egg, but he also provided the funding for the entire exhibition. In return, the Tretyakov agreed to host the Around the World Chess Invitational.

The tournament was set to begin the following morning, and the competitors were on hand with their families for the opening ceremony, an event more relaxed and social than the grandness of its name implied. Sir Reg was running a little late, so everyone mingled and ate finger foods as they admired the art, and a string quartet played Russian classical music.

Paris noticed Mother scanning the room and asked, "Still no sign of them?"

"No," he said, a concerned look on his face. Park Jin-sun and Dae-jung hadn't been at the photo op earlier, and now they were no-shows again. "I'm beginning to worry they didn't make the trip. Maybe the North Korean government changed their minds."

Just then, there was a murmur among the crowd as Sir Reg entered the room. He looked sharp in a tailor-made electric-blue suit and was greeted with a spontaneous round of applause. Jin-sun and Dae-jung were with him, and it appeared as though they were in the middle of a conversation as they walked.

"So that's where they've been," Mother said. "Reg is already making his play."

They were closely followed by four men in dark suits.

"Those the guards you were talking about?" Paris asked.

"My guess is Ministry of State Security," Mother said. "You can tell by the friendly smiles," he added sarcastically.

Sir Reg strode directly to the front of the room, and the string quartet stopped playing so he could speak to the crowd. The setting was intimate enough that he didn't need a microphone.

"*Dobryy vecher*," he said, using the Russian for "good evening." "I'm sorry I was running behind schedule. It's so lovely to see you. I'd like to officially welcome you to the Moscow Around the World Chess Invitational, sponsored by my company, Caïssa, and the fabulous Tretyakov Gallery."

Another round of applause.

"I'm so excited to be here with so many of you great

young players. You represent the future of chess, and tomorrow you'll play right where Anand and Gelfand battled for the world championship. Who knows? Someday one of you might be competing for that same title as well."

Paris scanned the crowd and saw a familiar face.

"Look who's here," he whispered to Mother.

Mother looked and saw that Sydney was part of Sir Reg's entourage. She had her camera ready and was standing off to the side with Tabitha. Mother breathed a sigh of relief to see that the plan seemed to be working so far.

"In a moment, we're going to post the pairings for the first round," said Reg. "But for now, enjoy the food, enjoy the art, and tomorrow we will all enjoy the chess." He turned to step away but stopped and added, "And remember, although you'll be playing here at the museum, we're going to present the medals Monday night at the KB5 concert, where you'll be cheered by tens of thousands of fans."

There was more applause, and Paris wondered if that was what Sir Reg's life was like, people clapping whenever he entered a room or said a few sentences.

The quartet resumed playing, and Reg started mingling with the guests and smiling for selfies. Mother saw this as an opportunity to work his way toward Jin-sun without being obvious. Recruiting an asset to flip from one country to another was a delicate procedure, and his goal tonight was simply to make a positive first contact.

"They're posting the pairings."

Paris turned to see that it was Antonia, the girl he'd met earlier in Gorky Park.

"Who knows," she continued. "Maybe we're playing each other in the first round. Let's go see."

Paris was as excited about the tournament as he was to be on a mission. He happily followed her to where most of the competitors were gathering around two large presentation boards.

"We're in group one," Antonia said, "with the highest-ranked players."

Dae-jung headed over to look at the pairings too, and Mother noticed that only one of the North Korean agents went with him, while the other three stayed with the father. That's who they were primarily concerned with protecting.

"Exciting, isn't it?" Mother said to Park. "This is the biggest tournament my son's ever played in."

"The same for mine," Park replied. "I bet he hardly sleeps tonight."

Park's English was flawless, and there was a friendliness to his tone that seemed to invite conversation, although his protection team instantly moved closer as they talked.

Mother was careful not to invade his personal space. He wanted the conversation to feel casual, almost accidental. He didn't even face Park directly, instead looking out toward the kids as they talked shoulder to shoulder.

"This is my first time in Moscow, and it's amazing," Mother said. "Have you been here before?"

Mother already knew the answer because he'd memorized Park's dossier, but he wanted to see how he responded.

"I went to university here," he replied. "This museum has always been a favorite of mine."

Mother noticed that one of the agents now looked perturbed at him, but he wanted to have a little more conversation, so he ignored that and pressed on.

"They're taking such good care of us," he said. "I can't believe they put us in a five-star hotel. My son and some of the other players are planning to meet for breakfast in the morning if yours is interested in joining them."

"He would love that," Park said. "Unfortunately,

we're not allowed to stay at the hotel. We're stuck at the embassy, which is like the flag that flies over it— one star."

Mother was surprised Park would make a joke like that. He was being critical of the government in front of the agents, which could lead to blowback. Stranger still, despite being negative, his tone and smile were as though he'd said something positive. The sentiments didn't match, and it took Mother a moment to figure it out.

He smiled back at Park. "They don't speak English," he said of the guards.

Park laughed like Mother just told him a joke before answering, "Not a word."

This was a positive development. Not only could the guards not understand what they were saying, but Park seemed to revel in taking advantage of the fact.

Before Mother could say anything else, however, his phone vibrated to signal the arrival of an emergency message from Monty.

He casually pulled the phone from his pocket and positioned himself so no one else could see it. He'd have only fifteen seconds once he'd opened the message before the app erased it.

Waterloo Bridge

Simon & Schuster paperback £21.00

Simon & Schuster was the name of a publishing company, so even if someone did manage to see or intercept the text, it would look like a simple reference to a book named *Waterloo Bridge* that cost twenty-one pounds. To Mother, however, the text was filled with extremely troubling information.

Waterloo Bridge was code for the British embassy, which meant that Monty, Kat, and Rio needed to go in for protection. Paperback was a reference to their cover story. If Monty had texted "hardcover," that would've meant that their cover was secure. "Paperback" indicated that it was soft and possibly compromised. The only positive in the message was Simon & Schuster, which was abbreviated "S&S" and stood for "safe and sound." Finally, the twenty-one was nine p.m. in military time. That's when he'd receive follow-up information.

It was just past seven, so Mother needed to wait nearly two hours before he learned any more. Until then, he had to act like everything was fine. He slipped the phone back into his pocket, and his mind raced through possible scenarios. If Monty's cover was blown, there was a chance the mission could be compromised. He did a quick check to make sure Sydney and Paris were okay.

Sydney was talking to Tabitha over by the Fabergé eggs, and Paris was with the other competitors looking at the drawings for the first round of the tournament. Here, at least, everything seemed to be fine.

Then the shriek of a security alarm filled the museum.

Waterloo Bridge

One hour earlier

MONTY WAS STILL IN THE BACKSEAT OF Yuri's cab when she got the call from the embassy. The voice on the other end was somber as it delivered the bad news. "I'm sorry to say that there's been a medical emergency back home."

"Oh my goodness," Monty exclaimed. "Who is it? What happened?"

"It's your father," said the man with a calming tone. "We don't know for certain, but we believe he may have had a heart attack. He's been rushed to Royal Edinburgh Hospital."

Monty sat quiet for a moment, stunned by the news.

"I—I—I don't know what to do," she said, her voice trembling. "This is such a shock."

"That's why we're here," he replied. "Come to the embassy, and we'll help you with the arrangements so you can get home quickly to be with your family."

"Of course," Monty said haltingly. "I'm on my way."

Monty's performance was completely believable, helped no doubt by the improvisational acting classes she'd taken during college as a member of the Oxford Imps. Her father wasn't really ill and had, in fact, recently competed in a triathlon. But she, Kat, and Rio were agents involved in an active operation, and precautions needed to be taken in order to get them safely out of the country without disrupting the mission.

Their confrontation with Nicholas Sorokin meant their role in Moscow was now over. But Yuri had managed to lose him on their chase through the city, which gave them a chance to catch their breath and follow proper protocols. Once Sorokin had gone the wrong way, Monty made a second call to the secret MI6 number to tell them that the temperature of the situation had gone from "very hot" to "warm," meaning there was still an emergency but no longer an imminent threat. She was told to wait for further directions.

Five minutes later came the phone call about her father's supposed heart attack along with the instructions to go directly to the embassy. This had nothing to do with Monty and everything to do with the FSB.

The *Federal'naya Sluzhba Bezopasnosti* was the Russian secret intelligence agency, and it monitored every single call from the British embassy and had closed-circuit cameras that recorded the faces of anyone who entered or exited the premises. Monty and the team now had a perfect explanation for arriving and abruptly changing their reservations to fly home immediately. MI6 even altered the admission register at Royal Edinburgh Hospital on the off chance someone checked for any mention of her father coming to the emergency room.

The embassy was located on the Smolenskaya Embankment in the Arbat district of the city. It consisted of four buildings, each between seven and ten stories high, which occupied two acres overlooking the Moscow River. Unlike much of the cold, sterile architecture nearby, the complex had a bright and modern feel.

There were even a pair of statues out front memorializing Sherlock Holmes and Dr. Watson, their faces made to look like those of the Russian actors who portrayed them in a popular television series.

There was nothing bright, however, about the windowless room where Monty, Kat, and Rio were taken after they arrived. It was known as a "SCIF," which was pronounced *skiff* and stood for *sensitive compartmented information facility.* It was the most secure location at the embassy, a room built inside another room with no connection to the outside world. Everything inside was battery-powered because there wasn't any electrical wiring, and no phones or computers were allowed within. This is where government officials talked when they wanted to be sure that the FSB couldn't eavesdrop.

The three of them were debriefed by Tru, who'd come to Moscow for a cyber security symposium, and an intelligence officer named Greg Miller, who was based at the embassy. Monty walked them through the encounter with Sorokin and their chase through the city.

"These maps seem to play a role, but I don't know what it is," Monty said

"Agent Miller might be able to offer some insight," Tru said.

"I don't know how they connect," said Miller, who was studying printouts of the two photos Monty had taken of the maps in the bookstore. "But I can tell you what they are. First of all, you have to understand that during the height of the Cold War, the Soviets had two simultaneous and contradictory approaches to mapmaking."

"What do you mean?" asked Rio.

"The maps that were made for average Russians in the nineteen sixties and seventies were borderline useless," he said. "Things were purposefully mislabeled or placed in the wrong locations. Rivers were moved, cities omitted, and roads sent in the wrong direction."

"Why?" asked Kat.

"It was all part of a state-sponsored misinformation plan," he said. "If the maps fell into the hands of the enemy—namely us Brits and the Americans—then we would be confused and lost should we ever invade Mother Russia."

"And the fact that it was also misinforming all the Russian citizens?" asked Monty.

"They weren't so concerned with that," said Miller.

"But these maps?" Rio said, pointing at the two printouts on the table.

"These are works of art," Miller said. "For decades

the Soviet military undertook a top secret operation to map the entire world with incredible detail. These maps were kept in secure locations and checked out from a vault. If one was destroyed, the ashes had to be returned as proof that it didn't wind up in enemy hands. If one was lost, the officer responsible was jailed." He looked up, and with a grim expression added, "Or worse."

"What's so special about them?" Rio asked.

"They were designed for military occupation," Miller said, "and they contain details necessary for tanks and armies. Details such as the dimensions of roads, the strength of bridges, and the location of specific buildings."

"If they were made during the Soviet era, they must be at least forty years old," said Monty. "We now live in an era of Google Earth and hyperaccurate satellite imagery. Surely they're out of date."

"In many ways, yes," said Miller. "But look at this map of Moscow. It includes tunnels that were built as an escape route to get agents out of the Kremlin. You can find no other record of that. And this one of London has a military research lab whose location is top secret and left off our maps to this day. That's why the Russians have never declassified the maps and is the reason Sorokin acted as he did. A satellite will provide you with a precise grid of every street in Moscow. But it has no way of detecting a secret bunker that was beneath those streets."

"Or a tunnel near the North Korean embassy," offered Kat.

"What's that?" Miller asked.

"We followed Sorokin to a park across the street from the North Korean embassy," Monty explained. "And we think he went underground there. It was immediately after he'd checked this map."

"Well, this is where the embassy is located," said Miller, putting his finger on the map.

"And this is the park," said Rio. "Look at that."

A line on the map indicated that a tunnel ran under the park and continued beneath the embassy.

"The nuclear materials were stolen from some kind of secret military base, right?" Kat said.

"Yes," said Tru. "It's called Kola-27."

"Would its location be listed on a map like this?" she asked.

"In great detail," Miller answered.

"So, you can see why there's so much at stake with this mission," said Tru. She turned to Monty, "Do you think Sorokin can connect you to Mother?"

"It's possible, but highly unlikely," said Monty. "Earlier today we followed Sorokin to a photo op in Gorky Park. Mother and Paris were there as part of the tournament."

"Did you communicate with him?" Tru asked.

"Yes," Monty said. "But briefly and without even making eye contact. Sorokin was nowhere near us and hadn't yet seen me. He'd have no reason to suspect."

"Are you certain?" Tru asked her.

Monty ran through everything in her head. "Positive. Mother's good."

"Very well," said Tru. "We won't scrub the mission. But the three of you are heading home right away. We've sent someone to collect your things from the hotel, and you'll be driven to the airport by an agent named Carey Cavanaugh."

"Who's that?" asked Monty.

"He's MI6," Tru said. "Although, officially he's listed as a family liaison officer with the embassy. It fits with the cover of your father being sick. He's arranged the new flights so that you can return home to be at the hospital. He's going to drive you to the airport and stay with you until you board your flight. He's very skilled, but you know that already."

"We do?" asked Monty, confused.

There was a knock on the door.

"That should be him now," Tru said.

She opened the door, and into the room stepped a man in a dark blue suit. He was clean-shaven, which is why it took them each a moment to recognize him.

"Yuri?" Rio said when he put it together.

"Oh my goodness," Monty said. "I never would've recognized you."

"That's the way it's supposed to be," Cavanaugh answered with a smile, his Russian accent now replaced by his British one. "Just like James Bond, no?"

Two Alarms

THE OPENING CEREMONY WAS GOING great until the sound of an alarm filled the Tretyakov. Most people froze as they tried to figure out what to do, but Mother had trained for emergency situations just like this. He'd studied the layout of the museum the moment he saw it on the schedule, and knew that there were exactly five access points for the gallery they were in. There were two corridors that led to other exhibit areas, an emergency exit in the corner, the door to a curator's office, and a stained-glass skylight in the ceiling.

He scanned them quickly and was looking at the sky-light when a second alarm sounded. This felt like an escalation and brought a gasp from the crowd. Mother spun around and saw that it was coming from the emergency exit, which was now wide open.

There was no indication, however, that any intruders had come into the room. This confusion continued for another thirty seconds, until someone closed the door and both alarms were turned off.

"Nothing to worry about," Sir Reg announced to the group, his voice raised to be heard over the commotion. "Nothing to worry about at all. Someone just got a little too close to the art and set off the security system."

There was relieved laughter throughout the party, and everyone went back to what they were doing before. All told, the interruption lasted roughly ninety seconds.

"Someone getting close to the art would explain the first alarm," whispered Paris, who'd headed straight for Mother at the sign of trouble. "But not the second."

"No," said Mother. "That was the emergency exit."

"Who used that?" asked Paris.

Mother did a quick scan of the room and realized that Park and his son were gone. "North Korean Ministry of State Security," he said. "They must've whisked the Parks out of the room the instant the alarm sounded."

"Wow," said Paris. "That was quick."

"It sure was," Mother answered. "They're not taking any chances."

Just then, Mother's phone vibrated. He looked at the screen and saw that someone was trying to AirDrop him a file. It was a feature that only worked if the phones were less than ten meters apart, which meant there could only be one source.

"What's up?" Paris asked.

"Not sure," said Mother. "Syd's sending me a file."

Mother turned and saw that Sydney was nearby adjusting something on her camera. He made the faintest of nods so that she'd know he'd received the message.

"Why don't you do a brush pass?" Mother said to Paris. "See if it's anything urgent."

"I thought we couldn't talk?" Paris asked. "We're not supposed to know each other."

"Yes, but she's here taking pictures at the party, and you're one of the competitors, so there's nothing suspicious about a polite interaction," Mother responded. "You should be able to say something quick without attracting attention. Just walk by and take your lead from her. If she stays quiet, so do you. But if she's got something to say, she'll know if it's safe to talk."

Paris nodded and started to walk across the room. Sydney noticed him and moved next to a table with small chess-themed desserts. It was the perfect place to *bump* into each other. She kept taking pictures as Paris studied the treats.

"I just sent a recording of a conversation," she said so quietly that only he could hear her.

"What is it?"

"Park arguing with his guards," she replied, "but it's all in Korean."

Paris nodded. "We'll have it translated straightaway."

He picked up a slice of bird's milk cake decorated with black and white squares like a chessboard and turned to head back toward Mother.

"By the way," Sydney added while she adjusted the focus on her camera. "It wasn't just *someone* who got too close to the art and triggered the alarm."

"Who was it?"

"Sir Reg," she said as she turned to walk away. "And it wasn't an accident."

Paris relayed the message to Mother, who spent the

rest of the event trying to figure out why Reg would set off the alarm. He was still working on it later when he exited his hotel and went for a stroll. It was almost nine o'clock, and he knew from the emergency text he'd received earlier that that was when MI6 would make contact with him about the situation regarding Monty, Kat, and Rio.

As was protocol, he walked for about fifteen minutes so that whoever was meeting him had ample time to make sure he wasn't being followed. Finally, he took a seat at an outdoor café near Lubyanka Square and ordered a cup of chamomile tea.

Three minutes later, a woman took a seat at the table next to him. He didn't have to look up to know who it was.

"Good evening, Tru," he said as he took a sip.

"This is rather cheeky, even for you," Tru said, more amused than annoyed. "You do know what that building is, don't you?"

Directly across the street from them was a massive building with a yellow brick facade.

"Come to think of it, I believe that's the KGB building," he said, referencing the Soviet-era security agency. "As well as the current headquarters for the FSB. What was that you used to tell me? '*Anyone can hide under darkness of night, but the cunning one hides out in plain sight.*'"

"True," she said. "But don't forget the bottom floor of that building is a prison for spies who get a little *too* cheeky. I'd hate for you to be taken there in the back of one of their black vans."

"I'll try to avoid them," he replied. "How are Monty and the kids?"

"Safe and sound on a flight to Heathrow," she answered.

"The text said her cover was soft. Anything I should be concerned about?"

"No," she replied. "You're safe for the time being. At least we think so."

"Now who's being cheeky?" Mother replied.

They continued to talk, and she gave him a quick run-down of the maps and what happened with Monty and Sorokin.

"I'm sending you a file," Mother said. "It's an argument between Park and his North Korean handlers. As soon as you can get it translated, let me know if there's anything useful in it."

"Roger that," said Tru.

"And something strange happened at the opening ceremony," Mother said. "An alarm went off, and the guards instantly whisked Park and his son away."

"Hardly strange," Tru said. "I'm sure it's standard protocol. They've got twitchy fingers, the North Koreans. If there's the slightest hint of trouble, that's what they're going to do."

"Exactly," said Mother. "The strange part is that Sir Reg is the one who set off the alarm. Sydney's certain he did it on purpose."

"Why on earth would he do that?"

"That's what I've been trying to figure out," he said. "I wonder if he's testing the North Koreans to see how twitchy their fingers really are."

Tru weighed this information. "Which means instead of convincing Park to change sides, he may just be . . ."

"Planning to grab him," Mother said, finishing the sentence. "Not a defection, but a kidnapping."

The Bolshoi

SYDNEY STOOD AWESTRUCK AT CENTER stage as she looked out at the Bolshoi Theatre, home to Russia's top ballet and opera companies. *"Bolshoi"* meant "grand," and it more than lived up to its name. The auditorium was ringed by five tiers of luxurious private boxes draped in red velvet. Imperial gold accents adorned everything from the ceiling mural to the ornamentation on the balconies and the stitching in the massive tapestry curtain. The centerpiece of it all was a gigantic two-ton gilded chandelier that hung above the audience and measured six and a half meters wide.

"It's all so breathtaking," she said as she turned to Sasha Sorokin. "You actually performed on this stage?"

Sasha nodded, her eyes full of life as she recalled the memory. "My sister and I danced in the corps de ballet for *Swan Lake* and *Sleeping Beauty*."

Sydney tried to imagine what that was like. "It must have been thrilling."

"A dream come true," Sasha said. "The crowds were electric."

Although the Sorokin sisters were still suspicious of all things Sydney, this at least resembled a friendly chat. Today the twins were in a better mood than usual because they were visiting some of their favorite Moscow haunts. In addition to providing security, they were acting as tour guides as they showed Tabitha around their hometown while Sydney captured the sightseeing for *All Roads Lead to Audrey*.

"How do I look?" Tabitha asked as she came onto the stage dressed in a black leotard and tights.

"Perfect," said Sydney. "Just like the photograph."

When Sydney found out they could visit the Bolshoi,

she had the idea of having Tabitha recreate a classic photograph of Audrey Hepburn, who'd trained as a ballerina before becoming an actress. Having Tabitha match Audrey's pose on ballet's grandest stage was perfect for the website, and a sign that even though her role as a journalist was a cover story, Sydney was taking it seriously.

After the photo shoot, the group visited some of the high-end shops and boutiques along Petrovka Street. This was also where Anastasia shared the story of an eccentric noblewoman that was so fascinating, Sydney had Tabitha retell it on video for the website.

"Hey, Team Audrey, it's Tabs, giving you the ultimate Moscow fashion tour," she said directly into the lens. "We're in front of Cartier, but not because I'm going to show you any jewelry or accessories. I want to tell you about a nineteenth-century celebutante named Anna Annenkova, whose house stood on this very spot. Anna was part of Russian nobility and was so worried that she might be unprepared for any sudden high-society happenings that instead of pajamas, she went to bed every night fully dressed in a ballgown with silk stockings and shoes. Talk about your fear of missing out."

Tabitha did it perfectly in one take, and when she finished, she flashed a humorous raised eyebrow.

"Got it," Sydney said, impressed. "You know, you're really good at that. You could totally be a television presenter. You're just so natural."

"I should be by now," Tabitha said.

"Why do you say that?" asked Sydney.

"My father's a billionaire, my mother used to be a pop star, and they both live for the spotlight," Tabitha answered. "I've lived my entire life in front of cameras. A tabloid cameraman snuck into the hospital the day I was born. Paparazzi followed me on my first date. And then there was that time I had the nerve to go for a jog despite the fact that my face had had a particularly bad acne breakout. The caption to that photo read, 'Tabs *spotted* in Hyde Park.' I guess it passes as clever to make fun of a fourteen-year-old girl."

"That's awful," said Sydney. "Totally unforgivable."

"Yes, but there's no stopping it," Tabitha replied. "So eventually I figured I should try to make the most of the situation. That's why I share so much on social and wanted to do this with *Audrey*. At least this way I'll have some say in how I'm presented to the world."

Sydney wondered if the wealth and fame was worth it. Tabitha could buy anything she wanted, but she couldn't have a normal childhood. Not that there was anything normal about traveling around the world on secret missions for MI6.

Next, they headed to Red Square, and on the way a man on the sidewalk called out something to them in Russian that angered the Sorokins. In a flash, Sasha grabbed him by the wrist and spun him around, twisting his arm up behind his back as he writhed in pain. She whispered something in his ear, and on the verge of tears, he said something that Sydney assumed was an apology. Finally, Sasha let go of his arm and he scampered away.

"Krav Maga," Tabitha said to Sydney. "You do not say anything inappropriate to these women or they will inflict pain."

Sydney knew they were trained, but seeing it in action was something totally different. It had been quick and merciless. "Good to know," she said to Tabitha.

When they reached Red Square, Sasha started telling them all about the Kremlin and St. Basil's. At 11:05, Anastasia broke away from the group momentarily to send a message on her phone. Sydney knew she had to be posting another picture for her cousin Nicholas, but there was no way for her to get close and see if it was St. Basil's or not.

When Anastasia returned, she interrupted her sister midstory and asked, "Who's hungry?"

"Now that you mention it," said Tabitha, "I could eat."

"Me too," Sasha said, ignoring the fact that she'd been rudely interrupted. "What are you thinking?"

"I think we should show them GUM," she said, pronouncing it *goom*.

"With ice cream after lunch," Sasha said, getting into the idea. "You cannot come to Moscow without having ice cream at GUM."

GUM stood for *Glávnyj Universál'nyj Magazín*, which translated to "Main Universal Store." Located directly across Red Square from the Kremlin, GUM was a shopping mall unlike any Sydney had ever seen. It was built in 1893 and featured an ornate facade nearly eight hundred feet long. Inside there were three tiers of stores, all topped by a magnificent iron and glass roof.

"I think I'm in heaven," Tabitha said when they entered. "Talk about your retail therapy."

"It's beautiful, no?" said Sasha. "All designer stores and luxury brands."

"I thought you were taking us someplace to eat," Sydney said.

"There's a cafeteria on the top floor with traditional Russian food," she said. "It's not fancy, but it's delicious."

Although it wasn't all to Sydney's and Tabitha's taste, the lunch lived up to the billing. The food was good and the atmosphere totally Russian. Sydney shot some great photos and a hilarious video of Tabitha trying different foods, like borscht and dressed herring.

Tabitha's reactions were priceless, and Sydney was surprised by how much she liked her. They were getting along well, and rather than a mission, it felt like she was just hanging out with Brooklyn. This realization made her feel a bit guilty, and she wondered if Brooklyn was back at Kinloch hanging out with Charlotte.

After lunch, they bought ice cream from a vendor on the main floor.

"Unbelievable," Tabitha said after her first taste.

"It truly is great," added Sydney.

"It's a traditional recipe mandated by the government," Sasha explained. "It requires the highest-quality cream, no substitutions. We came here every year on our birthday."

There was a large fountain next to the ice cream vendor, and Sydney took some pictures of Tabitha leaning against it. She was adjusting the lens when she noticed that Anastasia had slipped away. It took her a moment to figure out where she went, but then she saw that she was talking to someone on the other side of the fountain. She recognized the face instantly. It was Nicholas Sorokin.

27

Openings

IT WAS OVERCAST AND COOL AS MOTHER and Paris walked the mile and a half from the hotel to the Tretyakov. They decided to skip the shuttle bus because Paris wanted to work off some pre-tournament jitters and Mother wanted a chance to talk without worrying about who might overhear them.

"Did Tru send you the translation of Park's argument with his guards?" Paris asked as they cut across Red Square.

"At around four this morning," Mother said with an eyebrow raised. "I swear she does that on purpose."

"What were they quarrelling about?"

"The basic gist is that Park feels smothered by their presence. I believe the word he used was 'caged,' although some of that gets lost in translation. He argued that he went to uni in Moscow, knows the city well, and wants to be able to enjoy it. More importantly, he wants Dae-jung to be able to enjoy the fun parts of the tournament."

"You mean like the photo op in Gorky Park or breakfast with everyone at the hotel this morning?" Paris asked.

"Exactly," said Mother. "And considering he wasn't at either of those, you can guess who won the argument. The guard referred to Park as a *renegade*, which in this context sounded like quite the nasty name-calling. He also informed him that 'Dae-jung was here to win a medal, not to smile.'"

"Ouch," Paris said. "That's ridiculously unfair." A thought occurred to Paris. "I wonder if that's why they're presenting the medals at the concert. To make sure Dae-jung shows up."

"I think you're right," Mother said. "There's no way

they'd miss out on that. They'll want the photograph to show off Dae-jung."

"And if Reg is doing that to force their hand," Paris said, "then that indicates the concert may be where they're planning to grab him."

"That totally makes sense," Mother said. "But we still have to guard against it happening sooner. That could just be a fail-safe in case they can't get him any earlier."

"Excellent point," said Paris.

"You know . . ." Mother paused for a moment, trying to find the right words. "I hope I'm not guilty of the same bad behavior as the North Korean secret police."

"Why would you even think that?" Paris asked.

"Look what I put you all through," said Mother. "Yesterday, Kat and Rio were chased across Moscow by a Russian gangster. Meanwhile, you and Sydney are deep undercover trying to stop a crime syndicate from developing nuclear capabilities. And back in Scotland, Brooklyn doesn't even want to talk to me. I'd hardly call that expert parenting."

"You know what I'd call it?" said Paris.

"What?"

"Best. Summer. Vacation. Ever. We all love it. And don't forget, the only reason Brooklyn's angry at you is because she's not over here getting chased or going undercover along with the rest of us."

Mother threw an arm around Paris's shoulder and pulled him in close, giving him a quick kiss on the top of the head. "Thank you, son." They'd reached the Bolshoy Moskvoretsky Bridge, and a brisk wind picked up off the Moscow River. "How are you feeling about the tournament? Nervous or excited?"

"A bit of both," Paris answered. "I've always wondered how I'd do against elite competition, so I guess I'm going to find out. My fear is that I'll discover I have no business playing them."

"Don't forget that you did just win four tournaments."

"Yes," Paris said. "But not against players this good. Here I'll be happy if I can hold my own. I think my openings will be the key."

"Why's that?" Mother asked.

"Openings are about theory and memorizing variations to set up the board," Paris said. "I haven't studied them as much as the others have, which is why they're a weakness for me. My strength is the middle game, where attacking and creativity are key. If I can get there without making any big mistakes, I'll have a chance to do okay."

"That's exactly how I feel about Park Jin-sun," Mother said. "If I can get past his guards and really talk to him, I think I'll have a chance of convincing him to defect. But that's a big if."

"It sounds like a classic blockade," Paris said.

"What do you mean?"

"Barnaby Fitch taught me all about them," Paris said. "Except he was talking about pawns protecting the king, not secret police guarding a scientist."

"And how did he say you could beat the blockade?"

"There are several methods," Paris answered. "You can use a diversion to tempt them away to a different part of the board. My favorite, though, is the poisoned pawn."

"Oooh, I like the sound of that," Mother said.

"It's a risky tactic with a huge upside if it works," Paris said. "You leave a pawn unprotected and make it irresistible to pass up."

"And the poison?"

"What they don't realize is that you want them to move that piece because it makes them vulnerable to attack later on," said Paris. "I used it the other day against Rio. But in real life, not chess."

"How'd you do that?"

"He took the best spot on the couch, and I wanted it to watch the Liverpool game," Paris said. "So, I got myself a piece of pie and placed it on the table and walked away."

"And Rio stole your pie?"

"He thought he was pretty clever," said Paris. "What he didn't know is that I'd gotten two pieces of pie, and when he got up to get the one I put on the table, I looped around and got my spot."

"Nice," Mother said. "Does that mean he fell for it *rook*, line, and sinker?"

"Did you really just say that?" Paris asked with an eyeroll.

"What?" Mother said, feigning innocence. "I was just pointing out his *rook*ie mistake."

"Stop it with the chess puns," Paris said. "Just because you're a dad doesn't mean you have to use dad jokes."

"It's all part of the package, son. Or should I call you *mate*?"

"You're just going to keep going, aren't you?" Paris said, trying not to laugh.

"Day and *knight*."

The puns had finally stopped once they reached the Tretyakov and it was time to get serious again. The courtyard was filled with competitors and their families. The overall vibe matched Paris's blend of nervousness and excitement. Competing in an international tournament was always a big deal, but this setting made it seem even bigger. Unlike the gymnasiums or hotel conference rooms where tournaments were usually held, the museum was stunning and made up of several buildings, including one that looked like a castle and another that was once a church. It was the perfect location for a game that featured kings and queens, knights and bishops.

The tournament occupied two rooms that normally showcased special exhibitions. The top group played in the smaller of the two, where there were ten tables set up in a roped-off area. Paris's eyes were immediately drawn to a large scoreboard on the wall. His name was one of twenty on the list, each of which was accompanied by their national flag.

"Whoa," he said. "This just got real."

"Good luck," Mother said with a pat on the back.

"Thanks," said Paris. "And thanks for stopping with the puns."

"It was fun at first, but I got *board* with it," Mother said, which elicited a laugh.

Paris headed to the table where his match was set to

begin, and Mother went to the side of the room where several rows of folding chairs were set up for viewing.

Park Jin-sun was already seated in the front, and the North Korean agents had him totally boxed in, one on each side and two behind. Mother had no idea how he'd ever get close to him and wondered if he'd have to devise a real-life version of the poisoned pawn just so they could talk. He was about to take a seat when he got an unexpected assist from none other than Reginald Banks.

"Excuse me," Reg said to Park. "I need to talk to your associates. Can you translate for me?"

"Of course," Park said.

"Can you please tell them that only family members are permitted in the playing hall during competition?"

Park tried to hide his glee as he passed this information along to the head of his protection detail. The guard glowered and said something angrily in response. Before Park could even translate, Sir Reg beat him to the punch.

"I'm sorry if this is a problem, but I'm afraid it's non-negotiable. The rules come directly from the International Chess Federation," Sir Reg explained.

Park passed this along, but the guard seemed wholly unimpressed and showed no indication of moving.

Then Reg went in for the kill. "I'm afraid if you don't

leave, Dae-jung will forfeit, which I know will not please your government."

Watching nearby, Mother wondered if this really was a rule or merely Reg flexing his muscles. Either way, the guards reluctantly relented and got up from their seats.

"There's a lovely viewing room right across the hall," Reg said. "All the games will be broadcast there on closed-circuit television."

The guards left, and Mother gladly took a seat near Park, but not next to him. He didn't want to crowd him or seem obvious. Games typically lasted two to three hours each. He'd have plenty of time to make his opening move toward Park. Now, he slipped back into the role of father and watched proudly as Paris made an opening move of his own.

Breaking the Hex

MONTY, KAT, AND RIO WERE DRIVING HOME from the Edinburgh airport, having spent the previous night in London. The mood in the car was downcast as each wished they were still in Moscow on the mission.

"I know everyone's disappointed about what happened, but you really did some wonderful work," Monty said, trying to lift their spirits. "You should both be very proud."

"I'll be proud once I've cracked the St. Basil's code," Kat said, determined.

"And I'll be proud once Kat's completed charm school," joked Rio.

"Charm school?" Monty asked, intrigued.

"Yesterday Kat asked me to teach her how to be more charming," Rio said.

"It was a misguided moment of weakness," Kat replied.

"I LOVE this idea," Monty said.

"It's pointless," Kat said. "I'm a lost cause."

"No, you're not," Rio said. "In fact, I figured out the first lesson this morning on the plane from London. Are you ready for it?"

"Maybe later," Kat said halfheartedly.

"No, I want to be part of this," Monty said. "I think my charm skills could use some polish too."

Rio turned to Kat and gave her an expectant look.

"Fine," she said. "Let's hear it."

Rio smiled. "The first thing you have to do is learn how to KISS."

"I beg your pardon," Kat protested.

"Not *kiss* like that," said Rio. "KISS is an acronym with the four essential elements of *charmfulness*."

"I don't think that's a word, but I like where this is headed," said Monty.

"The *K* is for 'kindness,'" Rio said. "You always have to lead with kindness."

"That's easy," Kat said, a bit defensive. "I'm always kind."

Rio laughed. "You're *kindhearted* for certain. But you're often brutally honest."

"What? So I'm supposed to lie?"

"No," Rio replied. "But do you remember that time I tried to make waffles and got the ingredients mixed up?"

"Do I remember it?" she said sarcastically. "They were the most disgusting things I've ever tasted. I haven't been able to look at a waffle or pancake since."

"Exactly my point," said Rio. "You could've just said, 'Yes, I remember, but they weren't your best.'"

Kat realized what he was getting at and nodded. "Okay, I can see that."

"So, *K* is 'kindness' and *I* is 'interest,'" he said, continuing the lesson. "You have to be interested in the other person and what they are interested in."

"Okay, you see, right there, I don't think this is going to work," Kat said. "I am completely *un*-interested in most things that interest other people. It's like the ones who post pictures of their food on social media. Why would I care about anyone else's food?"

Monty laughed at this. "What do the *S*s stand for, Rio?"

"'Sensitivity' and 'sincerity,'" he answered. "You need to be sensitive to the other person's feelings and sincere in what you say to them. That last part is the most important of all. You have to be honest."

"But you just said—" she started to protest.

"I said you didn't have to be *brutally* honest," he replied, guessing where she was headed. "But you should still tell the truth. People don't like to be deceived."

"Kindness, interest, sensitivity, sincerity?" said Kat. "That's it?"

"Yes," Rio answered. "Those are the only ingredients you need."

"That's what you said about the waffles," Kat said, shooting him a look.

"Again, I understand that you did not enjoy the waffles," he said. "You no longer need to remind me of that."

"All right," Kat said. "Let me give it a try."

"This should be good," Monty said.

"I appreciate the thoughtful acronym that you've come up with for me," Kat said.

"Okay," Rio said. "That's somewhat like kindness."

"I find your approach to be . . . *fascinating*." She added a smile after saying that, even if it did look a bit unnatural.

"That's interest," said Monty. "Although, I question the sincerity a bit."

Kat gave her a look that said, *I'm trying my best here.* Then she turned back to Rio and said, "I am *sensitive* to the fact that this was not easy for you to do on short notice. And I *sincerely* think that three of your four examples are excellent."

"Three of the four?" he said. "Let me guess, *interest* is the one that's giving you trouble."

"Yes, but not for the reasons you think."

"Then why?"

"You know how I am about patterns," she said. "Kindness, sensitivity, and sincerity are all examples of qualities, while interest is an example of a feeling."

Monty was thoroughly amused as she said, "You must be an excellent teacher, Rio. Because I found that to be utterly charming."

"So did I," said Rio.

Kat smiled for the first time since before Nicholas Sorokin started chasing them through Moscow.

This improved mood lasted for the remainder of the drive home. When they reached the FARM and went inside, they were surprised by an aroma wafting from the kitchen.

"What's that smell?" asked Monty

Ever the food expert, Rio inhaled deeply and answered, "Chicken lo mein with sriracha sauce."

"That's very specific," Monty marveled. "But I was less concerned with the food than the fact that the house is supposed to be empty. Did we leave something out on the counter?"

Just then, Brooklyn exited the kitchen and was using chopsticks to eat from a takeout container filled with lo mein.

"Brooklyn?" Monty asked.

Brooklyn was startled and almost dropped her food. She looked at them and tried to make sense of the scene. "Aren't you guys supposed to be in Moscow for two more days?"

"Aren't you supposed to be at school?" Monty replied.

"For Saturday, they gave us most of the day off, so I thought I'd come work on the code." Then she gave a sheepish look and said, "Or, rather, I thought *we'd* come work on the code."

"*We?*" said Rio, confused.

"What's taking so long?" a voice called out. "I'm starving."

For Brooklyn, it was like watching two trains about to collide, and there was nothing she could do to stop them.

Charlotte walked into the room, and the color drained from her face the moment she saw the others.

"What's she doing here?" Rio demanded angrily.

"This is my house too," Brooklyn said defensively. "I can invite my friends over, can't I?"

"Of course you can," Monty said. "Although, I'm concerned with which part of the house you invited her to visit. Am I right to assume that you've been in the priest hole using Beny?"

"Yes," Brooklyn said. "And I know that's off-limits for civilians. But Charlotte was already part of MI6, so I didn't give away any secrets. She already knew all about it."

"Besides," Charlotte interjected. "We cracked the code."

"Wait, what?" Kat asked. "You solved the St. Basil's code?"

"Yes, we did," Brooklyn said, wide-eyed. "It's amazing. Wanna see?"

Kat couldn't believe it. The excitement of decrypting an unbreakable code momentarily eclipsed the uneasiness about seeing Charlotte at the FARM. Still, it was an awkward situation. Even though they went to the same school, they'd had virtually no contact since Charlotte left the team. This had been particularly hard on Kat. Despite her normal social awkwardness, they'd been very close. Charlotte's leaving was doubly difficult.

"Congratulations, by the way," Charlotte said softly as they went down the stairs. "About the Newton medal, I mean."

Kat nodded self-consciously as she processed the scene and replied, "Thanks."

They entered the priest hole to find two large maps laid out on the conference table. One was of Russia and the other Moscow. Nearly a dozen locations were marked by yellow sticky notes with names and dates written on them. Some also had blue stickies with more information.

"What do we have here?" Monty asked.

"Eleven locations," Brooklyn said. "Each one corresponds with a social media post of St. Basil's with the different-colored onion dome."

"And the additional stickies?" Monty asked.

"Crimes that happened at those locations within three days of the post going live," said Brooklyn.

"So far we've found five," Charlotte added.

"That's why I needed help," Brooklyn said. "Russian police records are a hot mess and beyond difficult to hack. It's taken two of us working nonstop for hours just to get those."

"What do the colors mean?" asked Kat.

"Yellow stickies are dates and locations; blue ones are information about the crimes," Brooklyn said.

"Not those colors," said Kat. "The colors in the code."

"Sorry," said Brooklyn. "You're going to love it because, the truth is, it's not nearly as hard as it seems."

Brooklyn took a seat at a computer, and the others crowded around her, although Charlotte kept a distance.

"Does everyone know what a hexadecimal is?" Brooklyn asked.

"I think it's safe to say that none of us do," Rio responded.

"Actually, I know," said Kat.

"Me too," added Monty, much to Rio's chagrin. "Sorry."

"It's a base-sixteen numbering system," said Kat. "Zero through nine, then A through F."

"Exactly," said Brooklyn. "They're used a lot in computing because one hexadecimal digit equals one half-byte of information, which is also known as a 'nibble.'"

"I'm sorry," said Rio, interrupting. "I thought you said this was simple. Nothing about this sounds easy. The only bites and nibbles I know involve food."

"You don't have to fully understand what a hexadecimal is," said Brooklyn. "Just trust me when I say that computers use them to keep track of colors. Every single color has a six-digit hex code that details the specific amount of red, green, and blue used in that color. There are more than sixteen million colors in all, beginning with 000000, which is the blackest of blacks and ending with FFFFFF, which is the whitest of whites."

The light bulb went off for Kat, who shook her head in disbelief. "That's brilliant," she said. "Six digits are perfect."

"Perfect for what?" asked Monty.

"Latitude and longitude," said Kat.

"Exactly!" said Brooklyn. "Super complicated to figure out, but once you do, totally straightforward."

"Still confused," Rio said.

"Let me show you," Brooklyn said. "Let's go with the picture that was posted a week ago." Brooklyn clicked opened the post the others saw Sorokin receive in the gift shop. "In this one, the onion dome is green and blue. But, in the eyes of a computer, it is two very specific shades of green and blue."

"How can you determine the hex numbers for them?" asked Monty.

"With this little tool right here," Brooklyn answered as she clicked on a program, and a small icon of an eye-dropper appeared on the screen.

"Where'd you get that?" asked Kat.

"It's from this graphic design program I've been using for art during summer school," she said with a smile. "All I have to do is tap the color with it, and I get this: 557125. Then I touch this color and get this: 375079."

"The North Korean embassy," Monty said, marveling at the discovery as she entered the numbers into an app on her phone. "That's spectacular. How did you figure it out?"

"I was working on an art project, and I went to change the shade of one of the colors," Brooklyn said. "When I did, I saw the hex number pop onto the screen, and it hit me. Total luck."

Kat shook her head. "Luck had nothing to do with it. It's magnificent."

"I wanted to be sure, though," Brooklyn said. "So I thought I'd check to see if those locations lined up with any criminal activity."

"The problem is that Russian police records aren't centralized," said Charlotte. "So you have to figure out who has jurisdiction and then hack into the specific systems, which are all set up completely differently. Not to mention in Russian with Cyrillic letters."

"And you've found crimes committed at some of them?" Monty asked.

"Five," said Brooklyn. "Some locations are completely clean. Some we haven't been able to tell for sure. And then there's this one." She pointed at yellow sticky in the far northwest corner of Russia, up in the Arctic Circle. "I think this one may have been a mistake."

"Why do you say that?" asked Rio.

"Because there's nothing there," she said.

"You mean no crimes?" he asked.

"I mean no *anything*," she said. "We checked a bunch of maps, and there's nothing there."

Monty thought about this. "I bet I know which map has something there."

"Which one?" asked Brooklyn.

"One of the top secret military maps that Nicholas Sorokin has in his back room," she said. "And if we checked it, I guarantee that this is the location of Kola-27."

"Where the nuclear warheads were stolen?" asked Kat.

"That's exactly right," said Monty.

Middle Game

IT WAS THE SECOND DAY OF THE TOURNAMENT, and despite his fears about being out of his league, Paris was more than holding his own. On the first day he'd won one game and drew the other. Now he was midway through his morning match, and even though he'd committed a major blunder during the opening, he'd used some creative attacking to capture key pieces and turn the board in his favor. He could sense a hint of desperation coming from his opponent, a boy from China named Li Ang.

"Your son's a good player," Ang's mother whispered to Mother.

"So's yours," Mother whispered back.

They were sitting next to each other, and their conversation consisted of seven hushed words, but judging by the glare from one of the officials in the blue tournament polos, it was as if they'd run screaming through the room. She didn't actually shush him, but she didn't need to. The look said it all.

It was against the rules for the competitors to talk while playing, and spectators were expected to remain equally quiet. The only noises in the hall were the sounds of pieces being moved and muted applause whenever a game would finish.

For Mother, this was a huge and unexpected problem.

At other tournaments, the parents tended to stay in a separate room and watch the matches on a monitor. This environment encouraged chitchat to fill the hours. Here, though, the parents didn't speak at all, which meant Mother didn't get a chance to strike up a conversation with Park to try to recruit him to flip.

To make matters worse, one of Park's guards was back in the picture and sitting next to him. Mother wondered if the North Korean government had lodged a complaint with the International Chess Federation or if Sir Reg had simply relented and made a compromise for one to be there instead of all four.

Mother sat three chairs away on the opposite side from the guard and was getting desperate. Just as Paris had reached the middle game of his match, Mother had reached the middle game of the mission and had nothing to show for it except a couple of hellos and a few friendly smiles. He needed to follow Paris's lead and begin to attack creatively, although, as it did on the chessboard, creative attacking in espionage came with heavy risk.

"When your voice cannot be heard, replace it with a silent word."

This was one of the Motherisms he'd taught the kids to remind them to think outside the box and solve problems with creative alternatives. But in this instance, it literally was his problem. He could not speak, so he had to find a way to communicate silently. But how?

There was no way to signal him or pass him a note without being seen by the guard. He needed to come up with something else, so he studied Park, looking for anything that might give him an idea.

At the tournament, the scientist had demonstrated

that he was a creature of habit. He always sat in the front row and remained in his seat until the round was completed. He had perfect posture, drank from a water bottle that he kept on the floor next to his right foot, and meticulously recorded moves on a narrow chess notation pad.

Pads like this were everywhere at tournaments because players were required to keep a record of each move using a method known as "algebraic notation." It was a simple system that assigned numbers and letters to the squares on the board, but something about the way Park did it struck Mother as odd.

Sometimes Dae-jung would move, but Park wouldn't write down anything. Other times, Park would scribble a notation while Dae-jung was still studying the board. Mother had noticed it the day before, but assumed it was some sort of quirk. It wasn't until now that he realized what Park was doing.

"He's recording a different game."

When Park momentarily set the pad on an empty chair between them to reach for his water bottle, Mother covertly studied the notations and was able to figure out which game he was transcribing. Slowly, an idea began to formulate, and by the time Paris had won his match, Mother had crafted a scheme that was incredibly bold.

And more than a little dangerous.

"Congratulations," Mother said to Paris as they exited the playing hall to go to lunch. "That was great. Your middle game was stunning."

"Thanks," Paris responded. "I was lucky to make it out of the opening."

"It wasn't luck; it was skill." Mother paused for a moment. "It was also inspirational."

"How so?"

"I'll tell you while we're eating," Mother answered cryptically.

They grabbed a couple of sandwiches from a catering table, went out the front of the museum, and found a bench overlooking a fountain in a nearby park. Once Mother was confident that no one could hear them, he said, "Now we can talk."

"Okay," Paris said. "How was my middle game inspirational? And please, feel free to lavish it with praise."

"It was utterly amazing," Mother said. "I thought you were doomed early on, but you turned the tables on him by being bold and creative."

Paris grinned.

"I realized I needed to use the same approach for communicating with Park," Mother continued. "And that's when I figured out how to talk to him."

"That's great," Paris said as he took a bite of his sandwich. "How are you going to do it?"

"I'm not," Mother said. "You are."

"Me?" Paris asked surprised. "When? Before or after my match?"

A wide smile formed on Mother's lips. "During."

Paris gave him a look of total confusion. "I don't understand."

"When do you play Dae-jung?"

"First thing tomorrow."

"That's what I thought," Mother replied. "That means this afternoon Park will be watching you. He charts the moves of Dae-jung's next opponent on one of these."

Mother pulled a folded piece of paper out of his pocket and opened it to reveal a blank chess score sheet.

"Big deal," Paris said, unimpressed. "Those are everywhere. They probably go over the game together during lunch or at night when they're back at the embassy. It helps him prepare for the next match."

"Exactly," said Paris. "So, this afternoon he'll be

recording all the moves in your match, which is how you're going to talk to him."

"I'm still lost," Paris said. "I can't talk while I'm playing."

"But you can communicate with algebraic notation," Mother said. "He's going to put down whatever you do, so he's going to write the message to himself. All you've got to do is play the chessboard like a keyboard."

"Wait a second," Paris said in disbelief as he was starting to understand Mother's plan. "You want me to make moves based on the words they spell in algebraic notation?"

"Yes, I do."

"In an elite tournament?"

"I'm afraid so."

"That's . . . ," Paris said, searching for the right exclamation.

"Bold and creative," Mother said.

"I was going to go with 'wildly outrageous.'" Paris's whole body sagged. "Not to mention that I'll get destroyed."

"Probably," said Mother. "Although, it doesn't matter how badly you lose. A loss counts the same in the standings."

Paris was crestfallen. "But I was playing so well. I've won two matches and I drew another. I've got a real chance at a medal."

"I know," Mother said. "And I hate to do it to you, but I can't think of any other way."

"What makes you so certain it will work?"

"I'm not," said Mother. "But I feel like it's our best chance to let him know that we can help him. To invite him to escape."

Paris ran through it in his head, hoping to find a reason to kill the idea.

"If this message is plain enough for him to see, won't it be plain enough for someone else to see as well?"

"That's definitely a risk," said Mother. "But I don't think anyone else will notice."

"My opponent will," Paris said. "I'm playing Antonia, and she'll track every move. So will the tournament official."

"Yes," Mother said. "But Antonia will use German notation, and the official will use Russian. To them, the letters won't spell out anything; it'll just look like you're erratic."

"So, they won't think I'm a spy, but they will think I'm a *patzer*," Paris said, using the term for an inept chess player. He thought for a moment and said, "What about Park? Won't his notation be in Korean?"

Mother shook his head. "No. I saw his sheets. He uses English."

"Why?" asked Paris.

"I don't know. You said there wasn't a strong Korean chess community, so maybe he picked it up from studying books in English. Maybe he does it because he's a *renegade* who wants to tweak the guards, in case they look over his shoulder and see it. But we don't have to know why, we just have to know that he does. And he's fluent in English, so he should understand."

Paris nodded. "You've got an answer for everything, don't you?"

"I wish," Mother replied. "If I did, I wouldn't need you to do this."

They were quiet for a moment, and Mother let Paris think it through as he took a couple bites of his sandwich. "Okay," Paris finally said. "It's just a little wounded ego. After all, it's Lucas Doinel in this tournament, not me. It's just a cover name. I'm a spy, not a player."

"You're both," Mother reminded him.

Paris nodded. "I'm on board with the plan. What's the message you want me to send?"

Mother smiled, proud of him on so many levels.

"We've got a limited alphabet, so we're going to need to be creative." Mother started to write the letters on a sheet of paper. "Let's see, we've *A* through *H* for the squares. And for the back row pieces . . ."

"King, queen, knight, bishop, rook," said Paris. "That's *K, Q, N, B,* and *R.*"

Mother wrote them all down.

"It's like we're playing Scrabble," he said. "Too bad we don't have Kat with us."

Together they started working out potential words, and forty-five minutes later Paris took his seat directly across from Antonia. He didn't say anything about it to Mother, but part of his resistance was because he'd been so looking forward to this particular match. He really liked Antonia and wanted to impress her with a good showing.

"Good luck," she said during their pregame handshake.

"Good luck to you too," Paris said, although he knew that she wouldn't need any at all.

Paris opened with one of his usual moves, so that it wouldn't attract attention, but after a few turns he moved his bishop and then his rook earlier than usual. Antonia looked up, surprised. They weren't moves she expected, but she knew Paris was a good player and assumed it was a clever tactic.

Back in the spectator section, Mother was keeping an eye on Park. The scientist also seemed surprised by Paris's recent moves, even more so when he decided to move his king soon after. In between the words, Paris used sound tactics as he tried to salvage the board enough so that he wouldn't lose before the message was complete. He managed to get all four words spelled out three moves before Antonia put him in checkmate.

Paris signaled his resignation by tipping his king over on its side and offering a congratulatory handshake.

"Good game," he said.

She gave him a look that was a mix of confusion and friendship. "Thank you."

"Sorry, I'm such a *patzer*," Paris added.

She smiled at the word, which was German and one she knew well. "Hardly. You just tried some things that didn't work."

After their handshake they walked out side by side as the observers clapped. Paris knew that he had done poorly as a chess player, but he hoped that he'd at least been successful as a spy.

Park had picked up on it after two words, and now he looked down at his score sheet, totally unsure what to make of it. To the guard sitting next to him, who didn't speak English or understand chess, nothing was out of the ordinary. They were just letters and numbers. But the message had been delivered.

BREAK FREE CAGED RENEGADE

Mother had included two references from the translated argument—"caged" and "renegade." He hoped that it would make sure Park put it all together.

Mother cleared his throat, drawing Park's attention. They locked eyes for just a moment, and Mother gave a slight nod and smile. Park's eyes opened wide. The message had been received, but he gave no indication of his response.

The Lads

"*THIS* IS WHAT I WANTED YOU TO SEE," Tabitha said as they walked through the tunnel and entered the stadium grandstand. "I call it 'the circus,' and it's one of my favorite things in the world."

Despite the fact that it was nearly midnight, the lights were all on, and Luzhniki Stadium was alive with activity as more than a hundred people worked to get ready for the KB5 concert, scheduled to kick off in less than twenty-four hours. Different crews were constructing the stage, building giant video display walls, and laying miles of cable. Sound engineers oversaw the audio gear, riggers dangled from scaffolding and adjusted lights, and the pyrotechnics team went through all the safety protocols as they set up the effects. The scene was rounded out by mellow seventies pop music playing over the speakers to give it all a chill vibe.

"It's amazing," Sydney said, soaking it all in. "They have to do this for every show?"

"Every single one," Tabitha said. "And as soon as the concert's over tomorrow night, they have to take it all down and load it back in the trucks."

"Amazing. How many trucks are there?"

"Forty tractor trailers loaded with more than three hundred fifty tons of equipment."

"And you know those numbers because . . ."

"I did a paper on it for school," Tabitha said.

"What was the assignment?"

"We were supposed to write about a family road trip," Tabitha said, trying to stifle a laugh. "So, I wrote about KB5's *Party After Midnight* European tour."

"Cheeky," said Sydney.

"Yeah," Tabitha admitted. "Not my most humble moment. But it got a good grade, and my teacher said it gave her a chuckle."

"By the way," asked Sydney. "Where are the twins? Isn't there always at least one of them on hand, lurking in the shadows?"

"They're probably checking in with security about tomorrow night," Tabitha said. "I know they're in the way sometimes, but they're just doing their job. Luckily, they don't need to hang with us in here because it's all safe. No one can get inside the stadium without one of these." She held up the identification credential that was hanging around her neck. It had her name, photo, and a hologram of the KB5 *Around the World* tour logo. "Here they let me roam a little."

This mission was unlike any that Sydney had ever undertaken. So far, she hadn't been chased by anyone, and there hadn't been the need to hide in a sewer or dangle from a building. She hadn't even handled any explosives. Instead, it had been filled with good food, expensive clothes, and glimpses into the worlds of luxury and entertainment.

All the while, she'd tried to keep tabs on Sir Reg, but he'd mostly been absent from the scene, popping in and out of the picture between business meetings. He never stayed long enough for her to learn much.

Her biggest discovery had been how much she loved creating content for *All Roads Lead to Audrey*. In addition to the pictures and video, she'd written four diary-style articles that had been posted on the site and well-received by *Audrey*'s readers. She wondered if this cover identity might one day turn into a possible career or course of study at university.

Tabitha checked her phone and smiled. "Look how many views and likes there are for the post about the Bolshoi," she said, scrolling on her phone and showing it to Sydney. "I think we're a hit."

Sydney smiled in agreement. "That's nice."

"How lucky am I that your editor stood up to up to my dad when he tried to replace you with Violet?" Tabitha shook her head. "I mean, she's my best friend and I love her to bits, but Jane Austen she's not."

Sydney gave her a surprised look. "You like Jane Austen?"

"I don't like her," Tabitha said. "I worship her. My favorites are *Emma* and *Mansfield Park*. What about you?"

"*Pride and Prejudice* makes me swoon."

Tabitha gave her the side-eye. "You seem surprised that I know the titles."

"A little bit."

"What? You thought because I was a spoiled rich girl, I didn't read books?"

"No," Sydney said, then she laughed and admitted, "Okay, maybe a little."

"I'm full of surprises, Ellie," Tabitha said. "You've but scratched the surface."

"Is that so?"

"In fact, I'm about to drop one on you that will make you swoon more than Jane Austen ever could."

"That's a high bar," Sydney said.

"Fine with me," Tabitha replied. "I love a good challenge."

Tabitha led Sydney down to the field level and through the organized chaos that was the build-out. The all-access stamp on the passes hanging from their necks got them past every checkpoint and into a VIP section backstage.

They went through a maze of hallways until they reached the fully tricked-out dressing room of the Russian national soccer team. It had been completely remodeled for the World Cup and was deluxe in every way. A paper sign had been taped to the door that read:

VIP LOUNGE

Before she opened the door, Tabitha turned to study Sydney's face.

"What?" Sydney asked.

"I'm taking mental pictures so I can compare them. This is *before.* . . ."

"Just open the door."

"Okay," Tabitha said with a Cheshire-cat grin. "Let's go inside."

"Tabs!" shouted a voice as they entered the room. "When'd you get here?"

Sydney looked up and saw the five members of KB5 playing video games and kicking back in sweet red leather chairs featuring the emblem of the Russian Soccer Federation.

"And there's *after,*" Tabitha said to a stunned Sydney.

"That's KB5," Sydney mumbled, totally tongue-tied.

"Top that, Jane Austen."

"Are we allowed to be here?"

"Of course we are," Tabitha said. "Come on, I'll introduce you to the lads."

For Sydney, the scene was beyond surreal. First, there was the setting. They were in a large room with jerseys hanging from the lockers that lined the walls.

In the center of the room, five of the world's biggest pop idols were treating it like their home game room, playing video soccer on a big-screen monitor. Music played from a nearby speaker, and junk food was piled everywhere.

"Everybody, this is Eleanor, but you can call her Ellie," Tabitha said.

"Hey, Ellie," said one of the boys playing the game, "I'm Roman."

"Isaac," said another.

"She knows your names, so you can forget about pretending you're humble," said Tabitha. "She's a reporter with *All Roads Lead to Audrey*, but she is one of us, so treat her like family."

"I get all my fashion tips from *Audrey*," said Roman.

"Hardly a good advertisement," chided Isaac.

"Are you the one who's been writing the articles about Tabs in Moscow?" asked Roman. "I loved the picture at the Bolshoi."

"You've read them?" Sydney said, amazed.

"Of course," he replied. "Food's over there, and you're free to grab a seat and watch me destroy Harrison."

"He's not going to beat me," Harrison replied. "I'm lulling him into a sense of overconfidence."

"Roman overconfident?" joked Leo. "Not exactly a long trip now, is it."

Sydney couldn't believe it. Just like that, she was part of the gang, hanging out and joking around with each other. She was living out the dreams of teenage fans across the globe. "So do you guys normally just hang out and play video games all night long?" she asked.

"We're shockingly dull," Leo offered. "But please don't write that in *All Roads Lead to Audrey*. After all, we've got a rep, and we're supposed to be the *Party After Midnight* boys."

"Moscow nightclubs aren't really our scene," said Isaac. "And a few hundred fans are camped out at the hotel looking for us."

"It's great for record sales, but not exactly relaxing," said Roman. "So we usually crash at whatever stadium we're at. Although, rarely are they as tricked out as this."

"Tabs," said Leo. "Why aren't you flying back on the plane with us?"

"What are you talking about?" Tabitha asked. "It's part of the story for *Audrey*. Ellie and I are both going to be there."

"Not according to the call sheet," he replied as he

handed her a multipage schedule, which included lodging and travel.

"This can't be right," Tabitha said as she read over it, her cheeks suddenly flush with anger. "Where's Ava's office?"

"Three doors down the hall," said Isaac. "But I think she's swamped with the build-out."

"Like I care," Tabitha said as she stood up and stormed out of the locker room.

Sydney followed and caught up with her just as Tabitha reached the office. A sign had been taped to the door that read AVA KNOX—ROAD MANAGER.

"What's this about?" Tabitha thundered as she opened the door without knocking.

Ava was in the middle of a phone conference, and even though she was in charge of the tour, she knew better than to pull rank on the boss's daughter. So instead of kicking Tabitha out of her office, she told the people on the conference that she would call them right back and smiled as she said, "Hey, Tabs, what's up?"

"Why'd you kick me off the plane with the band tomorrow night?" Tabitha demanded.

"I didn't," she said. "Your father did."

"What?" Tabitha asked, her anger suddenly tempered with confusion.

"He called me up this afternoon and said he needed to put two more people on the jet," Ava said. "I told him we were all full, and he said to move you two off the plane. I booked you first class on British Airways. It's fully luxe. I assumed he told you about the change."

"He forgot to mention it," Tabitha said, wounded. "Who did we get bumped for?"

"He didn't give me names," Ava said. "Just that it was a man and his son and that they were a top priority. I even offered to put them on the BA flight so you could stay with the band, but he said no."

This news was upsetting for Tabitha but enlightening for Sydney. Her eyes opened wide as she processed this information. Now she knew how Sir Reg planned to smuggle Jin-sun and Dae-jung out of the country.

Communications

ON THE FINAL DAY OF THE TOURNAMENT, Mother took Paris for breakfast at the same café where he'd met Tru a few nights earlier. They ordered *oladyi*, small Russian pancakes topped with blueberries and sour cream that tasted absolutely delicious. Midway through the meal, a black van parked a few meters from them and idled for several minutes with its engine running. No one got out or in and, like many of the vehicles in Moscow, the window tint was too dark to see inside. When it finally pulled away, Mother exhaled deeply.

"Well, that's a relief," he said as he watched it disappear into traffic.

"What is?" asked Paris.

"That huge building across the street is FSB headquarters, and I thought that van might be the secret police coming to arrest us," he said with the casualness that other people use to discuss the weather or the previous day's football scores.

"Was that a possibility?" Paris asked, stunned.

"Well, we did just invite a North Korean nuclear scientist to defect," Mother said. "The Russians don't care much for anyone spying on their turf no matter who the target is."

"I thought you said no one would see the message except for Park."

"Right," Mother answered. "But there was always the prospect that once he read it, he might alert his handlers, who would instantly notify the FSB."

"Funny, I don't remember you mentioning that prospect when you told me I had to play like a *patzer* and send the message," Paris said.

"Well, I didn't want you to worry," Mother said. "And now you don't have to."

"What makes you say that?"

"We've provided ample opportunity for a grab-and-go," Mother explained. "The long walk here, a table by the sidewalk, the headquarters across the street. I think we're all good."

"Wait a second," Paris said, incredulous. "Did you pick this café to make it easier for the FSB to abduct us?"

"Well, not *only* because of that," Mother said defensively. "I'd heard the *oladyi* were delicious, but . . . *yes*."

"Why would you do that?"

"I didn't want to go through the day constantly looking over our shoulders," Mother explained. "Now we know we're clear. If Park had told his handlers anything, someone would've snatched us by this point, and we'd be across the street in a cell instead of eating this yummy breakfast. I think it's better to know for sure, don't you?"

"I think it was better when I didn't even realize that it was a possibility," Paris said with a disbelieving laugh.

"I'll remember that for next time," Mother mumbled as he swallowed a bite. "Lesson learned."

After breakfast, they went straight to the British embassy, although it wasn't part of an escape plan like it had been for Monty, Kat, and Rio. They were scheduled for a photo op with the ambassador.

Dame Denise Hendricks was a career diplomat used to

high-level negotiations with foreign leaders. She had a PhD from the London School of Economics and was Britain's ambassador to the Russian Federation in Moscow. At the moment, however, she was serving as a decoy and providing Paris and Mother with a cover story.

"Welcome to the embassy," she said as she greeted them in an ornate room mostly used for receptions and press conferences. "I hope you're enjoying your visit."

"It's been great," Paris said.

"I hear you've been representing us quite well in the tournament," she said. "You've made everyone proud."

"Thank you, ma'am. I'm giving it my best."

"Why don't we sit down at the board and pretend to play so that Edgar can snap a few photos," she said.

An antique chessboard had been set up on a table nearby. It was a classic design from the mid-nineteenth century with pieces hand-carved out of rosewood by a London craftsman.

"This is a beautiful set," Paris said.

"It has quite a history," she said. "I'm told that it once belonged to Queen Victoria and was used in a match when George V played his cousin Tsar Nicholas II."

Paris instantly pulled his hands back, as if he wasn't sure he was supposed to touch the pieces.

"It's impressive," she said. "But there's no reason for you to be shy about it. Royal or not, you're a much better player than any of them."

Paris beamed, and they both laughed.

"Perfect," said the photographer as he snapped a picture. "We'll shoot some safeties, but that's the winner right there."

Sure enough, thirty minutes later, the picture of them laughing was posted on the embassy's social media accounts with the caption "British chess wiz dazzles ambassador."

It was the perfect cover story. If anyone questioned why Mother and Paris went to the embassy, all they had to do was check Twitter for an answer. This ruse bought them fifteen minutes to go into the SCIF, where Tru was waiting to brief them on the plan to exfiltrate Park and his son.

"We don't have much time, so let's get right to it." Tru had a sparkle in her eye as she talked, and it was evident that despite years at MI6, she still found this type of work exhilarating. "What's the latest on our nuclear scientist?"

"We delivered the message but still aren't sure of his answer," said Mother.

"Although, the fact we weren't kidnapped this morning is apparently a good sign," Paris said with a touch of snark.

"Very good, I'd say," Tru responded. "Did he take you to the café across the street from the FSB?"

"Yes," Paris said. "How'd you know?"

"He did it to me the other night," Tru said, smiling and shaking her head. "Twisted sense of humor if you ask me. As for Park, we have too many variables to work out to wait for his response, so for the time being we'll assume he's going to say yes. If he doesn't, we'll deal with that then."

"Do we have any idea what Sir Reg is planning?" asked Mother.

"A very good idea," Tru said happily. "Early this morning, Sydney sent word that he added two mystery passengers to a flight on his private jet, set to take off after tonight's concert."

"Dae-jung and his father?" asked Paris.

"Almost certainly," said Tru. "It's the perfect getaway. Reg already has a loose arrangement with the Russians as far as passport control is concerned, and there will be a mob scene of the band's fans at the airport that will make it easy to sneak them onboard amid the confusion."

"So does that mean Sir Reg has convinced him to join Umbra?" asked Paris.

"No," said Mother. "In fact, I'm almost certain that he hasn't. At least not yet. I've been watching every move Park makes, and Reg has barely paid attention to him other than at the museum that first night."

"Then how is he going to convince him?" asked Paris.

"The truth is, he doesn't need to," Mother answered. "He just needs to convince the North Koreans."

"What do you mean?" asked Paris.

"They have no reason to think that Reg is connected with Umbra; they just think he's a billionaire," Mother said. "If he snatches the Parks, the North Koreans will assume Park defected because he's been so difficult to them. They already think he's a renegade, so they'll think he's turned, which means he then couldn't go back even if he wanted to."

"That's exactly right," said Tru. "And we think it's going to happen tonight at the concert. All of you will be there for the presentation of the medals, and the crowd will provide the perfect cover to disappear."

"So do we try to get him out earlier in the day?" Mother asked.

"We considered that, but the same reasons that make

it ideal for Reg make it ideal for us," she said. "The crowd and confusion will give us an invaluable head start that we wouldn't have earlier in the day at the Tretyakov."

"But the stadium's huge, and the concert will last for hours," Mother said. "We have to make sure we get him out before Reg's people nab him."

"That's where Brooklyn comes in," Tru said with a grin.

"She does?" asked Paris.

"She cracked the St. Basil's code," Tru answered. "And yesterday, a picture was posted that told us exactly where it's going to happen." She showed them a map and put her finger on a spot in the parking lot southwest of the stadium. "The precise latitude and longitude of this location was embedded in the code. And that was confirmed an hour later when one of our agents followed Nicholas Sorokin when he rode his motorcycle there to scout it out."

"What's there?" asked Mother.

"This is where they park the trucks used to haul the band's equipment from stadium to stadium," she answered. "There are at least forty of them, and they're arranged like a maze. According to your itinerary, it's also where all the competitors from the chess tournament are scheduled to exit after the concert to catch the bus back to the hotel."

"Which makes it the perfect place to grab them and lose their handlers in the maze of trucks," said Mother.

"Not only that, but check this out," Tru said as she showed him a map of Moscow.

"This is one of Sorokin's Cold War maps?" he asked.

"Yes," answered Tru. "Monty snapped this before he chased her out of town. According to this, the parking lot is directly above a top secret tunnel that runs directly to the waterfront."

"So while the Russians and North Koreans are searching the parking lot, the Parks will already be racing down the river," Mother said.

"It's a smart plan," Tru said. "We just have to be smarter."

"And how do we do that?"

"We're still working on it," she said. "But the key is going to be Dame Denise Hendricks."

"The ambassador?" asked Mother, surprised.

"Yes," Tru said. "She has a fourteen-year-old daughter who's a rabid KB5 fan, so she was already planning on being at the concert. She'll have a limousine in VIP parking that is protected by her diplomatic immunity. We're working out a way to sneak Park and his son into the limo. Once they are inside, they're safe to get away from the stadium."

"And then?" asked Paris.

"They'll be transferred into a vehicle with a hidden compartment and driven across the border into Latvia," she said. "If all goes according to plan, they'll be in London late tomorrow night."

"But that depends on whether or not he says he wants to go with us," said Mother. "We're not like Umbra. We're not just going to kidnap him."

"No," said Tru. "But we're not going to let him fall into Umbra's hands. Do not forget that that's our top priority. Let us know as soon as you get his answer so we can plan accordingly."

It was just a fifteen-minute drive from the embassy to the Tretyakov, and when they arrived, there was no sign of the Parks. Paris went to chat with some of the other players, and Mother took his normal spot in the front row of the spectators' section.

He was relieved when Park walked through the door

but didn't know what to make of the fact that he sat far away from him and his normal seat. He didn't make eye contact, and there was no signal of any kind. Was this an indication that he didn't want to come?

Paris made his way over to the table for his match and was greeted by Dae-jung.

"Good luck," Dae-jung said as they shook hands.

"You too," Paris replied.

Paris knew that Dae-jung was better than anyone he'd ever played. He was determined to give him his very best game and opened with the Scotch gambit he'd learned from Barnaby Fitch.

This had worked against other players but didn't faze Dae-jung in the slightest. Paris quickly realized that he was almost certainly going to lose. He tried whatever he could think of to counter him, but he also took time to admire the beauty and artistry of Dae-jung's playing.

It was perfect and inspired, but then something strange happened. Dae-jung moved the same pawn twice in a row. That was something only a *patzer* did, not a great player. Paris looked at the board and then at Dae-jung, trying to make sense of it. It wasn't until he wrote the move down on his score sheet that he realized what had happened.

It hadn't been a mistake at all. It had been an answer. Right there on the sheet in front of him, hidden in the algebraic notation, four letters stood out, as clear as day.

FREE.

The Concert

AFTER BEATING PARIS IN THE MORNING match, Dae-jung finished off his tournament that afternoon against Antonia. Despite what most people thought, the word "checkmate" was rarely spoken at elite chess tournaments. Players at the top level could tell when defeat was inevitable. Rather than draw out the suffering, they typically conceded by tipping over their king and offering congratulations to their opponent. That's what Antonia did on the thirty-seventh move of their match.

"Very well done," she said as they shook hands. "You are an exceptional player."

"Thank you," Dae-jung replied. "So are you."

For Antonia, there was no shame or disappointment in losing. Dae-jung was clearly the best player in the tournament and had won every match he played. She had the second-best record, while Paris and Li Ang tied for third. All of them would receive medals that night at the KB5 concert.

British Embassy

Because computers and phones were forbidden in the SCIF, Tru had to set up shop in the embassy's situation room so that she could maintain contact with the three teams she had in the field.

The first one consisted of Mother, Paris, and Sydney, who were responsible for keeping eyes on the Parks and Sir Reg at all times. The second was a trio of agents who had Nicholas Sorokin under surveillance. And the third was the extraction team assigned to the ambassador's limousine.

Although their communication link was encrypted, there was always the concern that Russian intelligence might intercept a message, so they limited the amount of contact and spoke in code. At five o'clock, or seventeen hundred in military and spy time, Tru performed a scheduled check.

"Testing comms, one, two, three," she said into a microphone. "Identify if you can hear me."

"This is Luke," answered Mother.

"Copy Han," replied another.

"Leia is on the move," answered a third.

"Copy Obi-wan," Tru responded, her pulse quickening. "This operation is hot. We are a go."

Presidential Suite—National Hotel

Although they were staying in the same hotel, Sydney was in a regular room, while Tabitha was in a suite more luxurious than any Sydney had ever seen. It had three rooms, antique furniture, and fine art hanging on the walls. There was a piano in the sitting room and a balcony that offered panoramic views of the Kremlin, St. Basil's, and Red Square. In one of her posts for *Audrey*, Sydney had detailed a list of the Hollywood celebrities, rock stars, and members of royalty who'd previously stayed in the suite.

At the moment, however, it was the last place she wanted to be. They were already twenty minutes late, and there was no indication they were leaving anytime soon. She'd arrived half an hour earlier and still hadn't actually *seen* Tabitha. She only knew for certain that she was there because of the frustrated grunts and angry exclamations coming from the other room as she tried on different outfits.

"How's it going?" Sydney asked, trying to sound helpful.

Tabitha didn't answer so much as she growled.

She'd been in a funk ever since she found out they'd been bumped from the flight, and she'd taken out much of her frustration on Sydney. The surly, entitled Tabitha that Sydney had dealt with throughout the day was the spoiled princess she'd originally expected.

Now all Sydney could do was wait and hope that they didn't arrive at the concert too late to help with the mission.

Katpotnya District—Moscow

Carey Cavanaugh, the man Monty, Kat, and Rio first knew as the cab driver named Yuri, was one of the three MI6 agents tailing Nicholas Sorokin. They'd followed him in separate nondescript cars, rotating at regular intervals to keep from being spotted. They expected this would take them to the stadium, but at the moment Sorokin had led them to Kapotnya, an industrial district in the southeast corner of the city, filled with run-down factories and dominated by a gigantic oil refinery belching smoke and fire into the sky.

He'd ridden his motorcycle into an old warehouse surrounded by a razor-wire fence. All the agents could do was wait on nearby streets watching the potential exits. After more than thirty minutes, Sorokin drove out in a paneled work truck, and Cavanaugh alerted the others.

"Obi-wan, this is Han, do you copy?" he said into his radio.

"Roger that, Han. What do you have?"

"Vader is on the move and has changed vehicles," he said. "He's now driving a blue plumbing supply truck, and we are maintaining contact."

Presidential Suite—National Hotel

Sydney paced back and forth in the sitting room, trying to think of ways to hurry Tabitha. She resisted the urge to bang on the piano keys until she opened the door, opting to put aside her frustration and try to be understanding instead.

"Tabs, I know you're upset about the plane," she said through the door. "I am too. I mean, I was really looking forward to it. But the truth is, from the perspective of *Audrey*, the payoff for the story was always going to be the concert. As cool as the plane is, I'm not even allowed to take pictures on it, so it was only going to get a mention in the article. The photos and video of you backstage with the band are going to be epic." She paused, unsure if Tabitha could even hear her. "But we can only take those pictures if we're there."

Just then, the door to the bedroom opened and out stepped Tabitha, fully dressed with a smile on her face. She was wearing leather pants, ankle boots, a vintage tee, and a denim jacket. It was the exact same outfit she had picked out at the boutique in London on Sydney's birthday. Why it took that long to get back to where she started, Sydney didn't know.

"Okay, then, let's go," Tabitha said, as though none of the difficulty had ever happened.

"What do you mean?" asked Sydney.

"I mean, *let's go*," Tabitha answered. "I'm ready if you are."

"Don't we need to get the twins?"

"They're already at the stadium," Tabitha said.

"Really?" Sydney replied. "They watch every move we make for days, and now that it's time for the big event, they're gone?"

"I thought you'd be happy about that," Tabitha said. "There's a driver downstairs waiting for us. It's just going to be you and me."

"Great," Sydney said. "Let's go see an amazing concert."

Luzhniki Stadium—Loading Dock

After the chess tournament, the players went back to the hotel to change and have dinner. The mood was fun, and with the competition over, they were able to simply be kids and enjoy each other's company. The exception was Dae-jung, who'd been taken straight to the North Korean embassy.

Mother and Paris ate with Antonia and Ang, as well as their mothers, and they talked excitedly about participating in the medal ceremony. A bus picked them up at the hotel, and as they arrived at Luzhniki, Paris couldn't believe how many KB5 fans lined the barricades that blocked off the rear entrance. The fans couldn't see who was inside, so they started screaming at the bus in case the band was on board.

"You were right," Paris said to Mother.

"About what?"

"The Russians really are avid chess fans. Just listen to that crowd."

They both laughed, which was a needed release. Mother was still worried the North Koreans might change their minds and skip the concert.

The screaming died down when they got off the bus and the crowd realized that no pop stars were on board.

"Oops," Paris said humorously. "Maybe that cheering wasn't for us."

Mother breathed a sigh of relief when he saw the Parks and their handlers get out of a black SUV parked right behind the bus. Even so, he avoided any interaction with Park. He didn't want anyone else to suspect what was going on.

"All right, I need everyone to follow me," said Elena, one of the event's organizers. "We have to stay together as we go through security."

She was one of a half dozen tournament officials shepherding them at the concert. They were easy to spot because they wore the matching blue tournament polos.

"How are you feeling about everything?" Mother asked, more like a father than a secret agent.

"Excellent," said Paris. "This is my good-luck stadium."

"Is it?" Mother asked, puzzled.

"Luzhniki is where France won the 2018 World Cup," Paris said, grinning. "The karma here is very strong for me."

A pair of muscle-bound guards manned the door. When they stepped aside to let Paris and the others past, the crowd of fans erupted with jealous moans.

Garden Ring—Moscow

Rush hour traffic was bumper-to-bumper on the Garden Ring, the circular highway that looped around central Moscow. Although frustrating to drive in, the snarled pace made it easy for the three agents to tail Nicholas Sorokin.

Finally, the blue plumbing supply truck exited the highway, and they followed it to the area in the Luzhniki parking lot that had been coded in the most recent St. Basil's post. Sorokin flashed an ID badge to a security guard, who waved him into the otherwise closed lot. Everything was going according to plan.

Watching from his car, Cavanaugh made a call on his radio. "Obi-wan, this is Han. Vader has reached the Death Star."

Luzhniki Stadium—VIP Lounge

For the time being, at least, Tabitha's bad mood seemed

like a distant memory. She was backstage with the band and loved being part of the action. They were hamming it up as Sydney shot photos. At one point, she asked Tabitha to do an impromptu interview.

"Tabs here with none other than KB5 for a sixty-second exclusive interview backstage at their Moscow concert." She turned to Roman and, playing the part of a serious television journalist, asked, "We've seen the shows, we've watched the videos, we're dying to know, who in KB5 actually is the worst dancer?"

This led to an impromptu silly dance-off between Roman, Leo, and Isaac that was hilarious.

Rather than pick a winner, Tabitha turned to the camera and said, "It's too close for me to call. Tell me, Team Audrey, who do you think is the worst? We'll let your vote decide it."

"That's perfect!" Sydney said when she stopped the video. "I'm going to put that up right now."

Sydney quickly went to work writing up a post and adding a vote feature so that the *Audrey* readers could pick their favorite. But when she tried to post it, she didn't have a good enough connection.

"The Wi-Fi's terrible down here," Isaac said. "You've got better luck out in the hall."

"Thanks," Sydney said as she hurried out to the passageway, where she was able to post the video. She was just about to come back into the room when someone caught her eye. It was Sasha Sorokin, and the thing that Sydney noticed was that it was the first time she'd ever seen her wear anything other than all black. She had on one of the blue polos worn by the officials with the chess tournament. This was despite the fact that she'd had nothing to do with it. Moments later, she saw that Anastasia was wearing one too, and Sydney began to get an uneasy feeling.

She rushed back into the room and instantly picked up one of the itineraries that had everyone's schedule. It dawned on her that they'd been so focused on the fact that their names weren't on the passenger list for Sir Reg's jet, that they'd never checked to see whose were.

She found the flight information and saw that although Tabitha wasn't going to be on the jet, her security detail was. Sasha and Anastasia were both still scheduled to take the flight along with the mystery guests. Sydney's uneasy feeling became a real fear.

What if we have the wrong Sorokin? What if the twins are the ones who are going to snatch the Parks?

Luzhniki Stadium—Stage

The concert was about to start, and the crowd was already raucous when Sir Reginald Banks made what for the audience was a surprise appearance alongside two members of KB5.

"Hello, Moscow!" Roman said, eliciting a roar from the crowd. "We're just about to get to the music, but Harrison and I wanted to come out and say hello and introduce you to our friend—and boss—Sir Reginald Banks."

The crowd couldn't have cared less, but by having the two band members out, Reg was guaranteed a loud reception. He said hello, did a quick introduction, and then presented the medals for the tournament. They posed for a couple of pictures and hurried off the stage. All in all, it had taken less than two minutes.

At the end, Roman and Harrison hyped up the crowd to send the winners off with some real applause. Despite the crowd's lack of interest, it had still been a thrill for Dae-jung, Antonia, Ang, and Paris. And the pictures of them with thousands of people in the background were sure to look amazing.

Paris was so jazzed by the moment that, at first, he

didn't notice that the woman leading them offstage was one of the Sorokin twins.

"Follow me," she said, directing them. "I'll take you to your seats."

Luzhniki Stadium—Backstage Hallway
Sydney was desperately trying to get a signal on her phone so that she could send an emergency message to Paris and Mother. Finally, she saw the group walking nearby and raced toward them. She wasn't supposed to make direct contact, but she didn't see any other option.

Paris was at the back of the group, and when she caught up to him, it was hard to be heard over the noise from the stadium as well as from the fans chanting outside the wall.

"What's wrong?" Paris asked.

"The twins," Sydney told him. "I don't think Sorokin's the one we have to worry about. I think it's the twins."

"You think or you know?" Paris asked.

Sydney considered it for a moment and answered honestly, "I *think*."

Paris rushed ahead to rejoin the group and realized that both Sorokin sisters were now leading their group through the maze of backstage hallways. He had no idea if it was a trap or if they were just helping out, but he couldn't take the chance. The number-one objective of the mission was to make sure Umbra didn't get the Parks. There was no time to ask Mother for help. He had to figure out a solution on his own. He thought back to the opening ceremony at the Tretyakov and came up with one.

Up ahead there was an emergency door. On the other side of it were the screaming fans dying to get a backstage glimpse of the band. He hesitated for a second and then opened the door.

First, the alarm sounded, and soon a surge of KB5 fans rushed in from the outside and flooded the hallway. It was total chaos, and just as they'd been trained to do, the instant there was a hint of trouble, the North Korean agents closed ranks around Jin-sun and Dae-jung and rushed them out of harm's way.

By the time security restored order to the hallway, the North Koreans were all gone and on their way back to their embassy.

Paris watched in stunned silence, worried that he'd made a terrible mistake.

Lop Nor

Lop Nor Wild Camel Reserve, Xinjiang Uyghur Autonomous Region, China

EVEN THOUGH IT WAS THE MIDDLE OF THE day, the sandstorm was so intense that the driver had to wear night-vision goggles as he raced across the desert in a jeep specifically designed to withstand these harsh conditions. Next to him, his partner charted their course on a navigation device that blended thermal imaging technology with GPS mapping.

They were in northern China, near the Mongolian border, in the Lop Nor Desert. This was where scientists came to study the planet's last remaining herds of wild Bactrian camels. But these particular men were no scientists, and they had no interest in camels.

They were mercenaries working for Umbra.

They'd spent the last two weeks camping on an ancient lake bed so desolate and barren, it was known as the "Sea of Death." They'd been waiting for a storm like this, known as a "buran," to provide the necessary cover for their mission.

In addition to being home to the wild camel reserve, the desert was also the site of the Lop Nor Nuclear Weapons Test Base. This was where China tested and stored its nuclear weapons, and for at least six hours, the soldiers who protected the facility would be blinded by the storm. By the time it was over, the two men in the jeep would be gone.

So would three nuclear warheads.

Spag Bol

Aisling, Scotland

PARIS WAS IN A FUNK, ALTHOUGH HE WAS hardly alone. It had been a week since the City Spies had returned to the FARM, and it seemed as though everyone had second thoughts about what went down in Moscow. Kat blamed herself for tipping off Nicholas Sorokin. Sydney wondered if the glitz and glamour of hanging out with KB5 had caused her to miss what was going on with Sasha and Anastasia. But most of all, Paris questioned his decision to open the emergency door and set off the alarm.

They'd been in the midst of a huge operation involving MI6, the embassy, and multiple teams of undercover agents, yet he'd effectively erased it all with one split-second decision. A golden opportunity was gone. Park Jin-sun and Dae-jung were back in North Korea, and Reginald Banks was once again plotting ways to snatch them for Umbra.

What if I was wrong? Paris asked himself as he looked up from a chess book and stared out his window toward the North Sea. *What if everything was going perfectly, and I ruined it?*

"Hey," Sydney said, rapping on the half-open door, "can we talk?"

"Sure," Paris said, his mind still distant.

She closed the door behind her but got distracted by the messy state of Paris's room. There were stacks of books everywhere, multiple chessboards perched in unstable locations, and scraps of paper with illegible scribbling strewn across his desk.

"What are you doing?" she asked, trying to make sense of the scene.

"Studying chess openings," he said. "Right now, I'm deep into the Sicilian Defense."

"Did I miss a lecture in European history when Sicily

was attacked and defended itself by scattering junk everywhere?" Sydney asked.

"Did I miss the part where I asked for your opinion about how I keep my room?"

"Okay. Sorry." She held up her hands in mock surrender. "Don't get defensive. Or should I say, 'Don't get *Sicilian* defensive'?"

The joke was so bad it made him laugh, which snapped him out of his mood a bit. "What'd you want to talk about?" he asked.

"Brooklyn," she answered as she cleared a space among the books on his bed so that she could sit on the edge. "What do you make of the whole *friendship* between her and Charlotte?"

"I don't know what to think," he said. "But I have to say that I didn't see it coming."

"I don't like it one bit," she replied. "Charlotte's bad news."

"Yes, but is she really?" he asked. "I mean, I understand we have a history, but maybe we should give her the benefit of the doubt. After all, she was one of us."

"*Was,*" Sydney said emphatically. "But she left. With no warning. No explanation. Which means no benefit of the doubt. I can't figure out her scheme, but I'm sure she's up to something."

"Maybe she's just looking for a friend," he said. "Maybe they both are. Have you talked to Brooklyn about it?"

"I haven't had the chance," Sydney said. "She just got back from summer school last night, and she hasn't been very chatty. I think she's mad at me."

"Did you ever thank her for her birthday present?"

"No," Sydney admitted. "First, I was mad, and then came the mission, and then I forgot."

"So, in her mind, she got left behind on the mission and forgotten by her best friend," Paris said. "I wouldn't worry about it. All that's pretty fixable."

"Yes, but I'm still not happy about Charlotte," Sydney said. "How are you doing? You stopped beating yourself up about the end of the mission?"

"Not even a little," he said. "I keep running through it in my head."

"Don't," she said. "You did the right thing."

"I'm not so sure."

"Think of it this way," she said. "If you hadn't done it and the Sorokin sisters snatched the Parks, it'd be game over. But, as it is, we're still in it to win it."

"I guess so."

"Come on, it's time for dinner," she said. "Mother's making spag bol."

This put a smile on Paris's face, and they went down to the kitchen, where Mother was putting the finishing touches on his specialty, spaghetti Bolognese.

"That smells amazing," Sydney said as they entered the kitchen.

She grabbed a spoon and tried to sneak a taste of sauce, but Mother playfully slapped it away. "Not until we're at the table," he said, stirring the pot. "We're going to have a proper dinner for a change."

Rio, Kat, and Brooklyn were already there. Sydney tried to flash a smile at Brooklyn but got little in response.

"Where's Monty?" asked Paris.

"Running an errand," said Mother. "Which is good, because I wanted to have a talk with just the six of us before we eat."

"What type of talk?" asked Kat. "A mission briefing?"

"That can wait until tomorrow," he said. "This is a family meeting."

"What's that?" asked Kat.

"It's where we discuss things as a family," said Mother. "It's been a few months since the adoption, and I wanted to check in on some issues."

"Like?" asked Paris.

Mother put the sauce on simmer and turned to face everyone.

"I'm trying to find the right balance of being a father and being a spy. Sometimes I get it wrong, and I appreciate that you all have been understanding as I fumble through it. But I want to make sure that you know, being a father is what matters the most to me. The five of you, Robert, and Annie," he said, referencing his children with Clementine.

Mother hadn't said much about Robert and Annie since he came close to finding them in Australia, where their mother, who was also an agent, had been keeping them for safety a few months earlier. The others had avoided the topic because of its sensitivity, but since he mentioned it, Paris saw an opening.

"Speaking of Robert and Annie," he said tentatively. "Have there been any new developments?"

"None," Mother said. "I think Clementine knows we were close to finding them, so she's taken them deeper into hiding." He was quiet for a moment before adding,

"But I keep looking and searching and am confident that find them I will. I'm also comforted by the fact that, although I don't know why Clemmie has done what's she's done, I do know that she loves the children as much as I do and is ensuring that they are well cared for. Everything I learned in Australia indicates that they are healthy, happy, and safe."

"You know, if there's anything we can do to help . . . ," Sydney said.

"I do, and that means the world to me," he said. "Maybe after this mission, we'll have a little free time, and we can intensify the search."

"I'd like that," said Paris. "That is, if you'd trust me."

"Why wouldn't I trust you?" asked Mother.

"Well, I did just scuttle an entire mission by myself," Paris answered.

"You didn't *scuttle* it," Mother said. "You *saved* it."

"That's the father talking," Paris said.

"What do you mean?" Mother asked.

"The father in you, who wants to make me feel better, says I saved it. But the spy knows differently."

"Actually, the spy in me knows that you saved it too," Mother said. "I just spoke with Tru, and it turns out that Nicholas Sorokin left the scene almost immediately after he'd parked the plumbing supply truck at the stadium."

"Really?" said Paris.

"Why did no one tell us that?" asked Sydney.

"Because they didn't know," Mother explained. "They were focused on the vehicle and didn't realize he'd slipped out. It was only later when they were reviewing surveillance footage that they discovered he'd gotten into another vehicle and left."

"So, if Sorokin wasn't there . . . ," said Sydney.

"Then the plan wasn't for him to grab the Parks," said Mother. "All signs point to it being the twins."

"So I didn't mess up?" Paris asked hopefully.

"No, you didn't," said Mother. "And even if you did, it would've been all right. Everybody makes mistakes."

"That's such a relief," Paris said, letting out a deep breath.

Mother looked over at Brooklyn, who'd remained quiet the entire time. "Brooklyn, I can't help but think you're feeling a little left out."

"You noticed, did you?" she replied with a bit of an edge.

"I'm truly sorry you feel that way," he answered. "But it was absolutely the right decision for you to go to summer school. Your future, including how you do at school, will always be more important than any mission. Do you understand that?"

She nodded. "Yes."

"And don't forget that even though she wasn't *officially* on the mission, she still managed to break the code that MI6 said couldn't be broken," Kat interjected.

"That was mighty impressive!" Mother said as the others offered some hoots of celebration.

"Well, Charlotte helped," Brooklyn said modestly.

The mention of Charlotte changed the dynamic in the room from momentary celebration to uncertainty. There was an awkward silence until Sydney spoke up.

"I don't have much experience with family meetings," she said. "But are we free to discuss things openly and say what's on our minds?"

"Of course," said Mother.

Sydney shot a quick look at Brooklyn and then turned back to the face the others. "I don't think Charlotte should be allowed in the house."

"Why not?" Brooklyn asked. "She helped crack the code."

"It doesn't matter," Sydney responded. "You don't know her like we do. She can't be trusted."

"First of all, you don't know how well I do or don't

know her," said Brooklyn. "And as far as trustworthiness goes, I'm not so sure you're the best judge of that."

The two of them traded angry looks, but neither escalated the argument.

"I don't like it either," said Rio.

"Why not?" asked Mother.

"Because she left us," he said.

"What about you two?" Mother asked Paris and Kat.

"I'm not really sure how I feel," said Paris. "I've got mixed emotions about it."

"So do I," Kat admitted.

"I think you guys should give her a chance," Brooklyn said. "She misses all of you. Your friendship."

"She told you that?" Sydney asked with a sneer.

"Yes," Brooklyn answered.

"Well, she's playing some sort of game, then," Sydney said. "Because it was her decision to leave."

"Maybe that was a mistake," Brooklyn said. "Or maybe there's more to the story."

"Once again let me remind you that you don't know what happened," Sydney replied. "You weren't here."

"I'm sick of you telling me what I do and don't know," Brooklyn said. "I may not have been here, but as it happens, I know the whole story of why she left."

"Because she told you?" Sydney answered. "Again, it's all part of her game."

"No, because I figured it out and talked with Mother about it," Brooklyn said. "And then I talked to her about it too."

This caught everyone by surprise.

"You told Brooklyn but not us?" Paris asked.

"Not exactly," answered Mother. "Brooklyn figured it out, and I confirmed it."

"Why didn't you tell us?" Rio asked.

"Charlotte asked Monty and me to keep it a secret," he explained. "And I asked Brooklyn to honor our promise to do so."

"That's not right," Sydney said. "If we're a family, we all deserve to know. We shouldn't have secrets like that."

"I agree," Mother said. "Which is the reason I wanted to have this family meeting."

"You're going to tell us?" said Kat.

"No," Mother answered, "Charlotte is. She's coming for dinner tonight. Monty's errand is that she's picking her up right now."

"I think I just lost my appetite," Sydney said.

Brooklyn gave her a look. "So what? Now you don't want to know the whole story?"

Sydney didn't respond, she just sat there and stewed for a moment.

"I'm not going to force you to be here," Mother said. "But I think you should be. And I'd like everyone to have an open mind."

Fifteen minutes later the table was set, and the food was ready when Monty returned. "This certainly smells delicious," she said as she entered the room. "I've got company."

"Hi, everyone," Charlotte said meekly as she entered behind her.

"Good evening, Charlotte," Mother said. "So happy you can join us for dinner."

"Thank you," she said. She looked around the room at the faces, and the only friendly one she saw belonged to Brooklyn. She already regretted agreeing to come. "I really don't want to ruin dinner. I know how much everyone loves Mother's spag bol. But I've been trying to figure out how to say something to you all for a long time now." She paused. "I realize that I didn't leave on good terms."

"*Good* terms?" Sydney scoffed. "You didn't leave on any terms. You didn't even say a word."

"Sydney?" Mother said. "Let her talk."

"She's right," Charlotte said. "I didn't say anything before I left. And I didn't say anything afterward at school. I was too embarrassed."

"Embarrassed about what?" Rio asked. "You quit."

"Actually, I didn't quit," Charlotte said. "Mother kicked me off the team."

Suddenly much of the hostility at the table turned to confusion. Sydney turned an accusing eye toward Mother, but Charlotte cut her off before she could speak.

"Don't blame him," she said. "He did what he had to do, and I begged him and Monty not to tell you why. I pleaded with them to keep it a secret and just tell you all that I had quit."

"Why would you do that?" asked Kat.

"Because I didn't want you to know that I was a thief," she said. "I hacked into some banks and was planning on stealing a bunch of money. Millions of pounds. If I'd gotten caught, it would've been a disaster. I would've gone to jail. MI6 would've shut down the program. Everything would've been ruined. He had to kick me off the team. I didn't leave him any choice."

"You still could've told us," said Sydney.

"I realize that now," said Charlotte. "But at the time,

I thought it was better if you hated me, than if you knew what I really was. I was so embarrassed." She was on the verge of tears, which for Charlotte was unheard of. "But now I see that I was wrong, and I just wanted to tell all of you that I'm sorry."

For Charlotte this was a huge release, and she felt relieved. But, for the others, it spurred questions.

"What changed?" asked Paris. "Why tell us this now?"

"I got to hang out with Brooklyn at school," she said. "She's pretty awesome. And, um, she let me help her with the St. Basil's code." She paused for a moment. "And when I saw what I was missing out on, I realized how stupid I'd been."

"So, what does that mean?" asked Rio. "Do you want back on the team?"

Mother went to answer, but Charlotte cut him off.

"No," she said. "Mother and Monty have both been clear about that, and I agree. I've lost that right. That privilege. I can't be a spy." She looked up at the whole table. "But, if there's a place for it, I would like to be a friend."

Everyone remained quiet for a moment until Kat scooched her chair over a bit.

"Why don't you sit next to me?" she asked. "Like you used to."

"You'd be okay with that?" asked Charlotte.

Kat nodded.

"Why?"

"Everybody makes mistakes."

35.

Bertrand Dashiell Gibbs, Jr.

BRITISH AIRWAYS FLIGHT 39—MIDFLIGHT

THE CITY SPIES TRAVELED IN TWO SEPARATE teams to Beijing for the second half of Operation Checkmate. The first to go were Mother and Paris, who were headed for the last leg of the Around the World Chess Invitational. Years as a spy had trained Mother to take advantage of any opportunity to get sleep, so he'd nodded off early during the ten-hour flight. In the middle of the night, somewhere over central Asia, he awoke to find Paris poring over a chess book in the seat next to him.

The plane was only half-full, so they had a row to themselves, but Mother still spoke quietly to make sure he didn't wake any nearby passengers. "What are you doing up?"

"I need to study," Paris answered, determined.

"You need sleep," Mother said. Then he added one of his Motherisms. *"The mission's best that starts with rest."*

"I know. But I have to figure out as much of this as I can if I want to be a good player."

"You already are a good player," Mother said. "Extremely good."

"I thought so too," Paris said. "But then I sat across the board from Dae-jung and realized that I'm nowhere close."

"He's that talented?"

Paris nodded. "Spellbinding."

"What makes him so special?"

"It's hard to put into words," Paris said. "But when I was taking lessons from Barnaby Fitch, he said that your style of play should match your personality."

"You mean like if you're a cautious person, you should play cautiously? If you're daring, you should take risks?" asked Mother.

"Exactly," Paris said. "But when I went up against Dae-jung, I realized it was much more than just that. Playing him was like watching an artist work. It didn't seem like he was making moves that he learned from a book. He was just expressing himself creatively on the board. I don't know if that makes any sense. But even though we didn't speak during the match, by the time it was over, I felt like I *knew* him. And that's when I realized my problem."

"Which is what?" Mother asked.

"I don't know *me*."

"What do you mean?"

"I've been so many different people that I've lost track of who I truly am. Is the real me from Rwanda or Paris or Scotland? Am I Salomon Omborenga? Lucas Doinel? Antoine Tremblay? Or someone about to be invented in an office in Vauxhall Cross?" Paris shook his head.

Mother looked at Paris and studied his face, half obscured by shadow in the darkness of the plane. Neither spoke for a bit, and the only noise was the whine of the jet engine and the gentle hiss of the air vent.

"Bertrand Dashiell Gibbs, Jr.," Mother said.

Paris gave him a look, wondering if this was a name he should recognize. "Is that who I'm supposed to be next?"

"No," said Mother. "It's who I used to be a long time ago. My real name. My *identity*. Although, it sounds utterly foreign to me when I say it out loud."

Paris sat up straight, and his eyes opened wide. The mystery of Mother's true identity was a closely guarded secret and had been a frequent topic of discussion and guesswork among the City Spies. "Really?"

"I was Bertrand at church, Gibbsy on the football pitch, and Bertie at university. Quite unfortunate, that. I grew up at Number Twelve Arnold Grove in a part of Liverpool called Wavertree."

"Do you still have family there?"

"None," Mother said. "I was the only child of only children. My father walked out of the house when I was four, and I never saw him again. After that, it was just me and Mum."

"What was she like?" Paris asked.

"She was grand," said Mother. "She was a primary school teacher. She also taught piano lessons and helped out in a little community theater. And since there was no one to watch me, I was in all the shows." He laughed at the memory. "She did everything she could for me, and then she passed away the month before I graduated from St. Andrews. Such a shame. I would've loved for her to have seen that. She worked so hard to get me there."

"I'm so sorry," Paris said. "I wish I could've met her."

"She would've loved you right away. Your brain. Your heart. She would've thought you were perfect. She'd have taught you to play Beethoven. She said being able to play 'Moonlight Sonata' was the true mark of a gentleman."

For Paris, all this was amazing information. "Did you like being in the plays?"

"Loved it, especially the musicals," Mother said. "I got to shed the name of a man I despised and become Nathan Detroit, Conrad Birdie, Danny Zuko, you name it. Somehow playing all those roles prepared me to one day assume new identities for MI6."

"So which one's the real you?" asked Paris.

"I don't know," Mother said. "A mix of all of them, I guess."

"Isn't Danny Zuko the dreamboat in *Grease* with the slicked-back hair and the leather jacket?"

Mother laughed and nodded. "Okay, maybe all of them except him. I think I was a bit miscast in that role."

"So how did *Bertrand Dashiell Gibbs, Jr.* become *Mother*?" Paris asked.

Mother smiled at the memory.

"It was early during my training," he answered.

"They told me that I had to say goodbye to my old name forever, which was no problem. But they needed a name to call me by, and I drew a blank. I just couldn't think of one I wanted. So my trainer said, 'Who's your hero?' I'm sure he thought I'd pick a footballer or someone like Churchill, but I said the only thing that came to mind."

"Your mother," Paris said with a chuckle.

"They laughed too," Mother said. "But it stuck. I think they thought they were hazing me by calling me that. But I never minded. I just thought of my mum and tried to make her proud."

They talked some more about Mother's childhood, and somehow that made Paris feel more tethered to the world. Afterward, he decided to put his chess book away and got a few hours of sleep before they landed at Daxing International.

The ultramodern airport, known as the "starfish" because of its shape, was bright and open with sweeping white surfaces that looked like they were from a science-fiction movie. Unlike Moscow, passport control was fast and efficient, and not long after they landed, they were on a high-speed train racing toward the city center. Monty and the rest of the team would arrive on another flight later in the day.

"Do you still remember the lyrics?" Paris asked as they rode the train.

"To what?"

"The songs from those shows you did as a kid?"

Mother laughed. "Every one of them."

"Okay, here's the deal," Paris said. "If we pull off this mission successfully, you have to sing one of them to everyone back at the FARM."

"I said I was in the shows," Mother replied. "I didn't say I was good."

"Either way, it's bound to be entertaining."

"Fine," Mother said, nodding. "It's a deal. But what are you going to do?"

"Well, I'm not going to sing, if that's what you mean," Paris said. "But maybe I'll look into piano lessons so I can learn 'Moonlight Sonata.'" He looked up at Mother. "For Gran."

The Forbidden City

BEIJING WAS DEFINED BY CONTRADICTIONS.
It was old and new, distant yet inviting, sprawling but
somehow intimate. Here American fast-food restaurants
sold burgers and fries next to street vendors hawking
grilled scorpions, while modern nightclubs sat alongside ancient homes in alleys that dated back to the Ming
dynasty. Nowhere were the contradictions more evident
than at the Forbidden City, the massive palace complex
that stood at the heart of Beijing and for centuries repre-
sented the center of the Chinese universe.

Made up of innumerable buildings, including twelve separate palaces, and surrounded by an imposing ten-meter wall, it was bold and conspicuous yet still maintained an air of mystery. In that way, it was a fitting location to resume Operation Checkmate, which seemed straightforward but had so far been filled with unexpected twists and turns.

"There they are," Paris said excitedly to Mother as he waved to his friends.

Up ahead, Antonia and Ang were waiting with their mothers at the Gate of Heavenly Peace, which served as the Forbidden City's main entrance.

The group had planned a day of sightseeing at dinner on their final night in Moscow. Ang's mother, Jia-Hui, had offered to show them around. "I want you to see more than a chessboard when you're there," she'd said with friendly ease. "For Ang and me, Beijing is home, and we are proud of it. We do this whenever we have visitors."

Li Jia-Hui relished her role as tour guide and shared with them everything from symbolism and history to amazing facts and figures. "It was home to twenty-four emperors, spanning two dynasties, across a period of nearly five hundred years," she said as they approached the Hall of Supreme Harmony in the center of the complex. "I want you to look at the roof and tell me what you see."

"Yellow tile," said Antonia.

"Imperial yellow," Jia-Hui answered. "No one other than the emperor was allowed to use this color."

"Gargoyles," offered Paris, pointing out the rows of mythical animal figures that lined the ridges at each corner of the roof.

"They're called 'ridge beasts' and are designed to frighten away evil spirits," she said. "You can tell how important a building is by how many ridge beasts it has. This one has ten, which is the most of all."

"So, it must have been pretty important," Antonia said.

"Extremely," Jia-Hui replied. "This was the location for royal weddings, and it was here where emperors officially ascended onto the Dragon Throne."

"I like the sound of that," said Paris. "The Dragon Throne."

"Now, for a mystery," said Jia-Hui. "What's missing from the roof. Something that you'll find on roofs all around the world, but not on any in the Forbidden City."

This stumped everyone, and they were quiet until Mother said, "This is just a guess, but I'm going to go with birds."

Jia-Hui smiled and said, "That's absolutely right. There are no birds on any of the roofs in the Forbidden City."

"Why?" asked Ang.

"The roofs are specifically designed to be too steep and slippery, and the spines are built too wide for a bird's claw to grab hold of," she answered.

"Amazing," said Paris.

"And a good model for chess," added Jia-Hui.

Paris turned to look at her. "How do you mean?"

"It is better to prevent a problem from occurring than to deal with it after it happens," she answered. "You have to think ahead and plan accordingly."

For Paris, not only was the palace fascinating, but the afternoon provided a great chance to hang out with Antonia and Ang. He liked them both, and all three of them could relate to what it was like to play against Dae-jung.

"We are competing for second, no?" said Ang, and the others laughed.

"Certainly," answered Antonia. "I cannot beat him."

"I don't think anyone can," said Paris. "But we'll give it our best."

A few hours later they saw Dae-jung at the opening

ceremony. Reginald Banks had hoped to hold it on the grounds of the Forbidden City itself, but when he couldn't get permission for that, he opted for a private club on Tiananmen Square, overlooking the palace. After a performance of traditional Chinese music, he got up and welcomed the players and their families.

"It's wonderful to have you all here at the Beijing Around the World Chess Invitational," he said. "We had a stupendous tournament in Moscow and crowned an undefeated champion in Park Dae-jung. I'm very happy that he has come back to see if he can continue his winning ways. Let's hear it for him."

Everyone applauded, and Dae-jung smiled modestly and gave an embarrassed wave.

"In Moscow you competed amid priceless works of art at the site of a world chess championship," Reg continued. "It was quite the setting, but I wouldn't be who I am if I didn't try to outperform myself. Believe it or not, what we have for China is even grander."

"Where will the matches be held?" someone called out playfully from the crowd.

"Wouldn't you like to know?" Reg answered with a huge grin. "The site of the competition has been a great mystery, which seems fitting for our enigmatic host city.

I hate to break it to you, but I'm still keeping that secret tonight. It's part of the fun.

"Every morning, a bus will arrive at your hotel and take you to that day's setting. Each day will be different, and each location will be more magnificent than the last. We are going to celebrate the beauty and the history of this incredible city that mixes the ancient and the modern."

This brought a huge round of applause. Mother marveled at Reg's maneuver. It appeared to everyone that he was living up to his showman's history of always being bigger and bolder. But he'd also made it so that the North Koreans couldn't plan ahead. They'd have to arrive at the hotel like everyone else each morning in order to find out where the matches were being played that day. After being thwarted in Moscow, Reg was trying to control as much as possible.

"The first-round pairings are going to be posted in just a few minutes," he said. "So enjoy the music, have some delicious food, and let's all have a wonderful tournament."

There was more applause, and Sir Reg made a quick exit from the room as most of the players headed to the presentation boards to see the pairings.

Mother walked straight for Park Jin-sun. He'd not gotten a chance to talk to him at the concert in Moscow, and this was his first opportunity to try to explain what happened. As usual, Park was surrounded by the guards from the North Korean Ministry of State Security. Mother recognized them and knew that they didn't speak English. He and Park would have to appear as though they were having friendly chitchat so as not to arouse their interest.

"Hello," Mother said.

"Hello," Park said, trying to mask his anger. "Apparently, I misunderstood your message in Moscow. How disappointing."

"No," Mother said. "You didn't misunderstand. We just had to deal with some problems, but we've got those worked out now."

"Why should I trust you a second time?" asked Park, who chuckled as if Mother had just told a joke. "There is no halfway with this. If you can't deliver and I'm exposed, there will be tremendous consequences for me and my son."

"I understand," Mother said. "But the issue is complicated because we are not the only interested party."

Park turned to Mother. "Believe me, I am well aware of that," said Park. "And I don't think the other party has any *problems*. They just have promises and guarantees."

This was not good news for Mother. Not only had Sir Reg made his plans known, but Park seemed willing to entertain them. Just then the issue was further complicated when Reg came back into the room with a pair of generals from the Chinese army. They were in their uniforms and talked with Sir Reg through a translator.

"Jin-sun," Reg said to Park. "Why don't you get your son so we can go? This tour is going to be outstanding."

Mother watched helplessly as he tried to figure out what was going on.

Park turned to him. "Sir Reg has arranged with the Chinese army for Dae-jung and me to have a special VIP tour inside the Forbidden City. That's not usually allowed after dark, but it's amazing how much influence Sir Reg has. He does whatever he says he'll do. Simply amazing."

37

Tai Chi

EVERY MORNING AT DAWN, A GROUP primarily composed of local senior citizens gathered in the park surrounding Beijing's Temple of the Sun to practice tai chi, a quiet, peaceful martial art that promoted good health and meditation. The park was located directly across the street from the embassy of the United Kingdom, which explained why one of the seniors in the group was a six-foot-tall British woman with silver hair, who'd often used less peaceful martial arts to dispatch enemies as an operative for MI6.

"Good morning, Tru," Monty said as she took a position next to her. "Come here often?"

"Whenever I'm in town," Tru answered slowly, stretching out her words just like she stretched out her arms and legs.

As part of the meditative quality of the exercise, there wasn't supposed to be any talking during tai chi. But the two of them were in the back corner, removed from the group, and as long as they kept up with the movements and whispered, they could get away with a little conversation.

"Any reason we're meeting here and not in that secure building across the street?" Monty asked as she performed a slow sweeping movement known as "snake creeps through the grass."

"Several," Tru said, executing the same move. "For one, it's always good if you can release tension during a mission. For another, in a city with more than twenty million surveillance cameras, this little patch of grass is a rare location that none of them are pointed at. We've got a blind spot of about three square meters. But, most importantly, I'm not so certain how secure that building is."

"You think the Chinese are listening in on the embassy?"

"I know they are," Tru answered. "Just like we're listening to them. I can deal with that because it's how the game is played. My concern is Reginald Banks. He has ears everywhere. If he can get top secret files out of Russia, Saudi Arabia, and India, then his money certainly can purchase access across the street. Besides, everyone in there's running around and jabbering about Lop Nor."

"What's Lop Nor?"

"A desert up near Mongolia," said Tru, who was now moving into a posture known as "golden rooster stands on one leg." "It's a nuclear test site, and we've just learned that three of their devices have gone missing."

"That means weapons have been stolen in Russia and China," Monty said as she lifted her right arm and leg into the air as part of the golden rooster. "The same two places where Sir Reg has been spending his time lately."

"And you know how I feel about coincidences?" Tru said.

"I don't like them either," Monty responded. "Are we all set for the exfiltration?"

"Yes," Tru answered. "We're going to keep it simple this time. You get Park and his son to the airport, and we'll have a plane waiting. I'm not trusting any local assets. It's just our team."

The instructor leading the group shot Tru a look, and she nodded an apology. No more talking. They continued exercising for another thirty minutes, and Monty concluded that Tru was absolutely right. It was wonderful to release tension during a mission. She decided that she'd add tai chi to everybody's exercise routine when they got back to the FARM.

Afterward, Tru and Monty left in opposite directions, making sure to exit in a manner that no camera captured them together. Monty went back to the hotel to pick up Sydney, Brooklyn, Kat, and Rio so that they could head to northwest Beijing as part of their cover story. All visitors to China needed a visa that allowed them into the country. Mother and Paris got theirs through the chess tournament. Monty and the rest of the team were sponsored by China's most elite university.

"Hello, Monty," Ng Pei San said happily as she greeted the group near the picturesque main gate of Tsinghua University. "It's great to see you again."

"Great to see you too," Monty replied. "I'd like to introduce you to the FARM Fellows."

Pei San looked at the group and smiled. "Our future climate scientists. Monty's told me so many great things about you."

As far as Pei San knew, Monty's only job was as the director of the Foundation for Atmospheric Research and Monitoring. The two had met and become friendly when they were on the same panel at an environmental sciences conference. Pei San was a professor in Tsinghua's Department of Earth System Science, and her research centered on the serious pollution problems that plagued Beijing.

Impressed by the work Pei San was doing, Monty had volunteered the FARM's supercomputing power to help her research. In return, Pei San had offered to host them if they ever got the chance to come to China.

"It's great that you all are interested in studying our smog problem," she said as she showed them around the campus.

"What are the main causes?" Rio asked.

"Beijing is a huge and ever-growing city," she said. "The biggest polluters are the factories and power plants that burn coal, as well as automobiles. Add the fact that the surrounding mountains trap the air and that there are mammoth sand and dust storms that come in from the desert, and you have a bad recipe. Thank you so much for assisting with our research."

"It's our pleasure," said Monty.

Monty meant it. She really did want to help, and she was committed to using the FARM's resources for this important research. But she wasn't just being generous. Pei San was handing her a license to spy throughout the city.

As Tru had pointed out, there were more than twenty million surveillance cameras spread across Beijing. Most of them employed artificial intelligence and facial recognition software that tracked the movements of millions of people. If anyone did anything suspicious, police could swarm in within moments.

Certainly, it might catch the authorities' notice if they saw a group of kids snooping around. But now Monty and the team had a reason. They were collecting air samples all throughout the city in specially made canisters. Attached to the outside of the canisters were gauges and flow controllers designed to measure air quality. Hidden inside them, however, were listening and recording devices designed for spying.

Their mission assignment was to follow the tournament from a distance and look for anyone who might be working with Sir Reg to kidnap the Parks. If any Beijing police officers were to question their actions, all they had to do was show letters of explanation and permits from the university. They were basically free to go wherever they wanted in the city.

"Just a bit of warning," Pei San said as they started to leave. "The pollution index is not looking good. In a couple days the smog will be thick. So, if you're hoping to do some sightseeing, make sure you do as much of that as you can in the next two days."

"Thanks for the tip," Monty said.

As they walked across the campus toward the parking lot, Monty got a message on the phone. It was Mother telling her where the tournament was being played for the first day.

Monty read the text and turned to the others. "Who wants to check the air around the Winter Palace?"

Mutianyu

SIR REG MORE THAN DELIVERED ON HIS promise to provide extraordinary locations for the chess tournament. The first day was played in an idyllic courtyard at the Winter Palace, which dated back to the eleventh century. For the second, they were on a bus north of the city heading to their next destination.

They had no idea where they were going until Paris looked out the window and saw a sign that indicated what it might be. "Oh my goodness," he said excitedly. "I think we're going to play at the Great Wall."

Antonia, who was sitting next to him, couldn't believe it. "That would be incredible."

There was no greater symbol of China than the Great Wall, a series of fortifications that at one time stretched for more than thirteen thousand miles. While much of it was in various states of disrepair, there was a particularly well-preserved section an hour north of the city center.

This three-and-a-half-mile portion was known as the "Mutianyu Wall," and Sir Reg had arranged for the day's matches to be played on three different watchtowers, each of which came with spectacular mountain views.

"I've got to hand it to him," Mother said to Paris as they got off the bus. "Reg sure knows how to put on a show."

Although most of the players arrived on a pair of buses, Park Jin-sun and Dae-jung came in a now-familiar black SUV driven by their handlers. Since they'd been in China, Mother had had little luck getting time to talk to Park. He hoped that out here on the wall, things would be different.

"How are you feeling about the tournament?" Mother asked Paris as they waited in line for the cable car that carried visitors up to the wall. "Do you think your studying has paid off?"

"I'll have a better idea today," Paris answered. "I play Antonia in the second match. She beat me in Moscow."

Mother gave him a look. "She beat you because I made you send a coded message with your moves. You're not going to have to do that today."

"True," Paris said. "But there's no guarantee that I would've won anyway. She's an excellent player."

The cable cars held up to six people, and they boarded one with Antonia, Ang, and their mothers. Riding up in the air gave them a great view, and as they ascended to the top, Antonia looked out in wonder and asked Ang, "How many times have you been here?"

"This is my first time," Ang said. "I've always wanted to go, but it's been too far."

"Really?" she said, surprised. "But don't you live right in Beijing?"

There was an awkward moment until Jia-Hui explained, "There is another section called Badaling that is closer to our house. That's where we've always gone before."

"Yes," said Ang. "That's what I meant. Mutianyu is too far compared to Badaling. My English is not always right."

This struck Mother as odd. As far as he'd heard,

Ang's English was perfect. Still, he didn't worry about it because so much else was going on. He saw that the Parks were riding up in a cable car with their guards. Getting Jin-sun alone was going to be incredibly difficult.

In his first game, Paris was matched against a girl from Australia who hadn't been part of the Moscow tournament. He opened with the Sicilian Defense, which he'd been studying lately, and dominated the game from start to finish. When he was done, he came over to where Mother offered him a pair of congratulatory fist bumps.

"That was excellent," Mother said. "You do realize that you're currently undefeated."

Paris couldn't suppress his smile. "I may be aware of that," he answered coyly.

"Good," said Mother. "Because it's noteworthy."

"How's it going with Park?"

"Let's just say that, while you are undefeated, I am winless. I can't get him alone."

"Is he with Sir Reg?" Paris asked.

"No," Mother said. "Reg isn't even here. My problem today is Ang's mother." On the other side of the watch-tower, Li Jia-Hui was deep in conversation with Park Jin-sun. "It's like they're suddenly best mates."

"It makes sense," Paris said. "Dae-jung is playing Ang in the next round, and his father always scouts the competition."

"It still doesn't mean I'm not frustrated," Mother said. "Luckily, he plays you first thing tomorrow. That means he'll be watching your game against Antonia this afternoon. Hopefully I can get some time with him then."

"You're not going to make me send another message, are you?" Paris asked, mostly joking, but a little worried. "I'd really like to give her my best game."

"No," said Mother. "You've already delivered the message. All we can do now is wait."

Never one to make a subtle entrance, Reginald Banks arrived by helicopter just before the start of the second matches of the day. He strutted around the different watchtowers and posed for pictures with the players, his star power impossible to ignore.

"Impressive, no?"

Mother turned to see that it was Park Jin-sun.

"No," said Mother. "Expensive, but not impressive. People sometimes get them confused, but they're quite different."

With everyone's attention focused on Sir Reg, they were momentarily alone except for Park's ever-present guards.

"I'm not so sure," Park said. "It's amazing what you can buy if you have enough money."

"Can he buy you?" Mother asked.

"No. But he can buy information," Park said. "For example, he told me all about the plot to sneak Dae-jung and me into the British ambassador's limousine. And then to hide us in a compartment of a car while we're driven across the border to Latvia. He mocked it and said it was unworthy of a bad spy movie."

Mother was stunned. Somehow Reg had their entire plan from Moscow. "Does he know that I'm—"

"No," Park said. "He knew a lot, but he didn't know you were involved. He did not know about the message you sent. I have to admit, so far that's the only thing about you that's impressed me. He thought the British were just going to grab us and go."

For Mother this was a bit of relief, but he was still deeply troubled by the leak of information.

"You have to see this from my point of view," Park continued. "I don't want to go with him and his people, but I have to get out of North Korea. As soon as I make a move, I'm a traitor, which means the escape has to work. And how can I trust you to outsmart him when he knows your plans?"

By this point Reg was nearing them and they had to stop talking.

"If it isn't the proud fathers," he said, smiling at both of them. "How would the two of you like to go for a ride in my helicopter? The views of the Great Wall are magnificent."

"No, thank you," Jin-sun responded. "I appreciate the offer, but I'm here to watch the chess."

"Me too," said Mother.

If Reg was offended, it didn't show. "I love it," he said. "You both put family first, and that means everything." Then, quieter so no one else around them could hear, he added, "You must always put the welfare of your children ahead of everything else. Don't forget that."

There was an ominous quality to the way he said it, and Mother wondered if this was some kind of threat. If so, which of them was it directed to?

In the second game, Paris and Antonia played a spirited match that went back and forth until the end, when his attacking proved too much.

"Good game," she said, tipping over her king.

"You too," Paris responded. "I think maybe this was the most fun game I've ever played."

"Because of the setting?" Antonia asked.

"More because of the opponent," Paris answered as they shook hands. "And the quality of play."

As a treat after the round, the players all got to go down the mountain on a toboggan slide that zipped through the trees like a theme park ride. It lasted about five minutes, and everyone loved it, with the exception of the guards from the North Korean secret police. The wheeled sleds held only one person at a time, and they refused to let Dae-jung go, insisting that he ride back with them on the cable car instead. His father protested, and while they were arguing, Paris lifted a rope so that Dae-jung could slip to the front of the line and hop on a sled before they knew what was happening.

The guards yelled at Paris, but there was nothing that could be done about it except for one of them to hop on the next sled and follow Dae-jung down.

"Please tell Paris that I said thank you," Jin-sun whispered to Mother in the aftermath.

Room Service

PARIS AND MOTHER MIGHT HAVE BEEN IN the same hotel suite, but their minds were on different planets. Paris was sprawled out on the couch with a chess book, preparing for the next day's matches, while Mother absently sipped ginger ale and fretted about the mission.

He was troubled by the fact that Reg had known their plan in Moscow. What if the same was true again? What if he somehow knew the plan in Beijing as well? Mother had already sent messages to Monty and Tru to warn them about the threat, and now he was going over everything, trying to think of where they might be vulnerable.

"When's room service going to get here?" Paris asked.

It took Mother a moment to change mental gears and answer, "Should be any minute."

"Good," said Paris. "Because I'm starving."

"So am I," Mother said. "It was a long day today." He flashed a smile. "You did great."

"Thanks," Paris said.

"You and Dae-jung are the only two who've won all their matches so far," Mother said. "You know what that means, don't you?"

"If I can somehow beat him tomorrow—and I have no idea how I would do such a thing, but if I did—I'd be the champion. It wouldn't matter what happened in the last match, because the best he could do was tie me, and I'd have the advantage head-to-head."

"Impressive," Monty said. "Do you think you can you beat him?"

"Not a chance," said Paris. He flashed a grin and said, "But that won't stop me from trying."

Just then there was a knock at the door

"Finally," Paris said, hopping up. "We can eat!"

He looked through the peephole before opening it and was surprised to see that rather than room service, it was Park Jin-sun.

"It's Mr. Park," Paris said as he reached to open the door.

For an instant, Mother thought that maybe Park had gotten free from of his handlers and was escaping now.

Then Paris opened the door.

Not only was Park with the North Korean guards, but they were also joined by four members of the Chinese secret police. They all poured into the hotel suite, barking orders in Chinese and Korean. Mother didn't understand a word of what they were saying, but he got the gist.

"What's going on?" Paris asked.

"It's going to be okay," Mother said, trying to calm him. "Don't resist, but I think we're about to be arrested."

The Circus

AT THE SAME TIME PARIS AND MOTHER'S hotel room was being overrun by police, the rest of the City Spies were getting off the Beijing metro at the Olympic Park station. It was modern and new, with the ceiling designed to look like bubbles on the water's surface.

The five of them were on their way to dinner at a traditional Mongolian hot pot restaurant. According to the online reviews, the food was supposed to be delicious, although that wasn't the main reason they'd selected it.

They picked it because it was directly across the Olympic Green from Beijing National Stadium.

The building was known around the world as the Bird's Nest, and its striking architecture was actually two interconnected structures, designed to withstand a massive earthquake. The first was a giant red bowl that held the playing field and seating, while the second was a web of massive steel strips that resembled twigs and gave the stadium its nickname.

It was the only venue in the world selected to host both the summer and winter Olympics. It was also where the City Spies hoped to turn the tide against Sir Reg.

"This is where we go our separate ways," Sydney said when they exited onto the street.

"Are you sure you're okay with this?" asked Monty.

"Absolutely," replied Sydney. "It's just like when I used to sneak in and out of the Wallangarra School for Girls back home in Australia."

"Except there you only had to worry about the headmaster, and here there's the Beijing Police and the Ministry of State Security," Monty replied.

"You always know how to put a damper on things," Sydney joked.

"Just trying to remind you to be careful."

"Got it."

Sydney smiled and headed for the stadium while the others went toward the restaurant.

"I'll just be a jiffy," Sydney called to them. "You better save me some of that hot pot."

Although primarily a sports arena, the Bird's Nest sometimes hosted large concerts. In twenty-four hours, it would be filled with screaming fans who'd come to see KB5. As he'd done in Moscow, Sir Reg had scheduled the chess tournament to coincide with a concert, which meant the circus was back inside setting up for the performance.

Sydney approached the main entrance, where a pair of guards had things locked down. She unzipped her hoodie partway to reveal that an all-access concert credential was hanging from her neck. She'd kept it as a souvenir, but when she got home and studied it, she realized there was nothing that specified it was only good in Moscow. It was a VIP pass for the Around the World Tour; her hope was that it would get her past any checkpoints here just like it had at Luzhniki.

"Hi," she said to a guard as she held it up for him to see.

He mumbled something and waved her right through.

Much easier than Wallangarra, she thought. *There I had to climb over the walls.*

Her goal was simple. She wanted to find the master schedule listing everyone's hotel and travel arrangements. If Reg was once again planning on using his private jet, that would be included on the itinerary.

When she stepped into the grandstand, it reminded her exactly of the scene in Moscow. This was the circus Tabitha loved so much. More than a hundred people getting things ready for the show while soft seventies pop played over the speakers.

She knew that while some people traveled with the show, most of the workers were hired locally. That meant they wouldn't recognize her, which was exactly what she wanted. All she had to do was walk confidently, act like she belonged, and show her credentials to anyone who questioned her.

Once she reached the ground level, she headed toward the stage and then around back. It was the same basic layout as Moscow, and within minutes she was in the VIP section. Ideally, she didn't want to go into an office, where there was a greater chance of her being recognized. She'd hoped she'd come across a schedule lying around, but that didn't happen.

She approached the door marked VIP LOUNGE and wondered if the boys from KB5 were inside playing video games and eating junk food. There wasn't any noise when she pressed her ear against the door, so she cracked it open enough to see that the lights were out.

"They're not here yet," she happily whispered to herself.

The lights in the room were motion activated, so they turned on when she stepped inside. A stack of schedules was sitting on the table right in front of her. She grabbed one, stuck it inside her hoodie, and was about to leave when she heard a voice.

"It's Ellie, right? From *All Roads Lead to Audrey*?"

She turned to see that one of the band members was, in fact, there. Roman had been asleep on a couch and had awoken when the lights came on. Panic flooded her system, but she tried to remain calm.

"I'm so sorry, Roman," she said. "I didn't realize you were in here. The lights just came on automatically. I didn't mean to wake you."

"No worries," Roman said. "It's just that the jet lag has me turned upside down."

"Go back to sleep," Sydney said.

"Is Tabitha with you?" he asked.

"No," Sydney said. "I'm working on a different story this time."

"I saw the twins before I came in here and thought maybe she'd decided to come."

"The twins are here?" Sydney said, surprised.

"Even jet lagged they're hard to miss," Roman replied.

Sydney didn't expect them to be around, and the fact that they were worried her a bit. If anyone was going to know she didn't belong, it was them. She'd have to be more careful on her way out. "Could you do me a favor?" she asked. "Could you not tell them that you saw me?"

"Why? You doing something you shouldn't?" He said it with a sly smile that came across as a coconspirator, not an accuser.

"Hardly," she said. "But I'm kind of working on a scoop. It's totally good; you're going to love it, but they might not be happy if they find out I was down here."

Roman smiled. "My lips are sealed," he said. "Besides, for all I know I'm still asleep and you're a dream."

"Thanks," she said. "Don't tell the others, but you've always been my favorite."

"I'm everyone's favorite," he said in a way that was surprisingly charming. He laid back down on the couch, and she slipped back into the hallway and looked around to make sure the Sorokins were nowhere to be seen.

Interrogation

WHEN THE POLICE BURST INTO THE HOTEL room, Mother's initial reaction was as a father, not a spy. He was worried about Paris, and he rushed over to him and put a protective arm around his shoulder. Although one of the policemen was guarding the two of them, everyone else seemed more interested in searching the room. It was hard to make sense of it all because the police were speaking Chinese and the guards Korean.

"What are they looking for?" Mother asked Jin-sun, who was still standing at the door, shaken. "Jin-sun,"

Mother called out, trying to snap him out of it. "What's going on?"

"Dae-jung is missing," Park said.

"That's terrible!" Mother said. "What happened?"

Just then one of the North Korean guards came over and started questioning Paris. It was the same guard who'd yelled at him at the toboggan, and it seemed like that anger was carrying over.

"We don't speak Korean," Mother pleaded. "We don't know what you're asking."

"He wants to know if you've seen Dae-jung."

Mother looked at the guard and said, "No. Not since the Great Wall."

The guard stabbed his finger in Paris's chest and said something to Jin-sun.

"He wants to hear it from you, not your father," said Jin-sun.

Paris was flustered and didn't know who he was supposed to address. He swiveled his attention back and forth between them as he answered. "The last time I saw him was when I got on the bus after today's matches. How would I have seen him after that?"

"They think he's run away and want to know if you encouraged him or knew his plans," said Jin-sun.

"Of course not," Paris said.

Despite all the confusion, Mother noticed that Jin-sun had said *they* think he's run away. He wondered if Jin-sun shared the guards' opinion.

Just then, another person came into the room, but Mother was glad to see that it was just Li Jia-Hui, who'd been staying in the room next door.

"What's going on?" she asked Mother, trying to process the scene as the guards were turning the room upside down.

"Dae-jung has run away, and they've come here looking for him," Mother said.

"I'm so sorry," Jia-Hui said to Jin-sun. "Is there anything I can do?"

"Do you have any idea where he might be?" asked Jin-sun.

"No," said Jia-Hui. "But I'll check with Ang."

"Can you translate for a second?" Mother asked. "And find out what's going on? I think it's pretty apparent that Dae-jung's not hiding in my suitcase."

Jia-Hui got into a heated discussion with the police, and Mother was impressed by how firm she was with them. He knew that she was an attorney and wondered if that's why he wasn't intimidated. Finally, after the back and forth, she turned back to Mother.

"They say that they saw security footage of your son talking to Dae-jung at the Mutianyu wall," Jia-Hui said.

"Of course he did," Mother replied, exasperated. "And I'm sure there's footage of him talking to your son and a dozen other players."

Jia-Hui had another exchange with the police.

"They are looking for any clues that might help lead to Dae-jung," Jia-Hui explained. "They are worried about him."

Mother weighed this for a moment. "I'm worried about him too, but they're not going to find anything here. Ask them if we are under arrest."

Jia-Hui asked in Chinese, and the head policeman thought about it for a moment before shaking his head and answering, "*Bù.*" No. Then he continued talking, and when he was done, Jia-Hui translated for Mother.

"I know it's frustrating, but there's nothing you can do about it," Jia-Hui said. "These aren't just Beijing police. They're from the Ministry of State Security. They're going to stay as long as they want to. They've suggested we go out in the hallway and give them a little space. It will make it go faster."

Mother still had his arm around Paris and could tell that he was concerned.

"Yeah," said Mother. "Let's do that."

Mother, Paris, Jin-sun, and Jia-Hui all went out into the hall, and when they did, one of the police shut the door behind them. Mother knew better than to travel with anything that might connect him to MI6, but he was still worried that they might find something that was difficult to explain.

"Are you okay?" he asked Paris once they were in the hall.

"Yeah," said Paris. "Just a little shaken. Mostly I'm worried about Dae-jung."

"I'm going to go ask Ang if he knows anything about this," Jia-Hui said. "I'll be right back."

One of the North Korean guards had come out to watch them, but for the moment, Jin-sun and Mother could talk.

"Is it okay to speak in front of him?" Jin-sun asked, nodding toward Paris.

"Yes," said Mother. "Can you tell me what's going on? You didn't seem convinced that Dae-jung ran away."

"That's what they think," Jin-sun said. "But I know the truth. Reginald Banks has him."

"How do you know that?"

"He told me that he was going to give me extra incentive to go with him," Jin-sun explained.

"Of course," Mother answered. "That's why he was talking about the importance of family earlier."

"You want to impress me and make me believe in you?" Jin-sun said. "Find my son. Get him away from that man. Because tomorrow night, when all this is over, I'm going to go with whomever has him. I'm not picking you or Sir Reg. I'm picking Dae-jung."

That was as much as they were able to say before Jia-Hui came back with news to say that Ang had no information about Dae-jung. They stood nervously in the hall for another ten minutes until the police and guards came back into the hallway.

"You are free to go back into your room," Jia-Hui said, translating for him. "You want me to help you put things back?"

"Thanks, but we've got it," Mother said. "Get back to Ang. I'm sure he's upset by the news."

Mother shook his head as he surveyed the condition of the suite. It looked like it had been hit by a tornado.

He knew there was only one reason the police wanted them out of the room while they searched.

"It's going to be okay," Mother said. Then he leaned forward and whispered, "They bugged the room with audio and video. Understand?"

Paris nodded. He knew that that meant they couldn't discuss the mission at all.

"That's so sad about Dae-jung," Paris said, playing for the bug. "Why do you think he ran away?"

"I don't know," Mother replied. "Hopefully they'll find him soon, safe and sound."

He started putting clothes back into his suitcase and said, "Let's clean this up and get some rest. We've got a big day tomorrow."

He was saying that for the benefit of whoever was now listening in, but it was still true. The mission was coming down to a single day, and with the Chinese Ministry of State Security now involved, they had to be prepared for anything.

The Bird's Nest

THE FINAL ROUND OF THE TOURNAMENT was being played at the Bird's Nest. In addition to its playing field and grandstand, the stadium featured a deluxe VIP reception area on its sixth level, which had been converted into the players' hall. Afterward, it would open up onto a row of luxury suites for the concert. Sir Reg had control of all the pieces on the board, and this was where he planned to execute his endgame.

Mother and Paris were riding a giant escalator to the top floor when Jia-Hui and Ang came up behind them.

"How are you two doing today?" Jia-Hui asked.

"Still pretty shaken, to be honest," Mother answered. "How about you?

"The same," Jia-Hui answered. "Hopefully Dae-jung will come to his senses and return."

They reached the playing area and were surprised, and a bit hopeful, when they saw Jin-sun. He instantly approached the four of them. Mother noticed that only one of his normal guards was with him.

"Is Dae-jung here?" Paris asked hopefully.

"I am sorry, but Dae-jung is feeling sick today and couldn't make it," Jin-sun said, loud enough so that people standing nearby could hear.

"But . . ." Paris started to say something, but Mother cut him off. The *sickness* was obviously a cover story they'd chosen.

"I hope he feels better soon," Mother said.

Just then, Paris was approached by one of the Sorokin twins. For an instant he was worried that she had recognized him somehow, but she gave no indication of that.

"You are Lucas Doinel, correct?" she asked.

"Yes," answered Paris.

"I'm Anastasia, and I'm one of the tournament officials," she said. "Because Dae-jung is ill, he has to forfeit his match to you. That means you won't play this morning, but you'll still have a match this afternoon."

Paris processed this for a moment and answered, "No."

"I'm sorry?" Anastasia said, surprised.

"I believe you've misinterpreted the rules," he said.

"In what way?" asked Anastasia, slightly peeved.

"Dae-jung only forfeits if I show up but he fails to," Paris answered.

"Which is exactly what has happened," she replied.

"Except I have to be in the players' hall when the match is set to begin," he explained. "That's five minutes from now. If neither of us is here, then the match is ruled a draw."

Even amid all that was happening, Mother, Jia-Hui, and Jin-sun were all touched by this declaration.

Anastasia, however, was baffled. "Do you realize that if you simply stay in the room, you will win the game and with it will be the champion of the tournament?"

Paris stood up straight and looked right into her eyes. "Do you realize that I have absolutely no intention of winning anything that way?"

It was a standout moment, and Mother couldn't help but think of the conversation he'd had with Jin-sun the previous day. "See what I mean when I say there's a difference between expensive and impressive?" He paused a moment and nodded toward Paris. "That's impressive."

Mother turned to Paris and said, "Let's get out of here before the matches begin."

As they started to leave, Paris turned to Ang and said, "I look forward to this afternoon and the chance to play you."

"So do I," Ang said.

Paris and Mother strode straight for the escalator.

"We've got a few hours," Paris said. "Where are we going?"

"We're going to find Dae-jung and get him out of the country," Mother said confidently.

"I like the sound of that," Paris said.

The escalator ride was long, so Mother had a chance to turn and face Paris.

"By the way," he said. "The next time you're trying to figure out who you are . . . I want you to remember that. Because what you just did . . . that's your answer right there."

Orange Alert

JUST AS NG PEI SAN HAD PREDICTED, THE smog level was particularly bad on the team's final day in Beijing. The city's environmental bureau had declared an orange alert, second only to red among the four colors in its air pollution warning scale. There was a hazy quality to everything, and many people wore masks or bandanas to protect their faces.

The team was collecting air samples outside the Bird's Nest while they waited to meet up with Mother and Paris.

"I can't believe how bad this smog is," Rio said.

"Look on the bright side," said Monty.

"There's a bright side to air pollution?" asked Rio, incredulous.

"Twenty million surveillance cameras," Monty said. "If we're making a run for it with Jin-sun and Dae-jung, it might come in handy if they can put bandanas over their faces without attracting suspicion."

"That *is* a bright side," Rio said.

Brooklyn was off to the side, trying to set up a collection canister, and Sydney saw an opportunity to possibly ease the tension that had continued between them.

"Need a hand?" she asked with a friendly smile. "That valve can be tricky."

"I've got it," Brooklyn said curtly. "I know what I'm doing."

"I'm sure you do," Sydney said. "I was just trying to help."

"Because why?" Brooklyn asked. "I'm suddenly inept?"

"Don't be ridiculous," Sydney said. "I wanted to help because . . . you're my friend." She paused for a moment before adding, "My best mate."

Brooklyn gave her a skeptical look. "I think you may

be confusing me with a spoiled rich girl who lives in London."

Sydney fought the urge to snap back and said, "Tabitha was just part of a mission. That's all. I had to play my part."

"Really? Because I heard she gave you some ridiculously expensive shoes for your birthday," Brooklyn replied. "I didn't hear this from you, mind you, but I still heard about it. That sounds more like a friend than a mission."

"Actually, they're sandals," Sydney said. "And they are amazing. Truly exceptional." She gave Brooklyn a sweet look and said, "But nowhere near as nice as this."

Sydney reached her finger just below the collar of her shirt and pulled out the dolphin necklace Brooklyn had given her for her birthday.

Brooklyn's eyes lit up. "You like it?"

"I love it," Sydney said. "I've hardly taken it off since I found it. . . ." She shot Rio a look and added, "*Hidden in a pile on a table in the hall.*"

"Again," Rio said. "It's not my job to be your delivery service. If you two can't figure out how to talk to each other, that's on you, not me."

This got a laugh and helped ease the mood.

"That's true," Sydney said. She turned to Brooklyn and added, "I know it's too late, but thank you. I absolutely love it."

"It *is* too late," Brooklyn said as she cracked a smile. "But I'll let it slide."

"I've got an idea," Rio chimed in. "If you really want to make it up to her, you can give her those sandals. You know, to prove that it was just part of the mission and not because you wanted them."

"Shut up, Rio," Sydney said. "No one asked your opinion."

"No, but that would be nice," Brooklyn said. "You wouldn't have to give them to me. Just let me wear them every now and then."

It almost pained Sydney to say it. "Okay, sure. You can borrow them."

"Does that go for all of us?" Monty asked playfully.

"No," Sydney announced. "Only Brooklyn."

"Excellent," Brooklyn said as she winked at Rio.

"What about you, Kat?" Sydney asked. "Do you have any input on how I should make it up to Brooklyn?"

Kat snorted. "I lost interest in this little drama weeks ago. I've got other things to think about."

"Such as?" Sydney asked, amused.

"These trucks, for one," said Kat.

They were overlooking a parking lot filled with the semitrucks that carried the concert stage and equipment. Kat was fascinated by the sheer scope of it all.

"What about them?" Monty asked.

"It takes all those trucks to move the equipment for the show?" she asked. "And every time they have to unload and load them?"

"Yeah," Sydney said. "Tabitha told me all about it. She said it was forty-something trucks carrying more than three hundred tons of equipment."

Kat shook her head. "And these trucks drove all that from Moscow."

"I guess so," said Sydney.

"Those are some impressive logistics," Kat said. "I'd love to see that math."

Brooklyn said, "Just another teenage girl who looks dreamily at KB5 and thinks . . . *math*."

Even Kat laughed at this.

Sydney turned to Rio and said, "So help me, if your charm lessons change her, I will make you regret it."

"The last thing I would ever try to do is change Kat," Rio said.

"You are all aware of the fact that I am right here

and can hear you talking about me?" Kat asked.

The humor of the mood was broken when they saw Mother and Paris heading toward them. It was time to put their focus back on the mission.

"Are you two okay?" Monty asked the pair when they arrived. "Your messages were cryptic."

"Yeah, about that. We're pretty certain our room is under surveillance by the Ministry of State Security, so we couldn't exactly speak openly."

"Long story short," said Paris, "Sir Reg has kidnapped Dae-jung, and we've got to get him back or Jin-sun will go with them."

"Oh dear!" Monty said.

"Their plan is to take him on Reg's private jet along with KB5, just like they were going to do in Moscow," Sydney said.

"How do you know that?" asked Mother.

"I snuck into the stadium during the build-out last night and swiped a schedule," she replied. "Once again it has two seats being held for a pair of unnamed guests, who are almost certainly Jin-sun and Dae-jung. It also has the Sorokin twins listed. They're back in the picture."

"We know," Paris said. "We just ran into Anastasia."

"So this is what we need to do," said Mother. "We

have to figure out where Dae-jung is being held. Then you're going to get him while we finish the tournament and get Jin-sun. We'll all meet up at the airport and hopefully get out of here before anyone realizes what's going on."

"That sounds incredibly difficult," Monty said, trying to make light of the situation.

"Oh," Mother added sheepishly. "I also need to steal Brooklyn to come with us."

"Why's that?" asked Brooklyn.

"I'll show you when we get back inside," he answered. "It's one of those things that only you can do."

"Sounds good," Brooklyn replied, pleased to be needed.

"Can we get back to the part where we're supposed to find Dae-jung?" asked Rio. "In case you hadn't noticed, Beijing is one of the largest cities in the world. How are we supposed find him?"

"Does the concert travel schedule list where people are staying in the city?" asked Mother.

"Yes," said Sydney. "We could start there."

"They might hide him somewhere in the stadium," Mother said. "I can look while Paris is playing his last match."

"And I can help you," Brooklyn said. "Since you wanted me in there."

"What about Tru?" asked Paris. "She's in town. Can she get us help in the embassy?"

"Probably not," said Monty. "She's worried information might not be safe there."

"As we discovered was the case in Moscow," Mother added.

"Besides, everyone there is in panic mode over a place called Lop Nor," Monty added.

"Wait a second," Brooklyn said, surprised. "Is that up near Mongolia?"

"Yes," Monty said. "How on earth did you know that?"

"When Charlotte and I were working on the St. Basil's code, almost all the locations were in Moscow or the European half of Russia," she said. "But there was one way out in the desert in China just south of Mongolia. That's why there wasn't a sticky. The map didn't go that far. We figured it was a mistake because when we checked it out, the only thing there was a wild camel reserve."

"And a Chinese nuclear weapons site," Monty said. "A few days ago, three warheads were stolen from there."

They all weighed the magnitude of this, and Kat asked, "Do you know what that means?"

"That Lop Nor is somehow connected to all this?" said Rio.

"Not only that," Kat answered. "It also means the St. Basil's code isn't only used in Russia. It's used to signify latitude and longitude in other countries too. Including China."

Instantly, they all grabbed their phones and raced to open the social media account that was used for the code. The first one to get there was Brooklyn.

"St. Basil's!" she said. "There was a St. Basil's post yesterday."

"Which is when Dae-jun was kidnapped," said Mother.

"What are the colors?" asked Monty.

"Aqua and red," answered Brooklyn.

"Great," said Kat. "What are the hex codes?"

Brooklyn deflated. "I don't know," she said. "I don't have the color tool on my phone or laptop. It's just on the art program I use at school."

"We need to find that code," said Sydney.

"What about Tru?" said Paris. "Can she get help from the embassy? I'm sure they've got lots of computers there."

"If she's worried about information leaking, I certainly don't want to have them working on this," Mother said. "If Reg gets any hint we're onto him, they'll disappear."

"Then what do we do?" asked Rio.

"I know," Sydney said with a eureka smile. "Call Charlotte."

"What?" Rio asked, surprised.

"She already knows the code," said Sydney. "And she's at school where they have the program."

"I like that idea," said Brooklyn.

"You think we can trust her?" asked Rio.

"Totally," said Sydney as she turned to Brooklyn and gave her a nod. "I'll call her."

Paris asked, "What time is it in Scotland?"

"Three a.m.," answered Kat.

Brooklyn laughed. "At least we know she'll be home."

"Hello," Charlotte said groggily, answering the phone. "Is this somebody's idea of a prank?"

"No, Char, it's Syd," Sydney said. "We're in Beijing and we need your help."

"Well, now I know it's a prank," said Charlotte.

"It's not," Sydney said. She turned to the others. "She doesn't believe me. She thinks I'm pranking her."

Kat took the phone from her. "Charlotte, this is Kat. We need you."

"Sure," Charlotte said. "Anything. Whatever you need."

Kat explained the situation and told her that they needed the latitude and longitude from the St. Basil's post the day before.

"Okay," Charlotte answered. "It's going to take a couple minutes to access the computer lab."

"Quick as you can," said Kat. She went to hang up and then said, "One more thing."

"What's that?" asked Charlotte.

"Why don't you say it this time," Kat replied. "You haven't gotten a chance to in a while. I'll put the phone on speaker so everyone can hear."

Although she was nearly eight thousand miles away, Charlotte felt like, for the moment at least, she was right there with them. A part of the team.

"This operation is hot. We are a go!"

Endgame

Bird's Nest—Players Hall

ALL EYES WERE ON THE MAIN TABLE WHERE
Paris and Ang were playing the match that would determine who won the championship. Paris thought back to
when he was sitting across the board from Barnaby Fitch
at the Edinburgh Chess Club. They were discussing end-
games, the final phase of a match when there are fewer
pieces remaining and therefore fewer possible moves.
This was when the game shifted from tactics to strategy,
and the goal was to put your opponent in zugzwang.

"What's that?" he'd asked Fitch.

"It's German for 'the compulsion to move,'" said Fitch. "It's when any move your opponent makes weakens their position."

He'd just put Li Ang into zugzwang. He wasn't quite to checkmate yet, but Ang had no good options. If Paris maintained the pressure, he'd take the match and the tournament.

Once he'd done that, the only remaining moves would be between the City Spies and Reginald Banks. They question was, would they be able to put Sir Reg in just as difficult a situation?

Hutong District

The *hutong*s were alleyways located a short walk from the palaces of the Forbidden City. Often cramped and crumbling, they dated as far back as seven centuries and formed a labyrinth of humble homes, shops, and restaurants. They were Beijing's original neighborhoods, and while most had been destroyed in the quest to modernize the city, some still remained.

It was here, among the maze of twists and turns, that Charlotte had sent the team. She'd deciphered the code, and the coordinates led them to a *hutong* near the city center. Now they'd reached a crossroads where two alleys intersected, and Monty was checking their location with an app that gave precise latitude and longitude.

"Which way do you think we should go?" Sydney asked.

"I hope it's this way." Rio pointed down an alley to where a vendor was selling grilled chicken skewers. "That smells delicious."

"Sorry, but your stomach's going to have to wait," Monty said.

She pointed down a cobblestone passageway about ten feet wide that ran between two rows of houses. Along it were several mopeds and bicycles, and up ahead a pair of old men sat around a wooden table playing a board game known as *"xiangqi,"* which was often referred to as Chinese chess.

"I know we're in a hurry, but . . . ," Rio started to say.

"Don't even think it," Monty interjected. "We do not have time for you to run down and buy a chicken skewer."

Rio nodded. "I just thought we might get one for Dae-jung."

"Sure you did," Monty said with a laugh.

Ang was also at a crossroads, but he had no good options. He surveyed the board and realized he had no chance to win. Paris had maintained the pressure, and the best Ang could do was prolong the inevitable for a few more moves.

"Before I concede," he whispered to Paris, "I want to be the first to congratulate you. You did not make a single mistake."

"Thank you, Ang," Paris replied. "You played extremely well."

"You know this makes you champion," added Ang.

"I think we both know who the real champion is," Paris said.

Ang made it official by tipping over his king. They both stood and shook hands as the room erupted with applause.

In the spectators section, Mother and Jia-Hui stood clapping.

"Congratulations," Jia-Hui said. "Your son's a deserving champion. I realized that this morning when he refused to take the forfeit."

"Thank you," Mother said. "I just hope everything works out with Dae-jung."

"Me too," she said. "Still, we should go out tonight

and celebrate two great tournaments. We'll get Antonia and her mother as well. I know the perfect restaurant."

"I appreciate it," Mother replied. "You've been a wonderful host for us in Beijing. And you were very helpful last night with the police. But as soon as the medal presentation is over, we're taking the express train to Daxing and hopping on a flight home."

Jia-Hui nodded and said, "I understand. Maybe one day Ang and I will be in London and you can show us around."

"Edinburgh," Mother corrected. "We're up in Scotland."

"Right," said Jia-Hui. "My mistake."

Ministry of State Security Facility—Xiyuan, Beijing

The Ministry of State Security was housed in an ultra-secret compound in northwest Beijing. Here, a young analyst was listening to the surveillance tapes from Mother and Paris's room. Mostly, he heard the pair discussing various chess strategies and their concern for Dae-jung's welfare. But one comment caught his attention.

"I need to use the computer for a moment," Mother's voice said on the recording.

"Can't I finish watching this video first?" asked Paris. "It's a classic endgame I'm studying."

"I'll be quick. It's just that I forgot to make the new hotel reservations."

The analyst paused the tape and checked the time on the recording. It was 11:37 p.m.

He instantly pulled up the Internet traffic from the hotel and went to the exact same time. In a matter of minutes, he saw that Mother had reserved two rooms at a hotel in at Tokyo's Narita airport.

Next, the analyst accessed the information from when Mother and Paris had entered the country. According to their visas, they were supposed to stay in Beijing for an additional day before flying to London.

Since there was no way Mother could be in two places at one time, the analyst placed a call to his superior.

Hutong District

The deeper the team traveled into the *hutong*, the more interesting they found it to be. Some alleys were so narrow that two people couldn't walk side by side, while others were wide enough for groups of kids to hang out and play. At one point they came across a spirited game of ping-pong being contested on a table made out of plywood lying across two stools.

The coordinates from the code brought them to a doorway with two large wooden gates. Their red paint was faded and peeling, and their hinges had aged so that now there was a slight gap between them. Two stone dragons, one on each side, guarded the entry, and a tiled eave hung overhead.

"This is it," Monty said as she double-checked the app. "Dae-jung should be in there." She peeked through the gap and saw an empty courtyard.

"Quiet and alert," she said to the others. "We've got one chance at this."

The gate had no lock, so she pushed it open to reveal that the courtyard was surrounded by four separate buildings. Originally, this had been a grand home with each building reserved for a different generation of the same family. But now it had been split up into four separate residences with the courtyard used primarily for storage.

"He's in one of these," Monty said.

They broke up into pairs, with Kat and Monty going around one side while Sydney and Rio went around the other.

They found what they were looking for in the house farthest from the gate.

"Look who it is," Kat whispered to Monty as she nodded at a window.

Inside they could see a man eating out of a bowl with chopsticks while he watched television. Even though his face was turned the other way, Monty recognized him instantly.

It was Nicholas Sorokin.

British Embassy

The diplomatic delegation of the United Kingdom had long since outgrown the tight quarters of its embassy and much of the staff had moved to a separate, newer facility a half-mile away. However, whenever Tru was in Beijing, she liked to set up shop in the older, cramped building. This was in part because it gave her closer access to the ambassador, but more because it was across the street from her favorite tai chi park.

One of the negatives of working from the "main building," as it was called, was that she had to scrounge up a workspace and share an assistant with a defense attaché. The assistant's name was Elizabeth, and she worked in an office with several other aides.

Tru poked her head into the room and said, "Elizabeth, I need you to check on something for me."

"Of course, ma'am, what is it?" the assistant asked.

"I requested a charter plane be fueled and ready at Daxing airport," Tru said.

"Yes, ma'am," Elizabeth replied. "I've called back to confirm and everything's good."

"Excellent, dear, but there's been a change of plans. I need the pilot to file a new flight plan."

"Going where?"

"Narita International Airport. Tokyo."

Bird's Nest—Backstage

Paris and Mother were lined up backstage along with Ang, Jia-Hui, and Jin-sun. Once again, Sir Reg was going to present the medals before the KB5 concert, and they were about to go onstage. Paris had won, with Ang finishing second. Jin-sun was there because, despite missing the final day, Dae-jung had still finished in third place. Reg had insisted he be there to accept the award on his behalf, and Jin-sun was not about to go against the man who held his son in captivity.

The phone in Mother's pocket buzzed, indicating that he'd received a message. He knew that it would disappear fifteen seconds after he opened it, so he made sure to get somewhere he had a good view.

It read: Found him. Set to exfil.

Jin-sun saw his reaction and gave him a hopeful look. Mother didn't say a word. He just nodded.

Bird's Nest—Road Manager's Office

"It's essential that tonight runs perfectly," Reg said to Ava Knox, the road manager for the concert tour.

"Of course, sir," Ava replied. "Always."

"Everything's set for the plane?"

"Yes," she said. "Beijing traffic is terrible, so I arranged a helicopter for you and your guests."

"Excellent," Reg said.

Just then his phone rang. He smiled when he saw who it was.

"What do you have for me?" Reg asked.

"MI6 has chartered a jet to leave from Daxing airport," said Reg's source in the British embassy. "A total of five passengers heading to Tokyo."

"The Brits are so predictable," Reg said. "Sometimes I'm embarrassed that we're from the same country. We need the details on the plane."

"I'm sending them to Anastasia right away."

Hutong District

The team was at the entrance to the courtyard, trying to devise the best way to get Dae-jung out of the house and away from Sorokin. Peeking through the windows, they'd learned that the only two people in the house were Sorokin, who was still watching television, and Dae-jung, who was being held in a bedroom.

"How do we get in?" Sydney asked.

"Not through the door," said Rio. "Sorokin's right there."

"True," said Monty. "But I'm worried about the window. With that old hardware, we won't be able to slip into the bedroom and get Dae-jung. It will make too much noise."

"Well, there's got to be a way," said Sydney. "I mean, we were able to break into Sir Reg's mansion, and it had state-of-the-art security."

The mention of this brought a smile to Kat's face. "Yes, we did." She looked up to the roof where there was a chimney. "Ho, ho, ho."

British Embassy

Tru put her suitcase into the rear of the Range Rover and got into the passenger seat. The embassy staff driver turned to her and said, "Ma'am, aren't you going to ride in the back?"

"I'm not the bloody queen," she answered. "I can ride in the front seat like an adult."

"Yes, ma'am," the driver said as he fought the urge to smile. "Where to?"

"Daxing airport," she said.

As soon as the SUV drove away, a message was sent to notify Sir Reg that she was on the way.

Hutong District

The key to the plan turned out to be the ping-pong ball. Or rather three ping-pong balls that the team purchased from the two kids playing on the makeshift table in the alley. From her love of all things explosive and incendiary, Sydney knew that a ping-pong ball was the perfect ingredient for making a particularly effective smoke bomb. Three would massively increase the amount of smoke, which is exactly what they needed.

She scavenged the rest of the ingredients from some items they picked up at a small gift shop, and now she had climbed up onto the roof and waited as the others got into place. Her phone buzzed, and she looked at the message from Monty.

ALL CLEAR.

Sydney lit the smoke bomb and dropped it down the chimney. She knew that Sorokin was in another room watching television; by the time he noticed the smoke, there would be so much of it that he wouldn't be able to tell where it had come from. Hopefully, he'd assume that the wiring in the old house had caught fire and they needed to get out.

She tiptoed across the roof and took a spot just above the door.

After a few minutes, they heard Sorokin cursing in Russian as the house filled up with smoke. Soon after, he came out the door with Dae-jung, and he'd just stepped into the courtyard when Sydney jumped on him from above. It was a direct hit, and as he staggered farther into the courtyard, Monty attacked him with a flurry of Jeet Kune Do moves to knock him out cold. Meanwhile, Rio grabbed Dae-jung by the arm and started to run toward the alley.

When Sorokin finally came to, there was no sign of anyone, and the gates had been chained shut.

Bird's Nest—Backstage
Mother got the text from Monty right after the awards

had been presented. The group was backstage, about to head up to the luxury suite to watch the concert. He scanned the area and saw a straight, clear path to an exit and stopped walking.

"You ready?" he said to Jin-sun.

"What do you mean?" Jin-sun replied.

"I mean, are you ready?" Mother replied. "We've got Dae-jung, so it's now or never."

Jin-sun's eyes opened wide. "I'm ready."

"Good."

Mother looked down at his phone and pressed send on a message. It was only one word: SHOWTIME.

Bird's Nest—Computer Room

Brooklyn had spent the last few hours in a small computer room that connected straight into the servers for the stadium. She had also hacked into the system that controlled KB5's concert tech, just like she had the night of Tabitha's birthday party. As soon as she got the text from Mother, she began an encore performance.

Bird's Nest—Backstage

This time, Brooklyn had a lot more fireworks to play with and a direct line not only into the concert grid, but to all the systems used by the stadium. First, the pyro started going off and the lighting effects kicked in. There was instant pandemonium backstage, and after about ten seconds of it, all the backstage lights went out.

"Go," Mother said to Jin-sun and Paris.

Soon, the three of them were sprinting toward the exit, hoping they were visualizing the path properly.

Bird's Nest—Corridor Outside Computer Room

A team of security guards raced to the computer room to see if they could figure out what was happening. They were so focused on where they were headed and so certain of what a computer hacker might look like that they ran right past the twelve-year-old girl in the KB5 concert shirt.

Bird's Nest—Backstage

For Sir Reg, the perfect night was quickly turning into a nightmare. He'd just left the stage when the pyrotechnics had started to go off. There was confusion backstage just as there'd been at Tabitha's birthday party. He was still trying to find someone who could fix the situation when Anastasia rushed over to him.

"There's been a problem," she said, raising her voice to be heard over all the confusion and the fireworks.

"You think?" Reg shouted angrily.

"Nicholas called," she said. "He was attacked—"

"Speak up," he demanded. "I can't hear you."

"Nicholas was attacked, and Dae-jung is missing," she said louder.

Reg was ready to explode, but he was still focused on the end result. He didn't need Dae-jung, but he did need his father.

"Get up to the luxury suite immediately and find Jin-sun!" he commanded. "Then get him to the helipad right away."

"What about his guards?" asked Anastasia.

"Deal with them," he instructed. "I don't care how."

Olympic Park Metro Station

"Amazing job," Mother said to Brooklyn as they rendezvoused outside the metro station. He was with Jin-sun and Paris, and each of them wore a bandana over their mouth and nose to fight the smog and bedevil the facial-recognition software used by the secret police.

"It was tons of fun!" Brooklyn said happily.

"This is your team?" Jin-sun said, looking stunned. "Children?"

"Much better than any team Sir Reg can muster," Mother said proudly.

Helicopter

A helicopter carrying Sir Reg and the Sorokin twins raced through the sky over Beijing heading for Daxing airport. Unlike the chess players in the tournament, he was unwilling to concede, no matter the status of the board. He decided to put a new, powerful piece into play and called his good friend within the Chinese Ministry of State Security.

"General Chan, this is Sir Reginald Banks," he said into his phone. "I hope I'm not bothering you, but I have a matter of urgent need that I believe is a threat to your national security."

"What is it?" asked the general, alarmed.

"I'm afraid, sir, that it's my own government," said Banks. "MI6 has a spy plane about to take off from Daxing airport, and they've recently run an operation on Chinese soil. You might want to stop it."

Sir Reg gave him the specifics of the plane. Interestingly, this information lined up with a report that had come earlier in the day from an analyst.

Daxing International Airport

An elite team of six Ministry of State Security agents boarded the plane that had been chartered by the British embassy. According to information they'd received, they expected anywhere from five to eight passengers on board.

As it happened, there was only one.

"Hello, boys," Tru said pleasantly as she took a sip of champagne. "How can I help you?"

Departures

BEIJING WAS SUCH A SPRAWLING CITY that its two biggest airports were fifty miles apart. While everyone was looking for Jin-sun and Dae-jung at one, the City Spies had taken them to the other. It was a move inspired by Paris and Mother's discussion of the poisoned pawn.

The finishing touches were his hotel reservations in Tokyo and Tru's demand to have a plane fueled and ready to fly there as well. It all came together too perfectly to resist. By the time any of them figured out what had happened, they'd all be safely in the air with the Parks.

"Here's your identification," Mother said, handing Jin-sun a pair of blue passports as they walked through Terminal 3.

"Why are they from Canada?" asked Jin-sun.

"If anyone's looking, they'll be looking for British ones," Mother answered.

The whole group was booked on a Royal Dutch Airways flight to Amsterdam. Although they normally split up when traveling, Mother wanted them out of China as quickly as possible. He also thought the large group would confuse anyone looking for them. Sir Reg and the MSS didn't know about the rest of the team.

They were almost at the checkout counter when a voice called out to them.

"Stop right there."

When they turned, everyone was surprised to see who it was. Everyone, that is, except for Mother, who'd had his suspicions.

"Ms. Li," Paris said, confused. "What are you doing here? Where's Ang?"

"Her name isn't Li," Mother said. "And Ang is not her son."

"What do you mean?" asked Paris.

"She's with the Ministry of State Security," Mother said. "No doubt sent to the tournaments to spy on Jin-sun."

"When did you know?" asked Li.

"I started suspecting it when you showed us around the Forbidden City," he said. "When you told us why there were no birds on the roofs, Ang seemed amazed, but surely you would have told him that story once before. Then, when he said he'd never been to the Great Wall, I realized that he wasn't from Beijing."

"No, he's from Shanghai," said Li. "But he's a great player, and that's what I needed."

"But I wasn't certain until last night when you spoke to the police," Mother said. "One of the police officers referred to you as *dà jiê.*"

"'Big sister,'" she said, translating. "So you speak Mandarin after all."

"No," answered Mother. "But I've watched a lot of spy and police movies from Hong Kong, and that's the term they always use to address a woman who's a superior. That was your team last night, right? They work for you."

"Impressive," said Li.

"But not impressive enough for you to take the bait and go to Daxing?"

"That was clumsy," Li said. "It was too specific. It felt like you wanted to make sure I knew where you were headed. That's when I began to think you might be onto me."

"So what happens now?" asked Jin-sun.

Li had a pained look as she said, "Now you and Dae-jung come with me, and I'll return you to the North Korean embassy."

"No," Paris pleaded. "You can't do that! That can't be how this ends."

"Certainly, we can make some sort of arrangement," Jin-sun said. "You are aware of the consequences we'll face."

"I am truly sorry about that, but my hands are tied," said Li.

"Actually, they're not," said Paris. "You can turn around and walk away."

"But I can't," said Li. "North Korea is China's ally. If I do what you suggest, then I will face serious consequences too. Do you know how hard it is for a woman to work her way up in the Ministry of State Security? My every move is scrutinized."

Dae-jung sighed. "It's zugzwang," he said, looking at it from a chess perspective. "You have no good move."

"No, I don't," said Li.

Jin-sun took a breath and said, "What if you just take me? I am the prize they want. I will suffer the consequences. But there's no reason to punish my son. He's innocent." He turned to Mother. "Will you take him? Will you raise him?"

Mother was stunned; Jia-Hui was torn; and Jin-sun was desperate.

It was an impossible situation, and nobody knew what to say.

Except for Kat. She decided that this was going to be her moment.

"No," she said firmly. "You'll raise him, because you're both coming with us."

"That can't happen," said Li. "I won't let it."

"Yes, you will," Kat said. "I want to be kind and show an interest in what you're going through."

"What she talking about?" Paris whispered to Rio.

"I think she's trying to charm her," Rio answered.

They exchanged equally worried looks.

"I am sensitive to the fact that you are in a difficult

situation," Kat continued. "But I sincerely believe that you'll do what's right."

"And what makes you think that?" Li asked.

"For one thing, you're alone," she said. "You figured it out, but you didn't tell anyone. You let the MSS send people to the wrong airport. That's because you don't want to send them back."

"That's an excellent point," Mother said.

"But most of all," Kat said, "you're good at your job, and it's hard for women to rise through the ranks at the Ministry of State Security. You want to get promotions and be a hero. You want to be celebrated for being good at it."

"All of which will happen when I take them into custody," said Li.

"You haven't let me finish," Kat said. "I can give you something bigger. I can make you an international hero. You will be promoted and praised, and you will get all the credit, even though I'm the one who did the work."

Mother and Monty shared a look. They had no idea what she was talking about.

"But here's the problem," Kat said. "If you stay here and take them into custody, you'll miss out on a much bigger prize. And when your superiors find out that you did, you'll never be forgiven."

"And what is this amazing prize?" Li asked, calling her bluff.

"Six stolen nuclear devices," Kat answered. "They were taken from Russia and China. They are in Beijing, but they won't be here for long. You're going to have to pick which prize you want more. You can arrest these good people and send them back to North Korea, where they will suffer greatly. Or you can prevent six nuclear devices from winding up in the hands of terrorists, saving untold lives in the process."

"Kat?" Mother said. "Do you really know where they are?"

"I do," Kat said. "I've been trying to wrap my brain around it all day, and I just figured it out."

"You're bluffing," Li said.

"I'm not."

"And how do I know that?"

"Because I'm not good at lying," she said. "And I'm not good at talking people into doing things. But I am exceptional at putting together puzzles."

"And if you tell me where they are, how do you know I won't still arrest them?"

"I am just going to have to take your word."

The silence was long, but eventually Li answered. "Where are they?"

"They're in one of the trucks used to transport the equipment for the KB5 concerts," Kat said. "There are forty of them. They're about to be loaded and will pull away very soon. You need to seal off the parking lot around the stadium and start searching."

"What makes you think they're there?" Sydney asked.

"The plumbing truck," Kat explained. "On the last night in Moscow, Nicholas Sorokin drove a plumbing supply truck to the stadium and left it. Why?"

"He was trying to fool us, wasn't he?" asked Rio.

"No," said Kat. "He had no idea we were there. He received the code and left the truck for a reason."

"The nuclear warheads were in the truck," said Sydney, getting it.

Kat nodded. "He drove them there to be loaded onto one of the trucks. *That* was his mission."

"And the three that were stolen from Lop Nor?" asked Monty.

"I imagine they were loaded onto one of the trucks when they drove from Moscow to Beijing. They would've driven right through Mongolia and the desert."

"You're right, Kat," Mother said. "That's exactly where they are."

Li was paralyzed as she tried to think of what she should do. She looked at Kat and tried to read her. She started to move and then pulled out her phone and made a call. She started speaking to someone in Mandarin as she sprinted toward the exit.

Everyone else just stood there staring at Kat.

"When did you put this together?" Sydney asked.

"Just now, while we were standing here," Kat said.

"How?" asked Paris.

"I've been thinking about the trucks ever since I saw them earlier today. I realized you could hide anything in there. And then I noticed him."

She pointed to where a plumber was fixing a water fountain.

"He made me think of the plumbing truck, and I figured it out."

"All in the middle of a confrontation with everything on the line?" Monty said, shaking her head.

Kat shrugged. "Someone had to do something."

46

The First Day of School

DESPITE COUNTLESS PERFORMANCES AT the West Liverpool Community Theatre, Mother had never received an ovation quite as enthusiastic as the one he got at the FARM when he performed a medley of songs from the musical *Grease*. This was to pay off the deal he'd made with Paris in Beijing. His hair was slicked back, he wore a leather jacket, and in addition to singing, he did the full choreography.

Monty laughed so hard that tears streamed down her

face as she said, "That is the single greatest thing I have ever seen."

"Isn't it?" said Brooklyn. "Like beautiful and terrifying at the same time."

"Who knew he could sing?" asked Rio.

Afterward, they had dinner, and he told them all about a boy named Bertrand Dashiell Gibbs, Jr. He also told them lovely stories about his mother.

"Your gran was the most amazing woman I've ever met," he said. "And she would have adored each of you."

A week and a half later, the students of Kinloch Abbey returned to school for the autumn term. All of them gathered in the chapel to hear welcoming speeches from Dr. Graham and some members of the faculty.

They also heard a poem, written especially for the occasion by the school's poet laureate.

"Good morning," Paris said as he stood at the podium. "It's so nice to see so many friendly faces. Including some who it feels like I haven't seen in quite some time." His gaze drifted over to where Charlotte was sitting, and the two of them shared a brief smile. "We will spend the year being curious and looking not only for answers, but also questions. Because the questions are what enlighten us. Here's one that I wrestled with all summer long.

"Who am I?
Am I the blood within my veins?
The heart that always strains, to ease the
pains of others?
Am I the name that I've been given?
Does that explain why I am driven?
Does that honor my father and my mother?
What is it that you find, when the stars
somehow align?
And begin to define the essence that is mine?

"Who am I?
I am brother, I am son
I am many, I am one
I am more than I can comprehend
And forever I'm your friend."

UK EYES ONLY

Secret Intelligence Service/MI6

Vauxhall Cross, London, UK

Project City Spies (aka Project Neverland)

Self-evaluations prepared by individual team members

BROOKLYN

NAME: ~~Sara Maria Martinez~~

COVER IDENTITY: Christina Diaz

BIRTHPLACE: Vega Alta, Puerto Rico

RECRUITED: Brooklyn, New York

SOMETHING I LOVE: *Mofongo con camarones.* It's a delicious Puerto Rican specialty made with mashed plantains and shrimp. The best is from a café in Washington Heights. When you eat it, you're so full, you feel like you can skip your next few meals.

SOMETHING I MISS: Ice-skating at Prospect Park in Brooklyn. A neighbor gave me her skates when she outgrew them, and I instantly fell in love with the sport. There are two rinks in the park; one of them is covered and has a neat design on the ceiling. They're both free on Monday afternoons.

SOMETHING I'M PROUD OF: Monty gave me this great idea about writing fan mail to women in technology. I can't believe how many have replied. Now, I have an amazing collection of inspiring letters from scientists and engineers, including one from an astronaut and another from a Nobel Prize winner.

PARIS

NAME: ~~Salomon Omborenga~~

COVER IDENTITY: Lucas Doinel

BIRTHPLACE: Kigali, Rwanda

RECRUITED: Paris, France

SOMETHING I LOVE: I volunteer with a youth soccer league in Kinloch and help out with a team of six- and seven-year-old girls who are fierce and wonderful. Their Scottish accents are hilarious when they call out for Coach Loo-kas.

SOMETHING I MISS: The Museum of Natural History in Paris is free on Sundays, so that's when I would go and look at all the great dinosaur skeletons. My favorite is the triceratops.

SOMETHING I'M PROUD OF: I've never been prouder of anything than I was of Brooklyn when she saved the day on our mission in Paris. She was brave and daring and saved countless lives without hesitation despite the fact that she'd had limited training. She's already a legend.

SYDNEY

NAME: ~~Olivia Rose~~

COVER IDENTITY:
Eleanor King

BIRTHPLACE: Bondi
Beach, Australia

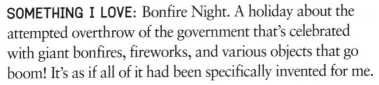

RECRUITED: Sydney, Australia

SOMETHING I LOVE: Bonfire Night. A holiday about the
attempted overthrow of the government that's celebrated
with giant bonfires, fireworks, and various objects that go
boom! It's as if all of it had been specifically invented for me.

SOMETHING I MISS: Freshwater Beach. Don't be fooled
by the name; Freshie's prime oceanfront. This is where
Duke Kahanamoku first introduced surfing to Australia
and where I first got up on a board. It's still my favorite
place to catch a wave because it's not as crowded as Bondi
or Manly, which are both nearby and filled with tourists.

SOMETHING I'M PROUD OF: When I'm picked to be the
alpha on a mission. It's the ultimate compliment that
Mother, Monty, and the rest of the team trust me to make
decisions when everything is at stake. It means they believe
in me, and I'll do anything not to let them down.

KAT

NAME: ~~Amita Bishwakarma~~

COVER IDENTITY: Supriya Rai

BIRTHPLACE: Monjo, Nepal

RECRUITED: Kathmandu, Nepal

SOMETHING I LOVE: My favorite number is 73,939,133. It's the largest right truncatable prime number. That means if you successively remove the rightmost number to create 7,393,913 and 739,391 and 73,939 and 7,393 and 739 and 73 and 7, each number is still a prime.

SOMETHING I MISS: Living in a world without bagpipes. This so-called "musical" instrument is played at events throughout Scotland, and every time it's painful. What's the difference between bagpipe music and a fight between a cat and a badger? Fur.

SOMETHING I'M PROUD OF: This team. I believe in logic and order, but there is nothing logical about a group of five kids from around the world who go on spy missions for MI6. We do great things with no recognition or reward other than the knowledge that we're doing what's right.

RIO

NAME: ~~João Cardozo~~

COVER IDENTITY: Rafael Rocha

BIRTHPLACE: Rio de Janeiro, Brazil

RECRUITED: Copacabana Beach, Brazil

SOMETHING I LOVE: The look of amazement on someone's face when I've performed a magic trick and they have no idea how I did it.

SOMETHING I MISS: Samba music. For six days every year, Rio de Janeiro is like no other place on Earth as the city is overtaken by Carnival. There are parades on the streets, and the nonstop sound of samba music fills the air. Whenever I feel sad, I put in my earbuds and listen to it with my eyes closed, and that helps.

SOMETHING I'M PROUD OF: I didn't tell anybody, but I set a goal for myself to make the headmaster's academic honors list. To do that, you need top grades in every class, and I had never even come close. It was incredibly hard, especially in math and English, but I made the list for the most recent term. Monty baked me a batch of *queijadinha*, a Brazilian dessert made with coconut. Yum.

Acknowledgments

I am so fortunate to be supported by the friends, colleagues, and experts who make up Team City Spies. They help with everything from plot twists and research questions to grammar dilemmas and spasms of creative anxiety. They even respond to emails with the misleading subject line of "One Quick Question."

Leading the way is the one-two punch of editor Kristin Gilson and publisher Valerie Garfield. They make Aladdin a wonderful place to write books, and they are joined by an incredible squad that includes Lauren Hoffman, Emily Hutton, Victor Iannone, Cassie Malmo, Beth Parker, Tiara Iandiorio, Rebecca Vitkus, Chelsea Morgan, Alyson Heller, Nicole Russo, Caitlin Sweeny, Michelle Leo, Amy Beaudoin, Anna Jarzab, Alissa Nigro, Savannah Breckenridge, Erin Toller, Beth Adelman, and Jeannie Ng. Also, huge thanks to Lisa Flanagan, who performs the audiobooks (sorry about all the accents), and Yaoyao Ma Van As, whose amazing illustrations you see on the covers and in the dossiers.

Rosemary Stimola is both a great friend and an amazing agent, and I am honored to be part of the Stimola Literary Studio, where I am supported by Allison Hellegers, Peter Ryan, and Nick Croce. I'm also indebted to the delightful Clementine Gaisman and Alice Natali at ILA and Jason Dravis at the Dravis Agency.

I'd like to thank Pete Karagianis and Daniel Lucas of the United States Chess Federation for their insights into major chess competitions, as well as Keyes Rodriguez for his impressions of what it's like to play in one.

For an understanding of all things Moscow, ranging from daily living to the Russian language to a better understanding of the workings of international diplomacy, I am indebted to Julia Gaber, Molly Thomasy Blasing, Marina Hess, and retired ambassador Carey Cavanaugh. Also, Greg Miller's excellent journalism and his willingness to answer my questions about the Soviet Union's secret mapping program were extremely valuable.

I learned much about Beijing and Chinese culture from He Jia Hui, Mason Seay, Matt Allen, and Jeff Axelrod. Likewise, I want to thank Sheila, Sally, and Ben Averbuch for all things UK, and Elizabeth Eulberg for her daring undercover reconnaissance mission along Kensington Palace Gardens.

Speaking of reconnaissance missions, I am truly grateful to Michael Morell, former Deputy Director of the Central Intelligence Agency, for sharing his expertise of the spy business.

I am beyond lucky to have many very smart friends who are willing to answer my phone calls and share their knowledge. These include Delle Joseph (French), Jeff Truesdell (journalism), Jim Bassett (environmental sciences), and Marieke Pelemen (art history). I'm also thankful for beta readers, including Mary Beth Morell, Elizabeth Vanos, and Clay Hobson, as well as a great group of writing friends who somehow managed to keep the laughter going, even during a global pandemic.

Most of all, I want to thank my incredible family, who make everything possible and worthwhile.